WOODMILL HIGH SCHOOL

RAZORBILL

RUMOUR
Has It

Real love.

Real life.

The real thing . . .

www.girlheartboy.com

RUMOUR
Has It

ALI CRONIN

razor
bill
PENGUIN

RAZORBILL

Published by the Penguin Group
Penguin Books Ltd, 80 Strand, London WC2R ORL, England
Penguin Group (USA) Inc., 375 Hudson Street, New York, New York 10014, USA
Penguin Group (Canada), 90 Eglinton Avenue East, Suite 700, Toronto, Ontario, Canada M4P 2Y3
(a division of Pearson Penguin Canada Inc.)
Penguin Ireland, 25 St Stephen's Green, Dublin 2, Ireland (a division of Penguin Books Ltd)
Penguin Group (Australia), 707 Collins Street, Melbourne, Victoria 3008, Australia
(a division of Pearson Australia Group Pty Ltd)
Penguin Books India Pvt Ltd, 11 Community Centre, Panchsheel Park, New Delhi – 110 017, India
Penguin Group (NZ), 67 Apollo Drive, Rosedale, Auckland 0632, New Zealand
(a division of Pearson New Zealand Ltd)
Penguin Books (South Africa) (Pty) Ltd, Block D, Rosebank Office Park, 181 Jan Smuts Avenue,
Parktown North, Gauteng 2193, South Africa

Penguin Books Ltd, Registered Offices: 80 Strand, London WC2R ORL, England

penguin.com

First published in Razorbill, an imprint of Penguin Books Ltd, 2012

001

Set in 13/15.25 pt Garamond MT Std
Typeset by Palimpsest Book Production Limited, Falkirk, Stirlingshire
Printed in Great Britain by Clays Ltd, St Ives plc

British Library Cataloguing in Publication Data
A CIP catalogue record for this book is available from the British Library

ISBN: 978-0-141-34063-0

www.greenpenguin.co.uk

Penguin Books is committed to a sustainable
future for our business, our readers and our planet.
This book is made from Forest Stewardship
Council™ certified paper.

ALWAYS LEARNING   PEARSON

For Jon

Prologue

'Six pounds fifty,' said the surly dude with the poly-ester polo shirt and eye-contact issues. I gave him the exact money, flashed a radiant smile to thank him for the impeccable service and took my vat of popcorn (salt and sweet mixed, *bien sûr*) and bucket o' pop over to the others.

Donna – bezzie – and her cousin Marv were waiting by the steps up to the screens, chatting to three boys I'd never seen before.

'Supplies,' I said, plonking the stuff down on the floor. 'Sorry: I only got three straws.' I looked at the new people. One of them, a really tall guy with dark wavy hair who was wearing drainpipes and a black blazer, said, 'Sharing straws. Cosy.'

Not a hint of a smile. Oh well, I knew my limits. No point wasting my time. Shame, though. He was fit.

'Oh, sorry, Ashley,' said Marv. 'Aiden, Jamie, Dylan.' He pointed to each in turn. I guessed they went to the same school, which is to say not our school. Donna and I go to Woodside High; Marv goes to Corlyns on the other side of Brighton.

They all nodded hello, except for Dylan – he of the sharing-straws comment – who barely looked up.

I said hey and we all trooped up to Screen Two for a couple of hours of ghosts and gore and explicit sex scenes.

Thank the baby Jesus for fake ID, as the Bible probably doesn't say.

'Well, that was lame,' said Marv, as we left the building.

'Are you kidding? I was petrified,' I said, hugging myself to keep warm. There had been something wrong with the heating in the cinema and it was freezing outside. Good thing I'd worn my duffel. Well brought up, see.

'Oh God, that bit with the eyeball in the mirror,' said Donna, clutching her throat.

'Yeah, but c'mon, it wasn't anything we hadn't seen before,' said Aiden. Or Jamie. I couldn't remember which was which.

'I enjoyed it,' offered Dylan, pulling a thin scarf out of his bum pocket and tying it round his neck. 'Horror's all about clichés.' His scarf had tiny skulls and crossbones on it.

I shrugged. 'I could see a gizzardy eyeball a million times. I'd still let out a bit of wee every time.'

Marv laughed. 'Don't watch the *Saw* films then.'

'Oh, I have.' I tapped the side of my nose. 'Incontinence pants.'

Oop . . . was it . . .? Yep, I think even Dylan might have cracked a smirk.

Donna cocked her head. 'Ah, Ashley. Such a lady.'

I offered up a smile and did a little curtsy. Not easy when you're wearing hobnail boots and the tightest jeans known to (wo)man. At least there was no chance of bits-revealage, the vibe being more hammock gusset than camel toe. Not that I cared much either way.

Anyway. We ambled along for a bit, comparing favourite horror film gory bits, then discussing why we recognized the actress who played the first to be bumped off (answer: she used to be in *Neighbours*) and finally sharing a bit of shock-horror at the fact that so many shops already had their Christmas decorations up. Which brings us neatly to . . .

'Actually, our friend Ollie's already organized a Christmas party,' said Donna. She turned to Marv. 'The one who had the bonfire-night party?'

He nodded. 'Yeah. That was a laugh.'

'Come, if you want,' I said. 'More the merrier and all that.' I sneaked a look at Dylan. Not my fault: my eyes made me do it. While he wasn't quite retching with disgust, he didn't seem thrilled at the idea either. Marv looked questioningly at Jamie, Aiden and Dylan, who must have sent some kind of testosterone telepathy back, cos then Marv said: 'Yeah, why not.'

And so it began, but possibly not in the way you think. *strokes chin mysteriously*

1

I hardly ever came to the Year Thirteen common room. It was too busy and it smelled weird, like feet, and sandwiches that had been wrapped in clingfilm, but you could make a cup of tea for free so it was where I came when I was skint. And I *was* skint, ever since my mum had stopped paying me to work at her poncey bridal boutique. Economic climate, blah blah. There wasn't even a more-free-time silver lining to this tale of woe, cos I still worked there. I just didn't get paid. Was I a mug? Quite possibly.

'So. About Dylan . . .' said Donna. I watched her doing the gaping-mouth crazy-eyes-at-the-ceiling thing as she put in her contact lenses.

'Oh, riiight. So that's why you nearly trod on a dog on the way to school,' I said, not purposely avoiding the question.

Donna blinked and rubbed the corners of her eyes. 'Yeah, well. I overslept. And I'm not going out with my glasses on, am I?'

'You look lovely with your glasses on.'

She looked at me sceptically. 'Right.'

'Oop. Kettle boiling.' I went over to the scabby worktop and reached to get two mugs down from the cupboard. They were chipped and stained with months of dried-on tea, which, in this place, passed for sparkly clean. Teabag in each, splosh of milk (it was on the turn – again, it could have been worse), quick stir and squeeze, bags in the bin, and I was back in my scratchy-yet-squishy common-room chair ready to analyse Dylan. Not that there was much to analyse.

'Yeah. Fit,' I said airily, recalling his long legs and lush hair, and not exactly feeling what I'd describe as airy. 'If only he'd have stopped yakking. Couldn't get a word in.'

Donna laughed. 'I know. He was weird, no? Marv reckons he's just shy.'

So Donna had been talking about Dylan with her cousin. Did she like him? I got a sudden flash of the green-eyes, which I just as quickly pushed away.

'You fancied him though, right?' Don took a smug sip of tea. She knew me too well.

I shrugged. 'Out of my league, babes. I might as well fancy Robert Pattinson . . .' I paused. 'Uh, did you? Fancy him?' We didn't usually fancy the same type, but you never knew.

She wrinkled her nose. 'Nah. You know my rule about cardigans.'

'He wasn't wearing a cardigan!' I protested, although

personally I like a boy in a floppy cardi. In my experience it's an item of knitwear that confounds stereotypes when worn by a boy, although obvs it has to be worn with the right amount of irony. Let it be known: cardi wearers are good in bed.

Don sniffed. 'Yeah, he was. Under the blazer.' She shook her head. 'Not my type . . . But *definitely yours . . .*' She sang the last two words.

I smiled. 'Like I said: out of my league.' It was gutting, really. All weekend after the cinema I'd kept thinking about him. I'd be watching telly or on the loo or trying to get to sleep and there he'd be, leaning nonchalantly against the wall of my mind, one skinny-jeaned leg crossed over the other. Well, that wasn't *all* he did. And lots of times he was naked.

Anyway.

'Don't be a pussy,' said Donna. 'You can have anyone you want. You've had most of the boys in this school, for example.' She smiled prettily. Bitch.

'Piss off,' I said merrily. 'And, anyway, there's a whole heap o' difference between them and . . . him. He's beautiful.'

Don put her hand on my knee and cocked her head earnestly. 'As are you, Ashley. As are you.'

I shoved her hand off. Very funny. 'Sasha's the beautiful one,' I said, draining my tea just as the beeps for next period went.

'Uh-huh.'

Donna could eye-roll all she wanted but the facts spoke for themselves. My perfect big sister was beautiful to my OK; good to my naughty; kind to my evil. *C'est*, unfortunately, *la vie*.

'Anyway, Marv reckons they're all coming to Ollie's party,' continued Donna as we paused at the door before she turned left to theatre studies and I turned right to media studies. 'You never know . . .'

Right. You never know . . . but you usually do. I put Dylan out of my mind and spent the next couple of hours working on my media studies coursework.

We had to make short documentaries. I was loving it. Like, really loving it. And, without wanting to sound like a complete wanker, there was a chance it could change my life. Unlike most of the others, I hadn't already started my uni applications. Donna wanted to be an actor; Cass was going for law at Cambridge, among others; Sarah wanted to do history of art; Ollie fancied music; Jack was going to do sports science . . . which left me and Rich floundering. I don't think Rich had a scooby what he wanted to do with his life and, until recently, neither did I. So I decided I wasn't going to go to uni. Not yet, anyway. It seemed kind of ridiculous to spend all that money on doing something I didn't care about just for the sake of getting a degree. Mum and Sasha were shocked and appalled, *bien sûr*, but it was my life. And, anyway, it had paid off: I'd found something I could be really passionate about. I'd done my research and I'd decided to apply to do film at Southampton, Bournemouth, Falmouth and East Anglia. As yet, nobody knew, and they never would unless I got a place. And I needed this documentary to complete my applications.

I'd decided to focus on people who'd had near-death experiences. This was a subject close to my thankfully still-beating heart, since I'd almost drowned swimming in the sea in Devon last half term. (Long story.) I thought using it for coursework might stop me having nightmares about it. It was kind of working. And, of course, Dylan had taken over my dreams for the past couple of nights, to *très* pleasing effect.

I'd already come up with a few real-life stories from local papers and crappy magazines, hidden among the stupid 'I Botoxed my armpits' and 'My husband's cheese fetish' sort of stories. One or two of them were right on the money. Reading their stories had made me realize just how dull mine was. I'd stopped breathing, then started again. End of. The time from when I got in the sea to when I woke up in hospital is just a blank. It's as if less than a second passed between the two events. But these people saw lights, watched themselves from above, lost all fear of death, etc. I wish I'd had all that.

I was engrossed in some old lady's story from the website of our local paper (about her house being bombed when she was a kid in the Second World War), when someone shoved my desk.

'Hey!' I said, ready to have a go, but it was just Sam. He didn't like me, although he used to. We'd once hooked up at a party. Truly, I'd never have gone there if I'd thought for a moment he *really* liked me. And the only reason I laughed when he told me he did was because I genuinely thought he was joking. Anyway, two years on and he still couldn't look at me without scowling. I tried a friendly smile, but he ignored me and walked to his desk, a book about Dungeons and Dragons under his arm. Mmm, sexy.

Dylan on the other hand . . .

Sod it. I had nothing to lose except my dignity, and that went long ago. Looking around quickly to check that Matt, our teacher, wasn't in sight, I logged on to Facebook. It was only a matter of time before school blocked it, but for now we were free to socially network to our hearts' content. Facebooking in class time, however, was a major no-no. We're talking withdrawal of Internet privileges. So I was furtive furtive, quickly finding Dylan in Marv's friend list and sending my own request. If he'd accepted it by the time I got home, I'd message him.

But first I had the rest of the day to get through. I had just enough time before the end of the lesson to fire off a quick email to the editor of the newspaper with a message for the old lady, asking her if she'd let me interview her about her experience, then I went along to the canteen for lunch, as always, and where, as always, Donna, Ollie, Jack and our other friends Sarah, Cass and Rich were sitting at the fourth table from the left, roughly in the middle of the room. Don't know why or how we'd picked that one – or even when – but on the rare occasions someone else was sitting there it was like walking into your bedroom and finding a stranger in your bed. And not in a good way.

'Still doing pack-ups?' asked Cass sympathetically, eyeing my hastily chucked together cheese-and-pickle sandwich, now limp after a morning in my bag. She hadn't bought lunch from the canteen either, but that was because she'd stopped at a deli on the way to school to pick up her usual £4 chicken-salad flatbread hold-the-mayo. She reckons it's because she doesn't like the crappy bread in the school sandwiches, and she has a point. But £4?

I nodded and took a bite of soggy bread and

sweaty cheese. It was edible, anyway. And Cass didn't need to look so sorry for me. Mum still had the shop and the house. We weren't on benefits quite yet.

'So I hear you had a good weekend,' said Sarah, peering at me saucily from behind her Ribena carton. 'Dylan, was it . . .?'

I shot daggers at Donna, who shrugged not at all guiltily. 'What? I didn't know it was a secret.'

That *what* was a secret? God, you admit to fancying one boy and it's Agatha Christie time.

'There's nothing to tell,' I said to Sarah. 'He's not for me.'

She shook her head. 'Ash, I have no doubt at all that you could have anyone you wanted . . . I've never yet seen a boy who doesn't fancy you.'

'Piss off!' I spluttered.

'It's true,' said Ollie seriously. 'I'd have you here and now if it was socially acceptable.'

'You'd have *anyone* here and now if it was socially acceptable,' I replied. 'No offence.'

He nodded amiably. 'Fair point.'

'But seriously, Ash,' said Rich, who was busy examining a spot on his chin using the mirror in Donna's eyeshadow compact. 'You really like him?'

I chucked my sandwich down on the table in mock outrage, where it instantly curled up at the edges like some fish corpse (the sandwich, not the outrage).

'What is this?' I demanded. 'You're never usually this interested in my love life.'

'That's cos *usually* you've already shagged them,' said Jack. 'This is new.'

Cheeky bastard. That's so not true, for the record. But all I said was: 'Yeah, well. He doesn't fancy me. End of.'

Dylan, Dylan, Dylan. If my friends hadn't made such a thing out of it I might have been able to put him out of my mind. But the bastards made sure he was installed good and proper, so by the time I got home that afternoon I was practically panting to get on the computer to check Facebook.

I slammed the front door and ran to the back room without taking my coat off, where, sitting straight-backed and serene at our computer, was my sister Sasha.

'What are you doing here?' I blurted. 'Why aren't you at work?' Fair questions. She didn't live at home any more, after all. And didn't she have a laptop/ iPad/iPhone/other assorted shiny, portable Internet gadgets? The 'executive home' she shared with her 'partner' (vomit) Toby in Kent, with its mini 'guest toiletries' in the 'guest bedroom en suite' and its taste-ful sofas and tastefully framed 'art' on the walls, was chock-full of the stuff. Technology coming out of its bright red-bricked ears. WiFi flowing invisibly from no less than three little blinking boxes attached neatly to the wall in the downstairs study, the loft room and in the garage. The garage FFS!

'Oh, hey, Ashley,' said Sasha, turning and smiling sweetly. 'I've got the day off. I've finally persuaded Mum to do her food shopping online so I'm signing her up with Ocado as it does Waitrose.' She turned back to the screen. 'It's by far the best, both ethically and in quality.'

Right. How fascinating. Kill me now if I'm going to find myself discussing supermarkets by the time I'm twenty-four. 'Well, are you going to be long? I need to use the computer.'

'About quarter of an hour?' said Sasha without turning round. 'I'll come and find you when I'm done.'

I made a face at her back and went into the kitchen to grab a snack. Monday wasn't one of Mum's shop's late-opening nights, but Mum still wouldn't be home till six, when we'd have pizza for tea. Monday-night ritual. On my way up to my room I stuck my head into the living room, where my little sister Frankie was watching TV. Most twelve-year-olds would be watching crappy American sitcoms on the Disney Channel or something, but she was sat in the lotus position in front of Mum's yoga DVD.

'All right, Franks?'

She held up a finger to tell me to wait, then placed the tips of her middle finger and thumb together and brought them in front of her, just like the skinny bird in the leotard was doing on the screen, breathed in deeply and chanted a long, slow, 'Ommmmm.' Then she paused the screen and spun round to face me, her hand-me-down school shirt and navy pleated skirt about as un-yogary as you could get.

I raised an eyebrow. 'Good sesh?'

'Yeah, brilliant. Apart from all the farting.' She gave me an unwavering gaze – the only sort she does, my crazy sister – and I laughed.

'Mum says it happens all the time in her yoga class,' she said reproachfully.

'Sure it does, Frankie-pank,' I said. 'Good day?'

She turned back to the screen. 'It was OK. Miss Baines said I had an unusual talent for mimicry.'

'Who were you mimicking?'

She pulled her legs back into the lotus position. 'Miss Baines.'

Of course. I turned to go, then stopped and said, 'Do you know why Sasha's here? It can't just be for Mum's Internet shopping.'

Frankie sucked her teeth impatiently. 'Dunno. Maybe she's had a row with Toby.' She clicked the DVD off pause.

Interesting, although I doubted it was true. Toby and Sasha were disgusting together, all little kisses and 'sweetheart' and 'darling'. I left Frankie to her 'omming' and went up to my room to change.

Ah, my room. Sasha gave it to me when she left home to go to uni. It was the best present she'd ever given me, by about a million miles. I'd spent a whole half term transforming it. I'd stripped off her Laura Ashley wallpaper and painted the whole room purple, except the dark-wood floorboards which I left as they were. Then I'd covered my bed with a couple of metres of this mental 1960s geometric-print fabric I'd found in Oxfam. I'd bought some slatted wooden blinds from Ikea and put those up in place of Sasha's gross floral curtains, and finally put my giant Kurt Cobain poster on the wall. There was nothing I could do about the disgusting fake-wood wardrobe – I couldn't afford a new one – so I'd moved it beside the door where at least you couldn't see it when you first came in. Who knew I was so creative? It was just how I'd imagined it, and I loved it. It was my space. I'd even put a bolt on the door, right up at the top so you wouldn't know it was there, although Mum had noticed almost straight away, with her mental mum-radar. I'd promised I'd never lock it at night, no sirree, so she let me keep it. Obviously I *had* locked it, but she'd never realized.

As always, the first thing I did when I got to my room was turn on my CD player, then close the blinds and turn on my bedside light. (I never used the ceiling light. I preferred to keep some things in the shadows. Deep, *non*?) Next, my school clothes were off and leggings and a mahoosive jumper were on. Relief. I'd just flopped on to my bed for a bout of staring into space when Sasha knocked on my door and poked her head round.

'Computer's free, Ashy,' she cooed. For the record, I hate being called Ashy.

I jumped up from my bed and followed her out of the door. 'You off, then?' I asked. She shook her head, her blonde ponytail bobbing perkily.

'I brought a chicken casserole for supper. Thought Mum deserved a break, you know? Something tells me she doesn't get an awful lot of help when I'm not around.'

I stuck my tongue out at her back. 'Yes, well. Sorry to spoil your fun, but Monday's pizza night. And it's tea, not supper.'

She shrugged. 'Tea, supper. Same difference. And it won't kill you to eat a home-cooked meal on a Monday.'

'My point is,' I said, through gritted teeth, 'Mum doesn't need a break because making a two-minute phone call to order pizza is not exactly hard work.'

'*Whatever*,' sang Sasha, running lightly downstairs, her perfectly manicured nails skimming the banister. I bared my teeth at her as she went into the kitchen to do her good-daughter deed for the day, then I speedily veered off into the back room. I pressed a key to bring the screen to life and quickly logged on to Facebook, where my stomach did a little lurch cos Dylan had accepted my friend request. Whoop! I bashed out a quick message. Well, I say 'bashed'. I spent ten minutes agonizing over the perfect wordage to make it seem like I'd just bashed it out. I ended up with:

> Hey. Good to meet you the other night. Xmas party details: it's on Sat 3rd Dec at the football hut on Bishops Lane – I think Cubs meet there too, if that was ever your thing. Dib dib dib. Ashley.

Oh, be still my splitting sides. But it'd do. I squeezed my eyes shut and clicked Send before I could change my mind. A glance at Dylan's profile told me there wasn't much to see. No status updates or Wall posts to speak of. I wasn't into revealing all on Facebook. Nice to know he had similar standards. I clicked on Info anyway, just to check, like, and almost laughed out loud when I saw his top music, films and TV programmes were pretty much a mirror for mine. You've got to respect a straight guy for having the guts to tell the world that one of his favourite movies is *The Wizard of Oz* (and I knew he was straight, before you go thinking otherwise, cos Donna had asked Marv), and I didn't know anyone else who dug *Family Guy* like I did.

Still smiling to myself, I opened another browser window and checked my emails. The editor of the newspaper had replied as well. Get me, all Ms Popular. She told me her assistant had contacted the old lady, who'd be happy for me to get in touch. Result. Well, no time like the present, *carpe diem* and all that. I picked up my phone and keyed in the lady's phone number.

'Good afternoon. Bridget Harper speaking.' She had literally the poshest voice I'd ever heard. She could have given the Queen a run for her money in the cut-glass stakes.

I cleared my throat. 'Oh hi, my name's Ashley. I think the editor of –'

But she interrupted me. 'Oh yes, hello there. You wanted to interview me about the war for a school project?'

Whoa, no flies on her. She must have been about ninety, but from her voice you'd think she was thirty years younger.

'Yes, if that's OK.'

'Of course. It'll make a nice change. Daytime television is not exactly uplifting.'

Hilarious. I arranged to go to her house ('I assume you're not an axe murderer, dear?') after school in a couple of days, and then quickly ended the call because – *ping!* – I had a reply from Dylan.

Hmm. Was he keen or just efficient? I opened the message with my heart doing little skipettes.

I'll be there! Dylan x

And there, *mes amis*, is the definition of short and sweet. Beaming like an idiot and with jumping beans getting jiggy in my stomach, I texted Donna:

Guess who just messaged
me on fb??

True to form, she called back within approximately 2.8 seconds.

'Told you he liked you.'

I shut down the computer and jogged back up the stairs to my room. I flopped on to my bed, but was too fidgetty. I got up and started pacing instead. 'Don't get excited. He just said he was coming to the party . . . Maybe he fancies *you*.'

She snorted. 'Get off. You know he doesn't.'

'Well, I'm not counting any chickens, babes, but I'll give it a go.'

'Good girl,' she said. 'So what did his message say,

exactly?' And we spent the next twenty minutes until Mum got home from work and called me for tea analysing those four words and an x till they were pretty much imprinted on my very soul. It was all good.

'This looks delicious, Sash,' said Mum, as she got the plates out of the cupboard. I sat at the table in my own little Dylan world while Frankie busied herself Frankie-ishly. She was doing a weird thing with her drink – trying to look at herself in the bottom of the glass or something.

'Sit down, Mum,' scolded Sasha. 'This is my treat. You just relax.' She handed me a bottle of white from the fridge. 'Ashley, pour Mum a glass of wine.'

'Please?'

She rolled her eyes. 'Please.'

I smiled and poured. Nothing could put a downer on my mood.

'So, the casserole is made with chicken from the organic farm down the road from us,' said Sasha busily, as she joined us at the table. 'And the vegetables are from the farmers' market.'

'What about the rice?' I asked, as I carefully picked out all the mushrooms. Horrid sluggy things. 'Grown by a blind, disabled lesbians' co-operative?'

'No, it's Waitrose,' explained Sasha. Not a hint of irony. I raised an eyebrow and tried to catch Frankie's eye, but she was examining the contents of her plate suspiciously. Apart from mushrooms, celery and duck, I'll eat pretty much anything. Frankie: not so much. She liked to know exactly what was in front of her. Even beans on toast had to be broken down into beans and toast. Side by side, not one on top of the other. Stews were food hell for Frankie.

'Mmm umm,' said Mum, rolling her eyes ecstatic-ally as if a mouthful of chicken and veg was just about the pinnacle of joy for her. Maybe it was. It'd been a while since she'd had a boyfriend.

I shovelled in a forkful. 'Yeah, really nice.' Well, it was.

'So, it looks like I might be promoted at work,' said Sasha, in the manner of someone trying to sound like she's making conversation when actually she's just doing a big old boast. 'My manager's moving on to one of the London offices . . . Obviously I haven't been there long, but my record's as good as anyone else's. I definitely have a chance.'

Sasha was an estate agent. Not much more I can say about that, except: *yaaaawn*.

'That's brilliant, Sash,' smiled Mum. 'You and Toby are doing so well.'

Sasha smiled and nodded as she swallowed her mouthful. 'Actually, Toby's up for a sizeable bonus this Christmas. I can't wait to see that cheque!' She rubbed her hands together. 'New kitchen here I come!'

This was how meals with Sasha always panned out. It was rare that me or Frankie got a word in, and normally by this point I'd be on the verge of sticking my fork through my hand to escape the pain of Sasha's mind-numbing blah blah. But not today. Today I had the prospect of Dylan. As she blathered on I smiled serenely while my mind ran showreels of him naked. Tra la laa!

The feel-gooditude carried over into school the next day, where there was a definite giddiness in the air, as if some invisible cosmic button had been pressed and – *bam* – the festive season had started. Or it could just have been the talk in assembly of all the Christmassy type shenanigans the school had planned. Whatever. It was festive cheerarama and among the people that mattered (well, us) the talk was all about Ollie's party, so after school Ol took us to the venue.

Normally we'd have got the bus, but that was before the Ian Incident. Long story short, he was a bus driver I once had a forty-five-minute thing with. I'd seen him most weeks for a few years and always thought he was fit – he wasn't much older than me – and we usually had a laugh. So when we got talking one time, when I was on my way to Donna's and he came on to me, I thought I might as well *carpe* the *diem* and have a go. It was a laugh, but that's as far as it went for me. Unfortunately he had other ideas, and started bombarding me with texts and stalking me on Facebook. God knows how he got my mobile number. Anyway, I hadn't caught a bus for months in case I bumped into him – even my friends had to avoid his usual routes because he always asked them about me. *C'est moi*: the misfit magnet.

So we walked, with Ollie and Jack – who'd managed to hire the hall at mates' rates cos he played for one of the football teams that used it – strutting ahead of us all king of the jungle, like they were a couple of rich kids who swanned around running nightclubs for the lulz, rather than two Year Thirteens with the keys to a footie hut.

'No pressure then,' I said under my breath after Ollie had spent ten minutes bigging the place up till it might as well have been the Moulin bleedin' Rouge.

'I know,' said Sarah. 'You don't think it's going to be all glossy and sporty with, like, big screens everywhere and horrible carpets?' She checked to make sure Ollie couldn't hear us, but he was deep in conversation with Jack. 'And what if it smells like the boys' changing rooms?'

I raised an eyebrow. 'You got intimate experience of that, have you?'

'Oh yeah, me and the Shattock love a tumble among the groin guards,' she deadpanned.

'Ugh, Sar!' Mr Shattock was big and hairy, and liked to wear short shorts. Like, scrotum-huggingly snug. He wasn't sadistic or sexist or any of your other PE-teacher clichés, but he was the least attractive man I had ever met. And that included my bad-seed Uncle Nige with the face tattoos and missing teeth.

We came to a sudden stop outside a low brick building with a metal roof. No worries on the glossy front, then. Jack unlocked the door and we all trooped inside.

It was a biggish rectangular room with scuffed wooden floors, a bar along one wall and space to dance. The walls were kind of yellowy-white with darker stains on them from, I guessed, when you were allowed to smoke indoors. Not a hint of Sky Sports. Yes, it was tatty and, while it didn't stink, you wouldn't want to sniff too hard, but it had potential.

'Hey, this is good!' I said. There were windows all down one side of the room. You could see the sea and the lights from the pier twinkling in the distance.

'Yeah, nice one, mate,' said Rich, checking out the bar appreciatively.

Cass stood in the middle of the room, chewing her lip and looking pathetic. Jack draped his arm round her shoulders. 'All right, isn't it?'

She smiled. 'Yeah. Really good.' I was just thinking that only patting Jack's hand could make her seem any more patronizing and less convincing, when she patted his hand. I swapped knowing looks with Donna and Sarah. It was blatantly obvious that Cass was worried about Adam, her dickhead boyfriend, and what he'd think of a scruffy hut as a party venue. Well, screw him, frankly. As far as I was concerned, Adam not liking something was a pretty freaking cast-iron seal of approval.

'C'mon, babes,' said Sarah, taking hold of Cass's hand and squeezing it. 'It's our last chance to party before all the exams and stuff next term.'

'Yeah, give yourself a break, lady,' added Rich, ruffling her hair. 'Even David Cameron kicks back every now and then . . . like, counting his money and shit.'

I gave him an 'Ooh, edgy' and he gave me the finger. Mature.

'Oi, Jack,' said Donna, seeing Cass starting to look stressed and got-at. 'What are the chances of you sneaking us a free celebratory drinkie?'

'No way!' spluttered Jack. 'There's probably CCTV everywhere.' I sincerely doubted it but, like everyone else, looked up at the ceiling. Nothing.

'Don't sweat it, honeys,' said Rich, pulling a hip flask out of his pocket. 'Have some of mine.'

Sarah's eyes went massive. 'Shit, did you have that

at school all day? What if there'd been a random locker check?'

He shrugged and smiled smugly. 'Well, there wasn't.' He sat down on the floor and we joined him in a little circle. It was pretty cool having the place to ourselves.

'What have we today, then?' asked Donna. 'Lemon liqueur? Cooking sherry?'

Rich looked at her witheringly. 'Baileys, actually.'

'Won't your parents notice Baileys going missing?' asked Cass, taking a sip.

Rich shook his head. 'My mum's got, like, three bottles in for Christmas. I just took a bit from each.'

Cass passed the flask to me. Baileys isn't my beverage of choice – you might as well drink brandy butter – but it was kind of perfect for the situation. Nearly the end of term, Christmas party season on its way . . . Dylan.

'Oh. My. GOD!' squealed Donna, suddenly spotting a large 1950s-diner-style jukebox next to the bar. She ran over and called back: 'Quick, I need 50p pieces.' We all had a rummage and offered up a few. 'Any requests?' she asked, as she scrolled through the options. But before we could respond she went, 'AGH, I haven't heard this one in ages!' then put one of the coins into the slot and pressed three buttons. Within seconds our ears were assaulted by an onslaught of sleigh bells.

'Ooh, I LOVE this one!' whooped Cass, clapping her hands, while the rest of us loudly protested.

'Don, what the hell?' I asked, hoping it hadn't been my money that had paid for this horrible piece of novelty Christmas shit.

Donna bashed the jukebox. 'NO! That's not what I chose!' She turned to us. 'It wasn't, I swear! I picked Dizzee Rascal.'

'Right. We believe you,' grinned Ollie. He jumped to his feet and grabbed Cass's hand. 'Dance with me,' he said, and he started leaping and jerking like someone had plugged him in. I've never met a boy who's as up for a dance as Ollie. Not even Rich who, not wanting to stereotype or nuffink, isn't necessarily the most heterosexual of people. Cass didn't need asking twice. You wouldn't think it to look at her, with her aura of neatness and good girl-itude, but Cass is a wicked dancer. The girl can bust moves with the best of them. Which, sadly, wasn't the rest of us. But we didn't care. The song wasn't halfway through before we were all bouncing around like loons.

'Whoop!' went Rich, grabbing on to the back of my jacket to start a conga. Cheesy choons need cheesy actions, and, anyway, who wants to be a party pooper? I grabbed Donna's jumper, she grabbed Ollie, who got hold of Sarah, who nabbed Cass, who grabbed Jack and *voilà*: we were in a mini conga of seven, high-kicking around the room and bellowing along to the music like we'd been possessed by the spirit of Christmas kitsch. Anyone spotting us through the window might well have felt the need to summon the men in white coats, but whatever. We were totally sharing a moment, man.

Afterwards we collapsed on the (none too clean) floor and lay starfished and heavy-breathing, letting the good feeling settle around us like feathers after a pillow fight. I closed my eyes and tried to block everything out except this moment. Tomorrow Mum was dragging me and Frankie to Sasha and Toby's for a 'pre-Christmas celebration meal' after school, where I'd feel out of place and fidgety. They were my family, but I didn't fit in. Alone with my best friends in a random building, discovering a real-life old-school jukebox, totally comfortable to look like idiots in front of each other: these were the kind of moments my life was about.

Thinking about tomorrow had broken the moment. I sat up and hugged my knees, the movement making the others look my way. We caught each other's eyes and smiled.

2

I tried not to be a moody cow in the car on the way to Sasha and Toby's the next day, but it was hard. I don't know why Mum kept insisting I join them on these family things. It's not as if I did anything except sit at the end of the sofa staring into space.

'I wonder what Sasha's making for dinner?' said Mum, in a valiant attempt at conversation. I shrugged and looked out of the window.

'Hope it's not that thing she made before,' piped up Frankie from the back. 'Why would anyone put apricots in a stew?'

'It's Moroccan, love,' said Mum.

Franks sniffed. 'That's no excuse.'

I smiled to myself. Thank God for Frankie.

Half an hour later we arrived at Sasha's house, which was nestled among the rest of the identical houses on the posh estate. I swear it was like a Lego town.

'Hellooo!' she sang, as she swung open the front door. She and Mum hugged and kissed, then she hugged Frankie and gave me a little wave from over

Franks's shoulder. Even though I'd never actually told her I wasn't up for huggage, she never went there. Fair enough. In her defence, I'd never been the most affectionate person in the world.

'Something smells good,' said Mum, as she handed Sasha her coat.

'It's Poulet à l'Orange,' she replied in a totally non-ironic French accent. I smirked at Frankie, who put her hands to her throat and mimed retching. Fruit and meat again: hilarious. At that moment Toby strode through from the kitchen, wiping his hands on his apron. (Yes, he was wearing an apron. It had 'Danger: Man Cooking!' written on it. I'm saying nothing.)

'Hello, hello,' he said, leaning in to give Mum a kiss on the cheek. 'Lovely to see you.'

'Come through to the lounge,' said Sasha. She turned to Toby. 'Sweetheart, will you bring the nibbles through?' He gave her a salute, winked at Frankie as if to say *I am SO satirical*, and strode back into the kitchen.

My sister's living room was huge, with massive maroon sofas, a wooden coffee table and nothingy pictures on the magnolia walls: a black-and-white poster of a tree in a misty field, a close-up of a rose, a photo of her and Toby on a windswept beach. A small Christmas tree sat on the table between the two sofas, and a TV was embedded into one of the walls. I happened to know it was cinema surround-sound, because Toby had told us approximately eighty-four times when they first got it. The whole room was almost supernaturally neat and tidy. As we all sat down, Toby came in juggling two bowls of crisps and a pile of small plates. 'Kettle Chips,' he said, I guess just to make sure that – God forbid – we didn't think they were your basic Tesco ready-salted. I took a handful and leant back on the sofa.

'Don't forget your plate.' Sasha held one out to me.

'Right. Thanks.' I took it and, with a massive effort of will, even managed not to roll my eyes.

'How was work today, Sash?' asked Mum.

'Not bad, actually. Still no news about that new job, but we've got four more properties on our books this week alone, so that's good anyway.' She smiled bravely. I can't say I was that sympathetic – it was her choice to become an estate agent during a recession, even if it was at a top-end place, selling multi-million-pound piles to bankers and company directors. I did kind of envy her being able to nosy around those mansions, with their indoor swimming pools and gyms and proper home cinemas like you see on *Cribs*, although the sucking up to rich people I could do without. I did enough of that myself at Mum's shop. Whatever I decided to do with my life – even if I did end up making films – I would never, ever treat people as if they were better than me just because they had money. Everyone's equal, that's my motto. Or would be if I had a motto, which I don't.

Mum nodded sympathetically. 'It is hard. I'm definitely getting more people making appointments, but so far that hasn't translated into a rise in sales.' And she and Sasha proceeded to talk business for the next ten minutes, while Frankie and I made faces at each other and took turns doing comedy yawns. I would have put the telly on, but I couldn't see the remote and I couldn't be bothered to get up to find it. Anyway, Sasha and Toby had about fifty million channels and I could never work out which button to press to get anything other than a snowstorm.

But then Toby came back in to announce that dinner was served, and we were saved. Sasha had really gone for it with the festive cheer in the dining room. There were streamers festooned around the ceiling and a huge Christmas tree by the double doors out to the garden. On the table was a salad bowl filled with glass baubles (bet you a million pounds she got that idea from one of her magazines) and Christmassy place mats with a cracker beside each one. Muted carols coming from the tiny state-of-the-art stereo on the dresser were the finishing touch. *sigh* How *lovely*, as Mum put it.

33

I mean, I didn't mind it. It didn't offend me or anything. I'm not a total tosser. It was just Sasha. She stood there with a smug half-smile on her face as if to say: *now THIS is how you do Christmas*. It just wouldn't have crossed her mind that her way was anything other than the right way. It was like the plate thing in the living room. Did she really think I was such a cretin that I couldn't manage a few crisps without spraying crumbs everywhere? A rhetorical question, obviously.

Anyway, *la la la*. Ignoring her, I sat down at the table, choosing the chair nearest the door.

'Oh . . .' Sasha bit her lip. 'No, that's OK.'

'What?' I asked, my arse hovering above the seat.

'No, it's fine. You were supposed to be sitting over here, but I don't suppose it matters.' She indicated a chair two further along from the one I'd chosen.

I raised an eyebrow. 'Sure it's OK?'

She nodded firmly. 'Absolutely. You go for it.' Okaaay. Exhaling loudly, I sat down and poured a large glass of wine, then started to fill the three other wine glasses. Franks had been given a tumbler.

'Not for me, thanks,' said Mum, covering her glass with her hand. 'I'm driving, aren't I?'

Sasha gave her a sympathetic look. 'Such a shame you can't stay over.' Toby appeared in the doorway carrying plates and she went over to take them from him, saying to me on the way, 'Ash, maybe it's time you started thinking about driving lessons? It'd be such a help to Mum.'

I cleared my throat. 'Great idea, Sasha. You going to pay for them, are you?'

She gave me a look. 'You could always save up.'

'With what? I work for free, don't I?' I cast my eyes to Mum. 'Not that I'm complaining.'

Sasha didn't respond to that, but took the opportunity of exchanging a meaningful glance with Mum on her way back to the kitchen. I didn't give a shit. They were always doing it.

Toby sat down beside me – presumably where Sasha had told him to sit.

'All right?' I asked, as he put his napkin on his lap and shuffled his chair closer to the table.

'Fine, thanks.' He gave me a brief smile, then turned his attention to Mum. 'Karen, has Sash told you about our holiday plans . . .?'

Great. I left them to it and picked up my cracker. I held it out to Franks and she peered at it doubtfully, like it might blow at any second.

'SAAAASH?' she yelled, without taking her eyes off it. 'CAN WE DO THE CRACKERS?'

Sasha ran from the kitchen to poke her head round the door. 'Give me two secs, OK? I'm just getting the potatoes out.'

Franks grinned at me and we posed, cracker at the ready.

'Oh, very funny, you two,' said Sasha, as she came in with the spuds. 'I don't think it's unreasonable to expect us all to be seated before we pull the crackers.' She was smiling, but there was a glint of steel in her eye. The girl was going to have a heart attack by the time she was thirty if she carried on like this. She needed to chill out.

And then I accidentally pulled the cracker. It must have been the world's most hair-trigger snapper ever, cos my arm involuntarily jerked and BANG, off it went. Scared the shit out of me. 'Oh. Sash. I'm really sorry. It was an accident, I swear.' I tried to look sincere but I couldn't help it. The look on her face was too much. She pursed her lips.

'Don't worry about it. I didn't really expect anything else, Ashley, to be perfectly honest with you.'

'Oh, come on. Take a chill pill,' I said, my cheeks aching with the effort of not laughing in her face. 'It's just a cracker.'

'Yes, thank you. I'm well aware of what it is.' She sat down and rubbed her forehead in agitation. Toby started stroking her back, but he didn't even look at me, leaving the job of having a go at me to Mum.

'Honestly, Ashley. Grow up,' she snapped. 'And

stop bloody giggling. It's infantile.' Ooh, long word from Mum there.

'Look, I'm sorry, Sasha. It really was an accident,' I said, widening my eyes as if that would prove my innocence in the whole affair. Crackergate, if you will. 'I honestly didn't mean to.'

She sat up straighter in her chair and flexed her shoulders. 'Apology accepted. Maybe I was being a bit precious . . .' She smiled brightly and ever so slightly like a scary housewife robot. 'Now, who wants potatoes?'

Phew, crisis averted. I rolled my eyes at Frankie, who giggled into her glass of OJ.

'So, Frankie, how's school?' asked Toby, twinkling away at my little sister. 'Did you sort out that business with your maths test being marked wrong?'

Weirdly, Toby and Frankie got on really well. They always had. Toby and I used to get on, but not any more, and for one reason or another he probably found it as difficult to talk to me as I did to him, but he was supposedly the adult in this scenario. A bit of small talk wouldn't have killed him. Anyway, my sister was an excellent cook (of course) and her orangey chicken was amazing, as was the chocolate mousse for pudding, so I was happy enough to sit and guzzle in silence while Franks flirted with Toby, and Sasha and Mum wittered on about whatever it was they wittered on about.

By the time we'd polished off coffee and posh chocolate mints it was half eight and, although we only lived about forty-five minutes away, Frankie was beginning to fidget. She was a bit OCD about being up past ten.

Mum patted her belly. 'Whew, I'm stuffed. Wonderful food as ever, Sash.'

'Any time, Mum. You know that. I wish we lived closer so I could help out a bit more.' She put her head on one side and smiled *comme une* saint. Mum smiled back and checked her watch.

'I suppose we'd better be off . . .'

Out in the hall, our coats appeared in Sasha's arms as if by magic.

'Thanks for dinner,' I said, all polite-like. 'Amazing food.'

Sasha put her hand on her chest as if she'd had a severe shock. 'Oh! Well, Ashley. I'm honoured! And you're welcome.'

Oh, piss off, you sarcastic bitch is not what I said, much as I wanted to.

Mum rubbed her hands together. 'So, we'll see you on Christmas Day!' Then, in unison, she and Sasha both squealed: 'Only twelve more sleeps!'

Give. Me. Strength. Christmas I could take or leave. Two was the magic number for me. It was only two days till Ollie's party: only two days till I'd see

Dylan again. The thought was enough to get me through the journey home.

But first I had my interview with Bridget. I hadn't realized how nervous I was. Just thinking about it made me need a poo. (Sorry, but it did.) The interview wasn't everything, but if Bridge came up with the goods I reckoned it'd definitely be worth a few extra marks for my project. I'd arranged to borrow a camera and microphone from school and spent the whole of the next day's media studies experimenting with positioning, light sources and sound, and generally making sure I knew exactly how to use it all without cocking up/looking like a tit. During the free period after lunch I worked out what questions I'd ask, and by the end of the day I was pretty sure I was sorted. But still, I felt weirdly nervous. This documentary had to be tickety-effing-boo if I stood any kind of chance of getting into film school. I wasn't used to caring this much about school work. It was kind of nice, if slightly stressful. A quick vodka and Coke would have sorted me out, but breathing alcohol fumes over your interviewee is possibly not best practice.

I bumped into Cass and Sarah on my way out of school.

'All right, Ash, how come you're round this side?'

(I usually left school through the teachers' car park cos it was closer to my house.)

I walked backwards for a bit so I could talk without stopping. 'Got to interview an old lady for my media studies coursework.'

'Oh. Right.' Sarah crinkled her forehead. 'How very committed of you, Ashley.'

I did a false little laugh. 'Yeah, well. Can't be a slacker all my life . . . Anyway, I'm a bit late so have a good night, yeah?' And without waiting for their answer I started sprinting in the direction of Bridget's road. I felt bad about keeping this film-school stuff from my friends, especially Donna, but the stakes were too high. I wasn't about to lay my soul bare for something that might never happen. Best just to keep shtum. She'd understand.

I'd printed out directions to Bridget's and left way too much time, so I got there twenty minutes early. Just long enough to really start shitting myself (not literally) about what was to come. I spent the time walking up and down the tree-lined avenue and going over the interview in my head. Or at least I tried to, but the big old houses kept distracting me. It wasn't quite dark and hardly anyone had drawn their curtains yet, giving me a Technicolor view of large living rooms, big soft leather sofas, colourful rugs and bookshelves crammed with books. It was that kind of road. Most of the houses had been done up, with new windows and Audis and 4x4s in the drive, but Bridget's looked rundown, with peeling paintwork and weeds sprouting through the paving in the front path.

With five minutes to go I rang the doorbell and waited bloody ages before I heard footsteps and fumbling on the other side. A textbook little old lady opened the door, complete with long white hair tied up in a bun. She would have looked like Mrs Pepperpot, except she was wearing trousers and a blouse and her face was caked in make-up. Every wrinkle was magnified a million times by the fact that it was grouted with foundation, and the muted pink lipstick would have been subtle if it hadn't run into the wrinkles around her mouth like felt tip on kitchen roll.

'Ashley, I presume?' she said, smiling and holding out her hand.

'Nice to meet you, uh, Mrs Harper,' I replied, shaking her hand. It was weird. I was feeling shy — there's no other way of putting it. And I was never shy. Maybe it was because I didn't know any old people — not proper ancient like Bridget, anyway. I was intimidated by both her massively long life and her closeness to death. Was that wrong of me? I dunno.

Anyway, she pooh-poohed my formality with a wave of her hand.

'Oh. Call me Bridget, dear. I would have to call you Miss Greene otherwise, and I can't be doing with that.' (Yes, my name's Ashley Greene. And no, I'm not a vampire. Can we move on?) *Cahn't be doing with thet.* I dug her accent, big time. She led me into the house and I noticed for the first time that she was leaning heavily on a walking stick.

Her house was incredible – like a museum of the Fifties. The wallpaper was peeling and had damp spots on it, and the carpet (complete with eye-spinning swirly patterns) was threadbare, but I loved it. I mean, this was proper old. The place was practically haunted with history and stories. You could imagine the sound of kids running through, and parties, and family jokes and arguments. The fact that it was so quiet now was kind of unbearably sad.

As if she'd read my mind, Bridget turned slowly round to face me and said, 'Obviously the house is far too big for one person, and the echoes can be a bit much sometimes, but I can't bear to leave.' She closed her eyes and smiled. 'Lots of memories . . .' She opened them again and looked at me, her eyes dark brown and clear and not at all like you'd imagine an old person's to be. 'I'm very lucky.' Or, in other words, *don't go feeling sorry for me just because I'm old. I've seen things you've never even imagined, girlie.* Or that's what I took her to mean. I liked her already.

Her living room wasn't as much of a museum piece, in that it had been kitted out with a big telly and an armchair that whirred and tilted so she could sit on it without bending, then whirred back down again until she was sitting with her feet up on a raised footrest. Next to the chair was a small table covered with books, a magnifying glass, a TV guide, a box of tissues, a pot of pens . . . and that's just what I could see. *Countdown* was on the telly, but she'd turned the sound off.

'You can film me here, if that's all right with you,' she said, as she shifted in her chair. She winced. 'I broke my pelvis a few years ago and it hasn't been right since, so sitting's just about all I'm good for these days.'

'No, that's great,' I said, starting to unpack my stuff. I paused and looked around the room. 'Would it be OK if I moved your lamps about a bit? I'll put them back, obviously.' I laughed nervously.

'You do what you like, dear.' She pointed the remote control at the telly and turned the sound back on, leaving me to faff about with the camera kit. 'Let me know when you're ready . . . Oh!' She put gnarly fingertips against her forehead. 'I haven't offered you a cup of tea! I'm terribly sorry. The kettle and what-not are in the kitchen – I'm afraid you'll have to help yourself.'

'That's OK, I'm fine,' I said. 'Um, unless you'd like me to make you one?' As soon as I'd said it I wished I hadn't. Offering to make a stranger a cup of tea in their own house is pretty freaking weird, even if said stranger is about two hundred years old.

But she clasped her hands together, her rings clacking. 'Do you know, I'd love one. How thoughtful of you.' She beamed at me, and suddenly I wanted her to like me, which sounds stupid but there it is.

'Carry on along the hallway – you'll see the kitchen,' she continued. 'Feel free to have a root around, although I think all the tea-making apparatus are already out. You might find some biscuits in a cupboard somewhere, although heaven knows how old they'll be. I used to buy them when my grandchildren came to visit, but my son and his partner moved to New Zealand a while ago.' She cleared her throat and scratched her eyelid. 'Anyway. Help yourself.' And she turned her attention back to *Countdown*.

Apart from the fridge, oven and an ancient microwave, the kitchen was a total time-warp. The units were covered in peeling orange vinyl and the wallpaper had a daisy pattern on it. There was even a larder with some ancient-looking packets and jars behind the cornflakes, bread, butter dish and tins of soup and beans. I had a quick snoop around while the kettle was boiling, but I wanted to get going on the interview so I bunged a couple of teabags in two mugs, sloshed in the water and milk (giving it a ginger sniff first) and carried them back through to the living room. I'd forgotten to ask Bridget if she took sugar, but I figured she'd have told me if she did.

A few minutes later I was ready to go. 'OK.' I cleared my throat and made sure my notes were assembled on the floor in front of me so I could read them without picking them up. I didn't want rustling noises on the film. I took a breath and pressed Record.

'Bridget, tell me about your near-death experience? It was during the war, wasn't it . . .?'

So Bridget told me her story. She spoke slowly and quietly, but her voice was clear as you like. She'd obviously told it before.

'It was in nineteen forty, Saturday, September the fourteenth,' she said. 'My sister Susan and I lived with our parents here in Brighton. It was about half past three in the afternoon. I remember Susan and I were playing cards, and she'd been getting cross with me because I wouldn't let her win even though she was younger than me. Unbeknownst to us, at that moment a German pilot was being chased by an Allied Spitfire right above Kemp Town, where we lived. The pilot thought he'd have a better chance of getting away if he made his aeroplane lighter, so he released all his bombs at once . . . Well, you can imagine the devasta-tion.' She stopped and took an agonizingly slow sip of tea.

'The first thing I remember is a pure, bright light surrounding me, and a feeling of utter calm. I started to follow Susan, who was walking away from me, but she looked back and shook her head. She looked quite cross, which at the time I assumed was still related to the card game. Next thing I knew, the light was replaced by a feeling of intense pain spreading through my body. I was confused and very fright-ened, but a nurse appeared and told me not to worry. She said a bomb had exploded in our street, flatten-ing our house, that I was in hospital and that I was extremely lucky to be alive.'

She stopped talking. Without looking at my notes, I said, 'And what happened to the rest of your family?'

Without pause, she said: 'Susan was killed, as was my mother. My father was out at the time and was unhurt. Fifty-two people died in all, including my best friend.' She smiled sadly. 'I lost my mother, my sister and my best friend in the space of a few min-utes, but that's war for you I suppose.'

This was so much more than a story about a near-death experience. I forgot about the camera and became . . . embroiled, I guess, in her sadness and the horror of what she went through. Of course, I couldn't help thinking of Frankie, and Donna, and what I would do if they died. Ignoring the wetness in my eyes, I said: 'I don't know what I'd do if that happened to me. How do you get through it?'

Bridget coughed and pulled a tissue from the box on the table beside her. 'You just do, dear. The grief never goes away, but over time one learns to handle it. Susan was twelve when she died and for a long time I felt terribly guilty that I had survived and she hadn't. I took some comfort from the fact that she probably felt no pain, as I had felt nothing while I was experiencing the bright light and whatnot.'

'What do you think the bright light was?' I asked.

She shook her head. 'I don't know. The rational part of me understands that it was probably chemical processes as my brain et cetera started shutting down, but . . .' She paused. 'I don't know.'

'Do you believe in heaven?'

She smiled. 'Now that's a big question, another to which I don't know the answer. I am agnostic, and I'm afraid that's as far as I can go.'

I checked my notes, but most of the questions seemed irrelevant now, and the others had already been answered one way or another. 'One last question. How do you feel about war?' I asked. 'Did your experience change your opinion?'

Bridget looked thoughtful for a moment. 'Well,

you have to remember that I was only fifteen at the time, and we were all taught to believe that Britain was strong and that we were all fighting together for our future freedom.' She waved a hand in ironic emphasis. 'So in that sense, yes, the scales rather fell from my eyes that day. But now . . .?' She shrugged. 'War is a fact of life.'

I switched the camera off and put it down on the floor beside my chair, then picked up my notes and pretended to look through them. 'I think that's everything.' I paused. 'Thanks, Bridget . . . I'm so . . .' I searched for a word that wouldn't sound completely wanky, but couldn't find one so stuck with my original choice, '*honoured* that you shared your story with me.'

'Well now, you're very welcome, Ashley. Thank you for letting me share it with you.' She smiled expectantly. I wanted to burst into tears and tell her that life is hard, and for her to shake her head and say she understood, and then for her to ask me to stay longer so she could tell me more about her life, but the interview was over. And, anyway, that would have been weird.

So I packed up my things, took the mugs into the kitchen and gave them a rinse, then said goodbye.

As I walked home I wondered what Bridget would be doing now. Would she be watching telly again, our conversation forgotten? Or would she be sitting in her silent room, thinking about the past? About me? The interview couldn't really have gone better, but for some reason I didn't feel happy. The only way I can think of to describe it is like the feeling you get when you think you've offended someone you care about, but aren't sure how. I should have been feeling excited about the direction my film was taking, but instead I trudged home and thought black-holey thoughts about death.

Next morning I sat in biology willing the clock to move. I'd persuaded Donna – star of A2 theatre studies and properly talented actor – to read some real near-death experiences in different accents, which I was going to use as voiceovers to photos I'd cribbed from books and magazines. I was meeting her in the editing suite (yup, editing suite – that's how cool *I* am) at lunchtime, but time seemed to be on strike. I could have sworn it was 9.15 for about twenty minutes.

But approximately 349 years later lunchtime at last rolled round, and I practically sprinted to meet Donna. She was already there, poring over the stories I'd given her to read, mouth moving as she practised the words.

'Oh, all right?' she said, the noise of the door making her look up. She held the pile of stories upright and banged it on the table, neatening the edges. 'Ready when you are.'

I felt kind of giggly at the idea of recording Donna speaking in funny accents, but she obviously didn't, so I didn't let on. It was profesh all the way.

'So . . .' I cleared my throat. 'What accents are you going to do?'

'Well, this one says she lives in London, so I'll just use my normal voice.' She held up the story at the top of the pile. 'Then I thought I'd do Scottish, Irish, Manchester and Posh for the others.'

'Wow, can you do all those?' I asked. I couldn't do a Scottish accent if you held a gun to my head.

'Yeah, course,' she said, looking scornful.

'OK. Well . . . let's do this.' I got the computer ready to record, then moved away so Donna could scooch up to the mic. 'Ready?' She nodded, and I reached over and clicked on the Record button.

'Four years ago I was involved in a car accident . . .' she began. It was her, but not. Her voice was older and softer – you could totally believe that this person had been through a traumatic experience. Halfway through, in the part of the story where the narrator talks about losing her mum in the accident, tears came to Donna's eyes and she choked up. I had to turn away and pretend to be making notes. She was brilliant, but the emotion embarrassed me.

Which I know says more about me than it does about her.

But, as Donna worked her way through the stories, I started getting excited. I started to let myself believe that my film was going to be good. Perhaps even really good. It was a dangerous place to be, but I couldn't help it.

'Thanks, Don, that was amazing,' I said, as she nailed the final story in one take (it was about a girl who nearly drowned, weirdly enough).

'No probs,' she said. 'Are we done? Can we eat now?' She stood up, stuffed her coat through her bag strap and flung her bag over her shoulder, putting about a gazillion-pounds'-worth of editing kit in serious jeopardy.

'Yeah.' I frowned at the computer screen as I saved and backed up the files. 'You go ahead. I'll see you there.' As she walked out the door I yelled after her, 'And get me a jacket potato with cheese, will you?' She gave me the finger behind her back, which I translated as *Of course, it'd be my pleasure.* Smiling, I logged off the computer and gathered together all the bits of paper that Donna had left strewn over the floor. A good day. And it was Friday. And tomorrow was Ollie's party. *smiley face*

3

Cass's bedroom looked like Katie Price's after a wardrobe clear-out. Fake fur and animal print everywhere. I think it was Donna's idea to dress up as bad-taste cave girls for Ollie's (not even fancy-dress) party. Totally a crappily disguised excuse to show some skin in tiger print, but hey, at least it was warm. Actually, now I come to think of it, it must have been Donna's idea, cos she's the one who spent hours on eBay bidding for cave-girly stuff. And we weren't entirely going the Jordan route. Like, I was wearing black Doc Marten boots and a zebra-print tutu, and I'd tied my hair into a messy topknot and wrapped a leopard-print scarf round my head. Granted, Cass had bought a tight little leopard-print number and matching heels, but she had Adam and his, shall we say, traditional sensibilities to think about. He didn't have to dress up to be Neanderthal. Ha ha.

Donna was looking fierce (I know, I'm on fire) in tiger-print wedges, black tights and a leopard-print playsuit, and Sarah managed to look chic (which was cheating, but she kind of couldn't look bad taste if

she tried) in a zebra-print shift dress. After a couple
of hours of whirlwind getting-ready action we stood
in what can only be described as awed silence in front
of Cass's mirrored wardrobe.

'We look amazing!' breathed Sarah, turning to the
side and smoothing her dress. 'My legs look so *long*!
Like, I'm never wearing anything but zebra print ever
again.' She lowered her voice to a dramatic whisper.
'It's . . . *magic*.'

'I think it's the length of the frock, babes,' said
Donna, laughing. 'You should do mini more often.'

Cass held her hair up at the back. 'Do you think
it'd look better like this?' she asked. 'I look kind of
boring.'

We all contemplated Cass's barnet, currently loose
and GHD'd to within an inch of its poker-straight
life. Donna chose an elastic out of the box on Cass's
bed and moved behind her. 'Why don't you tie it up
like this, then backcomb it?' she said, using her fingers to pull Cass's hair back into a messy ponytail.

'Yeah, then put loads of eyeliner on. With your
pale eyes it'll look amazing. Really dramatic,' I added.

She didn't look convinced. Sarah bumped her
gently with her shoulder. 'Go on, Adam won't be able
to keep his eyes off you.'

Cass's face lit up. 'You reckon?'

'Totally,' we all said seriously. It was tragic that

Adam was her barometer, but what could you do? So she let Donna work her magic. The effect was kind of startling. She looked tasteful and edgy at the same time – like herself, only fiercer. She looked in the mirror and instantly stood taller.

'See?' said Donna, folding her arms with satisfaction. 'Gorgeous.'

Cass blushed and smiled. 'Thanks, Don, you're so clever.'

'You know it,' said Donna briskly, although she was loving the compliment. 'Oop, someone's got a text.'

We all reached for our respective phones. 'It's me,' I said, then groaned. It was from the bus driver with designs on me.

> Jus thinking bout u!
> maybe go 4 a drink soon?
> Let me no whens a good
> time!!

'What is it?' asked Donna.

'Ian the Stalker,' I said. 'Wants to go for a drink.'

'Oh, super,' said Sarah, who was still turning this way and that in front of the mirror. 'You going to arrange that then?'

'Ha ha.' I deleted the message.

Donna lit up the screen on her phone to check the

time. 'Nearly half eight . . . Shall we?' And after a few minutes speed-tidying Cass's room (she did have another weakness after all: being a neat freak) we trooped outside. Linking arms, Donna-then-Cass-then-me-then-Sarah, we walked to the party. We pissed off a few people who had to walk in the road to get past us, but we were too hyped to care. And I couldn't freaking wait to see Dylan. That whole day the thought of it had been giving me these little jolts of excitement, even though I couldn't quite believe he'd actually turn up. Obviously I hadn't mentioned it to the others. I mean, Donna knew, but she was my best mate. I don't do full disclosure; that way, when it all goes wrong, you're in a position to look like you never cared that much in the first place.

'Wow.'

Sarah said it, but we all thought it. The inside of the football hut had been transformed from a scabby, sweat-stained drinking den into a Christmassy grotto. Someone had strung fairy lights around the room and across the front of the bar. There were tea lights in empty jam jars clustered in groups on the window sills, and mini Christmas trees covered in tiny white baubles sat at either end of the bar.

Ollie came up behind us as we stood admiring his venue. 'Like it?'

'It's amazing,' said Cass. She turned to him. 'Who did it?'

He didn't even try to look hurt that we assumed it was nothing to do with him. 'My cousin's an interior designer . . . Shiiit, look at you!' He'd only just noticed our outfits? No girl would ever take that long. He nodded appreciatively, his gaze lingering on Sarah's legs. She totally noticed, too, but she wasn't going there. She'd just got over a bad experience with some posh London student who'd only been after some no-strings sex. Which would have been OK if she hadn't lost her V-plates to him, then promptly fallen in love with him. Anyway, the upshot was that she was making up for her temporary lapse in judgement by swearing off all boys. Even this one, who was officially a lovely guy and, if you ask me, had a bit of a soft spot for our Sarah. I didn't get her at all but, y'know, pfft. Whatever.

Ollie called Jack and Rich over to admire our out-fits. Rich whistled through his teeth. 'Whit-woo, ladies,' he said. 'You . . . actually look totally stunning.' He smiled slowly as he took in the full effect of our animal-print onslaught.

I raised an eyebrow. 'No need to sound quite so surprised.'

'Well, when you're usually such dogs . . .' His gaze stopped at Sarah's legs. 'Whoa . . . What. Are. *They??*' She giggled happily and blushed.

Meanwhile, Jack was taking in the new sex-bomb Cass. 'You look amazing,' he told her, smiling almost shyly.

'Thanks. You look nice too,' she said, smiling back. I cleared my throat and looked around for Dylan. While I could obviously have spent ALL NIGHT LONG listening to my friends being told how fabulous they looked, I hoped the highlight of my evening was very much still to come.

'I don't think they're here yet,' said Donna, watching me crane my neck to look over the sea of people. God knows how Ollie knew them all. Maybe he didn't. She nodded towards the bar. 'Drink?'

Brilliant idea. Cass and Sarah stopped simpering long enough to tell us what they wanted, and we weaved through the masses – getting a few compliments of our own, thanks very much – to do the honours.

At the bar we leant on the counter, picking from the snack bowls that had been evenly spaced along it, I guessed by the interior-designer cousin. 'You look incredible, by the way,' said Donna, without looking at me.

I swallowed a mouthful of salted peanuts. 'So do you, babes. At least as gorgeous as Miss Monogamy and Saintly Sarah back there.'

'Yeah.'

'Yeah.'

And, having successfully put the world to rights, we got back to stuffing our faces while we waited for the fat old barman with the extrovert arse-crack to notice us.

'Do you think he comes with the place?' asked Donna, nodding at said dude.

'He must do. Who'd choose him?' Appearances aren't everything and all, but c'mon: the man was clinically obese. Every time he bent down to get something out of the fridge I was seriously worried it'd be the last thing he ever did. I didn't want a dead barman on my conscience, so next time he puffed and wheezed his way down to fridge-level, I shouted, 'While you're down there, can we get five Becks and two cranberry-juice mixers?' He nodded – and we got served next. I love it when a plan comes together.

'Nice work,' said Donna appreciatively, and we carried the drinks back to the others. Adam had turned up, and was slouched in his chair, legs spread like a football pundit. Great.

'Hi, Adam,' I said. 'What a rare treat.'

He shrugged. 'Yeah, well.' I waited for the rest, but apparently that was it. Oscar Wilde, eat your heart out. Donna and I exchanged a look and put down the drinks, but Cass already had one. She smiled apologetically. Adam always did this: went straight to the bar and bought himself and Cass a drink, thereby avoiding getting his round in.

''S OK, I'll have it,' I said, and glugged it in one. Waiting for Dylan was making me nervous.

'What do you think of Cass's outfit then, Adam?' asked Donna, sitting down beside him and leaning in companionably.

He sniffed and ran his hand through his hair. 'My Cassie always looks gorgeous, don't you, babe?' He patted his knee and Cass moved across to sit on his lap. Next he'd be asking her to lie down for doggy treats. (Hmm, *that* sounds ruder than I meant it to.) He stroked his hand up her thigh and under her skirt. Right up her skirt.

Rich put his head on one side. 'Hmm. Where have I heard this song before? I can't quite put my finger on it. Adam – can you put your finger on it?' Donna snorted into her drink and I turned away so Cass wouldn't see me laughing.

Ollie rubbed at an imaginary mark on the table. 'Tsch, this wood needs touching up. Anyone else got wood . . . that needs touching up?' And then we were all chortling away into our drinks, trying not to catch each other's eye in case we did full-on hysteria.

Adam took his hand out from under Cass's skirt and – I swear I'm not making this up – wiped it on his jeans, then pushed her off his knee. 'C'mon, babe, we're going. I didn't come here to have the piss taken out of me by a bunch of kids.' (Have I mentioned that Adam is all of twenty-one? Like, such a grown-up.)

'Aw, don't go, hon,' wheedled Sarah, grabbing Cass's hand. 'I was looking forward to us all having a dance.'

Cass opened her mouth to speak, but Adam cut her off. 'She's coming with me.'

And then suddenly, out of the blue and even further out of character, Jack banged his bottle down hard, so we all had to leap to stop ours from falling over. 'When are you going to stop being so controlling, mate?' (He said 'mate' exactly as if it was another word for 'you total and utter penis'.)

'I'm sorry, what did you say to me?' Adam put on that kind of mock-confused, wrinkled-forehead thing, which you just know is going to end up with someone getting punched.

Donna tried to step in, but Jack put his hand up to stop her. He looked Adam right in the eye and kept his voice super low and even. 'I said: stop being so controlling. She's a person, not your pet dog.'

Cass put her arm protectively round Adam's waist and said loudly, 'Don't talk to him like that.' Two high spots of colour had appeared in her cheeks, but I couldn't tell if she was angry or embarrassed or what. Anyway, it so wasn't like her to raise her voice and Jack kind of reeled back as if she'd slapped him. So Adam took his chance and went in for the kill.

'Piss off, pretty boy,' he snarled. 'I can't blame you for wanting to bone my girlfriend – she's hot. But ask yourself this: why would she want a boy when she can have a real man?' He turned his back on us and then, draping his arm heavily round Cass's shoulders so she was squooshed into his side, steered her away from the table and towards the door. She looked back briefly, longingly, but he jerked her shoulder and she turned away again.

Rich exhaled loudly. 'Whew. Nice guy.'

Jack had sat back down but was clenching his bottle so tightly that his knuckles had gone white. Sarah put her hand over his. 'You were right to say something.'

He tugged at his hair. 'What's she *doing* with him? She's gorgeous and funny and clever. And he's . . . he's just an idiot.' He shook his head and you just knew he was thinking: *And now she hates me*. The rest of us eyed each other over Jack's head. He'd been in love with her for as long as any of us had known him. Like, it was never said. But we knew. Cass knew too, although she pretended she didn't.

So Jack, the poor bastard, who could have had pretty

much anyone he wanted because he was a buff foot-
baller with brains and a sense of humour, had never
had a shag. He wanted the big event, when it happened,
to 'mean something', and he thought it would only
mean something with Cass. Which, apart from being
IMHO a pointless way to live your life, meant that Jack
was probably going to die a virgin.

Ollie drained his beer and wiped his mouth with
the back of his hand. 'You're right, mate,' he said.
'The man's a wanker. And Cass'll get over this. She
won't hold it against you.'

'That's what I'm worried about,' said Jack grimly,
and we all laughed. The corners of his mouth did rise
slightly then, but it was a little oasis of OK in a vast
expanse of meh. The boy was bummed. And not in a
good way. But he stood up and smiled bravely, rubbing his hands together. 'Anyway, moving on. Who
wants a drink?'

Ollie pounced on the idea. Last thing he wanted
was everyone remembering his party for Adam's
dickish behaviour. 'Same again. Cheers, mate.' We all
ditto'd that, except Sarah who, not being much of a
drinker, asked for a Coke.

'Oh, *poor* Jack,' sighed Sarah, as we watched him
join the bar jostle. Yes, poor Jack. I furrowed my
brow supportively but my mind had moved on to
more pressing matters. Like, where the hell was

Dylan? And right then, as if it was meant to be (and as if I believed in fate, which I don't), he and Marv appeared in the door like a couple of cowboy baddies entering a saloon. Tsch, where's some dry ice and dramatic music when you need it? I must have gone a bit meercat, cos Donna followed my gaze and gave me a none-too-subtle elbow in the ribs.

'Oi, oi, look who's here,' she said.

'Yeah, thanks for that. I had noticed.' My insides were doing a jig – I couldn't believe he'd actually turned up, but outwardly I just rolled my eyes at her. She gave me a Muttley cackle, then put two fingers in her mouth and produced an ear-splitting whistle. About three-quarters of the room turned to find out why their ears had just started bleeding, but thankfully only the two boys came over. And my stomach went a teeny bit liquid as I watched Dylan loping across the room, his hands deep in the pockets of his skinny jeans.

As he came closer I gave him the subtle once-over. Working from top to bottom, we're talking flowing locks – *bien sûr* – a loose plaid shirt with a long silver pendant over it – I love a boy who can wear jewellery – those jeans and, finally, amazing pointy-toe shoes that made him look like some crazy-ass Pied Piper. In short and to sum up: fit. FIT FIT FIT. I hadn't fancied anyone this much in ages. Years, even.

I sighed with a mix of desire and disappointed realism. Whatever Donna said, he'd be severely dating down if he got with me. Oh well: nothing ventured. Taking a deep breath, I downed my second beer and the last five centimetres of Sarah's discarded vodka cranberry, and prepared to be dazzling.

'Hey,' I said to both boys, doing eye contact and big smiles-a-go-go. 'Cool that you made it.' I nodded at the chairs recently vacated by Adam and Cass. 'Those are free.'

Donna introduced the boys to Ollie, Jack, Rich and Sarah, and they sat down, Dylan taking the seat next to me. Ee! As he lowered his long body into the chair he took in my clothes, giving me a Grade-A eyebrow-raise. I returned in kind. 'Was there something?'

He grinned. 'Nice outfit.' It was the first time I'd seen him smile. For such a tall, serious-looking dude, he had a ridiculously cheeky grin. Dimples and everything.

'Thanks, it is, isn't it?' I breathed, running my hands over my body camply. Then, in my normal voice, added: 'You don't look bad yourself. Love the necklace.'

'It's a pendant, actually,' he corrected me. 'Boys don't wear necklaces, didn't you know?'

I bowed my head apologetically. 'My mistake.' Then I gave him the wide-eye. It's something I once saw my mum do when she was chatting up Bob, a cool guy who ended up being her boyfriend. I was only seven at the time, but it was one of those moments that stay with you forever. He was a butcher, would you believe, and we were in his shop buying, I dunno, bacon or something – she always found an excuse. He made some joke and she looked straight at him, laughed and widened her eyes, just for a heart-beat, making them flash. I promise I saw him fall in love with her, right there. He suddenly looked at her intensely, almost confused – maybe even a bit sad at the potential for it all going tits up. Anyway, he was right cos they split up when I was twelve. It was a shame. I really liked him. I've used the wide-eye ever since.

Having caught Dylan in my tractor beam (joke), I slapped my hands on the table and stood up. 'Right. Are you dancing?' To which his response should obviously have been, 'Are you asking?' but he wasn't reading from the script, cos he just shrugged and said, 'No, thanks.'

Blown out at the first hurdle. Ouch. Luckily I was at the fuzzy feel-good stage of drunkenness so decided not to take it to heart, instead saying: 'Fair enough. Anyone else?'

Ollie was up straight away, of course, swiftly followed by Donna, who turned to Sarah.

'C'mon, babes, up and at 'em.'

Sarah looked unsure but Ollie dragged her up. 'You're not getting out of this, Millar.' Which left Jack to make conversation with Marv and Dylan. I wasn't too worried. Dylan just needed a few more drinks and a bit more attention from *moi*, and I was pretty sure the night would end in my favour.

By the way, in case you're thinking *Who IS this bint who loves herself so very much?* – I don't, basically. I'm under no illusions when it comes to boys and sex. I'm all-right-looking and I've got an all-right body, but I'm no beauty. I mean I'm funny, but if boys wanted funny then Miranda Hart would be a sex symbol. What boys want from me, and what I want from (most of) them, is a laugh and some rudey cuddles. Nothing wrong with that.

So, yeah, I was fairly optimistic that Dylan and I would end up Doing It. It was afterwards that worried me. I needed to somehow talk myself into not caring when he inevitably did up his trousers and loped off into the sunset. But given the option of sex with Dylan or nothing with Dylan . . . ? It was a no-brainer.

So I jumped on to the dance floor and busted some retro moves to the B-52s, Ollie and Sarah both singing all the words like their little hearts depended on it. I kept stealing glances at Dylan. I'm not the world's best dancer, but I love it, and IMO that counts for a lot. There's nothing more turn-offy than someone who takes themselves seriously on the dance floor, all sultry gurning and hair-flicking, so I concentrated on dancing like no one was watching, while hoping he was watching. Mostly he wasn't, but sometimes he was. One time he even caught my eye and smiled, so I beckoned him over. But he shook his head, wrinkling his nose in the universal sign for *Nah, not my thing*. It was agony having him so close yet so unapproachable, although I have to say that, with all the pretending I was having the best time *ever*, I did end up having a pretty good time.

After a while I realized there was someone dancing really close behind me, totally bursting my personal-space bubble. I turned to see a Year Twelve kid I recognized from school, although I didn't know his name. My Dylan-watch had meant I hadn't noticed him until he started dancing so close to me. I ignored him, which was apparently the green light for him to come and dance *right* in front of me.

'All right?' he bellowed.

I gave him a brief smile, then turned my back and bopped over to our table, shimmying in front of Dylan. He, Marv and Jack laughed as I turned round and waggled my bum in their direction, but Dylan made no move to stand up. My heart plummeted. It wasn't going to happen. Forcing the smile to stay on my face, I danced back to Donna, blanking the kid who was still hovering.

'Dylan's so not interested,' I shouted in her ear.

She frowned and shook her head. 'He's shy! Give him a chance.'

But five songs later Dylan was still deep in conversation with Marv and Jack, and he hadn't looked my way any one of the approximately fifty-seven times I'd looked his. And the Year Twelve kid was still buzzing around me like a slightly sweaty flea.

I rolled my eyes. 'Are you going to get me a drink, then?' (I still don't know why I asked. I thought I wanted him to leave me alone, but the words just came out.)

His face lit up. 'Yeah, what do you want?'

'Double vodka and Coke.' He licked his lips so I yelled, 'Don't get any ideas. It's not going to happen.' He shrugged, looking slightly miffed, and jogged off to the bar, leaving me on my own. Maybe I just liked the attention. At least *someone* was making the effort.

When he got back I downed the contents of the glass he handed me. The alcohol sluiced through my bloodstream like a knife and, suddenly, I was hammered. It felt like even blinking my eyes took ages, and as the music faded into a background fuzz the bass thudded through me like a tense heartbeat. I started dirty dancing, grinding my pelvis in front of the kid. In my drunken haze I thought jealousy might spur Dylan into action. It was the only weapon I had left.

'You're a hot dancer,' the kid shouted at me, sweat forming in droplets at the ends of his eyelashes.

'Thanks,' I yelled back. 'Your eyelashes are amazing. Like a girl's.'

He frowned slightly, unsure what to say to that one. I started dancing around him, snaking my arms above my head. I didn't care what I did or how I looked. There was no yesterday or tomorrow, only that moment. The kid plucked up the courage to put his hands on my waist, mirroring my moves and dancing with me. Actually, he was all right at it. And he smelled good. I began to enjoy being with him. The me-and-him-ness of it all. I couldn't take my eyes off the bit of collarbone showing where his shirt was open, the way it flexed as he moved. And then, suddenly, we were kissing. I let him guide me towards the back wall, where he pressed up against me. It wasn't loving or tender or even passionate. It was soulless kissing, but that's all I wanted. Mouth-to-mouth with tongues: a means to an end. I liked the heavy feeling of his body pressed against mine and, to be honest, I liked the feel of his erection against my stomach.

Oh, what the hell. I lightly pushed him away and started walking towards the door to the stairs. 'Come on, then,' I said over my shoulder, and he started following me. I caught Donna's eye on the way and she shook her head in mock despair. I ignored her. So what if the night always ended this way? A shag was a shag, and if Dylan wasn't interested – as he obviously wasn't – I had nothing to lose. Anyway, he was out of my league: I'd known it all along.

Downstairs, I dragged the kid into the Ladies, took him into a cubicle and locked the door.

As we stood bent over the toilet, the kid grunting away behind me like he was going for his own personal best, I felt less drunk and more like I was being used as a wank machine. Note to self: a space so small you can't even turn round is not the best venue for satisfying sex. The place was too quiet and it smelled of wee and disinfectant. All the intensity of the music and buzz upstairs had vanished. It was, in short, pretty much the worst sex ever. I didn't feel like an empowered woman taking what she wants, I felt like a hole with legs. It was shit.

'Cheers,' he panted when he'd finished, pulling off the condom and reaching behind me to drop it into the loo, the skank. 'I gotta hand it to you. You're as good as they say.'

I stopped straightening my skirt and swallowed. I could literally feel the blood draining from my face. 'Excuse me?'

'Well, word gets around that you get around.' He leered. 'But don't worry, it's all good.'

Suddenly my breath was coming in short panicky bursts. Was everyone talking about me? Did everyone think I was a slag? I put my hand to my throat and tried to calm down. I was this close to a full-blown panic attack, and I hadn't had one of those since the Devon sea in half term. 'Fuck you,' I said hoarsely, and I pushed past him, out of the toilets and bang into the chest of the guy I actually liked.

Dylan gently held my arms. My head was level with his chest. 'Hey, not so fast,' he said, smiling. God, it felt good to be near him. I wanted him to wrap his arms round me and hide me away forever.

I looked down, my eyes welling up with shock, hurt and disappointment, when that tosser emerged from the toilets, still fiddling with his flies like we were in an effing *Carry On* film.

He glanced at Dylan, then back at me. 'Maybe do it again some time, yeah?' he smirked. And, with a quick hoick of his jeans, he sauntered back up the stairs.

I closed my eyes in despair. Shit SHIT. Without stopping to look at the disgust – or even worse, indifference – that must have been written all over Dylan's face, I pulled away from him and headed for the stairs. At the top I made a beeline for the exit, but Rich intercepted me.

'Wait, Ash. Are you OK?'

I dodged to get past him. 'What does it look like?' But he kept blocking my way. 'Look, I don't want to talk about it. I just want to go home . . . Please, Rich.'

'All right, but I'm coming with you. Don't move.' He held his finger up and I nodded wearily. He sprinted back to the table to get his coat. I saw him exchange a few words with the others, who shot me concerned glances, and then he was back. 'Let's go.'

Without saying anything, we started towards my house. I was glad of Rich. I'm always glad of Rich, but you know what I mean. It was nice to have a boy with me and know nothing was expected of me, sexually. I leant into him gratefully. He understood exactly how to handle me when I was like this. I huffed mirthlessly to myself. Maybe he could give me a few tips, cos I'd done a pretty frickin' awful job of handling myself tonight. Stupid tears sprang to my eyes again as I thought about the feeling of Dylan's hands round my arms, and then what that disgusting kid had said. *You're as good as they say.*

Suddenly I was going to puke. Staring around wildly, I saw a bin and ran, reaching it just in time to heave a slurry of cranberry, vodka, beer and a hefty dose of regret on top of the fag butts, crisp packets and empty drinks cans. The perfect end to the perfect night.

Rich handed me a tissue. 'All right?'

I nodded and wiped my face. 'Sorry about that.'

'Don't be soft.' He hooked my arm through his and we continued along the dark streets in silence. Frost glistened on cars and garden walls, mocking me with its festivity. Stupid Christmas.

Outside my front door, Rich hesitated. 'You want me to stay over?' I plonked my head on his chest and nodded. Again, this wasn't new.

Inside, all was quiet, although it wasn't that late. Mum was always exhausted after a Saturday at work, and Frankie had her OCD thing about getting enough sleep. Anyway, a quiet house suited me fine. I turned to Rich.

'You want tea?'

He shook his head. 'Let's go to bed. You look wiped.' Nodding wearily, I dragged myself upstairs, where Rich used the bathroom while I got into my PJs. Then I went for a wee and half-heartedly brushed my teeth while he went into my room to strip down to his boxers and T-shirt, not that he was shy, and we got into bed. Rich held out his arm and I gratefully shifted next to him, resting my head on his chest. He lifted up my hand and gave it a quick kiss. 'Night night, dirty stop-out.'

'Night,' I mumbled, feeling safe in Rich's arms.

But Dylan – beautiful, unattainable Dylan with his cute smile and dry humour and elegant fingers – was the last thing that went through my mind as I fell into a sad, exhausted sleep.

4

I lost my virginity when I was fourteen to my boy-friend, Etienne. He appeared at the beginning of Year Nine – a vision in foreign shoes and skinny-side-out school tie – and disappeared at the end of it, although we'd split up by then. His parents, who were both doctors, had a year's contract at the hospital. His dad was a gynaecologist, which always made me nervous when I was round their house cos I kept thinking he could somehow imagine what my fanny looked like.

The point is that Etienne was my first, and he was cool. We liked each other, and I really fancied him. He made me laugh, and he liked the same music as me, and he had the most incredible smooth skin, which made a welcome change from all the pus-faced boys I was used to. We were like perfect opposites in skin colour, too. Where most black people are actu-ally kind of brown and most white people are actually kind of yellowy-pink, he was literally black and I was literally white. Ebony and ivory-tastic. And he spoke with a French accent. I rest my case.

So anyway. We'd been going out for a couple of months and we'd got pretty close to doing the deed a few times, but there was always someone around. Then one afternoon I got home from school and the house was empty. Mum had taken Frankie shopping and Sasha was staying at a friend's for the night. We took our chance and gave up our joint virginity on my bed, under the duvet, with The Doors on the stereo. It was pretty rubbish, but we got better, and then there was no stopping us.

We broke up when I got with someone else at a party. I was hammered on cheap cider and hardly knew what I was doing, and it was just kissing, but still. It was my bad, and I couldn't blame him for chucking me. I would have tried to get him back, but he pretty much immediately got with someone else too, so that was that. If I regretted stuff, which I don't, I'd regret cocking it up with Etienne. I still couldn't listen to 'Light My Fire' without thinking of him.

I couldn't honestly tell you how many boys I've shagged since then. I mean, I could, if I could be bothered to work it out, but what's the point? I remember the good ones, forget the bad. And it's not like I'm keeping a tally: that's not what it's about. I do it cos I like it. It's fun, and I can forget about every-thing and exist in the moment. I don't think I'm all

that, just cos I have lots of sex, but at the same time
I don't think I'm a slag. 'No boys were harmed in the
making of this picture' type thing. I'm just me.
Ashley Greene. And I've never pretended to be anything else.

So why did I turn up at school the Monday after
Ollie's party to find that suddenly I was slag of the
century?

It started immediately. Literally the moment me and
Donna walked through the gate a Year Eleven girl
eyed me up, narrowing her eyes bitchily, then whispered something to her friend.

'What was that?' asked Donna, shooting them a
quick evil.

'Dunno,' I said, shrugging. Honestly, it could
have been anything. I got a lot of snide remarks
about my clothes, not that I gave a shit, and today I
was wearing black lipstick. Just an experiment, and
I'd have to wipe it off before tutor group, but I'd
known when I'd put it on that the girls who don't
wear anything unless some magazine has told them
to would take offence. Like, what's it to them? I
couldn't understand it. (As it happens, I was with
them on this occasion. The lippie made me look like
a corpse.)

So me and Donna ignored them and carried on our merry way to the canteen for a fried-egg bap. But then this bunch of five Year Twelve girls stopped right in front of us, like they were challenging us to a rumble or something. I kind of giggled, which probably didn't help, but I'd suddenly pictured them pointy-toeing towards me and clicking their fingers *à la West Side Story* (it had been my nan's fave). Blatantly a funny image, right? But the girl in front, a mouthy type called Grace Simpson who had gem-stoned acrylics where her fingernails should be, didn't think so.

She jabbed the air in front of my face with a pointed finger. 'You're a whore.'

I raised an eyebrow. 'Enlightening.' I tried to push past them, but she grabbed my arm. 'Oi, get off!' I said, trying to pull away, but she dug her nails in. It bloody hurt, although obviously I didn't show it. My heart was beginning to pound a bit. I can stand up for myself, but I'm not into fisticuffs. Violence scares me, which is fair enough when you think about it.

'I said . . .' she said, pursing her mouth until it closely resembled a cat's arse, 'You. Are. A. Slag.'

Actually, she'd called me a whore, but I didn't correct her. Instead I made myself look bored and sighed, saying, 'OK, fine. I'm a slag. Can I go now?'

That set her off. Something clicked and she went mental, yelling at me like a banshee. It would have been fascinating if it wasn't so frightening. 'Where do you get off, dressing like a goth and thinking you can go around shagging everything that moves?' she screamed. She turned to the girl next to her. 'She thinks she's it, doesn't she?' Then, turning back to me, she started jabbing the air again, her face so close to mine I was showered with her spittle. 'You think you're *it*, you dirty, white-faced bitch.' (She was white too, by the way, just smothered in fake tan and foundation.)

Staring her out, I shot back: 'What exactly is your problem?' It was a genuine question.

'I'm not the one with the problem,' she spat back, and she turned on her heels and stalked away from us, her hangers-on tagging along behind. She waited till she'd moved a few metres away from me to launch her final word, presumably so as many people as possible could overhear her bellowing: 'And stay away from Billy Marshall.'

'You all right, babes?' asked Donna, as I stood rooted to the spot.

'Yeah. Fine,' I said, although I was shaking. I might have been a mouthy cow, but I wasn't hard. At all. If that girl had gone for me, I'd have dropped like a stone. I swallowed and turned to Donna. 'That was weird, right?'

'I know.' She wrinkled her forehead. 'Have you ever even spoken to her before?'

I shook my head. 'Nope.'

'Billy whatsit must be that boy you shagged at the party. Maybe she's his girlfriend,' she said.

'Well, she's welcome to him,' I said, picking my bag up off the floor, where I'd dropped it before squaring up to Grace. 'Come on, the canteen'll have run out of eggs if we don't get a move on.'

It was the weirdest thing. I never worried about what people thought of me. I figured if someone didn't know me, I didn't care what they thought because – duh! – they didn't know me, so how could they have an informed opinion? But suddenly my eyes were darting all over the place, checking for evils and whispered comments. The worst thing was not knowing what people from the party were saying about me. Grace and her lot hadn't even been there, so someone must have told them.

I tugged at my fringe and studied the dusty grey floor, wishing beyond anything that I'd never gone there. I hadn't even fancied that Billy tosser, and now just the thought of him made me want to puke.

'Uh, Ash, you sure you're OK?'

I looked up to see Donna staring at me quizzically

and I realized that I'd stopped dead in the middle of the corridor.

I sighed. 'It's just . . . well, it sucks being called a whore.'

She leant against the wall. 'Listen, don't worry about Grace and her lot. You've got me and Cass and Sarah, and the boys, and we still love you.' She nonchalantly chewed on a hangnail. 'Y'know, even though you're a slag.' She grinned and I punched her on the arm.

'Piss off, Dixon. DICK-son.' *Bring it on, beeatch.*

'Whatever.' She smiled serenely. 'Oh, by the way. You love Dylan.'

I gasped. 'Whoa. Below the belt, lady.'

She smiled again, more seriously this time. 'You do, though, right?'

'Doesn't matter anyway,' I said, starting to walk. 'Not after Ollie's party.'

'Hmm.'

Great. How reassuring.

Donna Dixon, number-one fan of the New Look tall section and owner of the bounciest bosoms in Brighton (honestly, you should see them – cars have nearly crashed because drivers are so mesmerized by their *boing*), had been my best mate since the start of Year Seven, when we were put next to each other in science. On the surface we weren't that alike. We were either side of the 'alternative' line, is how I guess you could put it. She wanted to follow fashion, I wanted to be different. She liked chart music, I was a fan of obscure indie. She wouldn't wear Doc Marten boots if you paid her – I wouldn't have been seen dead in a pair of Primark stilettos. But we had the same outlook on life, the same attitude. She was cool. A cool bird. I loved the bones of her.

I mean, Rich, Ollie, Jack, Sarah and Cass were cool too, especially Rich. I wouldn't have been without them. But Donna was the one I called when I was feeling shit, and the first one I wanted to tell when something good happened. That bollocks about friends being more important than boyfriends? It's so not bollocks. Take Cass. She and Sarah were supposed to be best mates, but while Adam was around Sarah would always come second. I reckon she knew that too. And she and Cass were almost torn apart by that thing with Joe, the posh London student.

So call me a slag if you want, but you won't find a more loyal friend.

Anyway. We finally got to the canteen, picking up two funny looks and one whispered comment on the way. They had indeed run out of eggs, so we got a couple of Snickers from the vending machine instead and hurried to tutor group.

'First person to give me a sympathetic look gets a smack in the mouth,' I said grimly, as we sat down with the others. 'I'm so not in the mood.'

Sarah leant across the table and stroked my hand, creasing her brow and sticking her bottom lip out. 'Poor widdle Ashy-washy.'

Aw, Sarah. She could be perfect sometimes. (Slightly gullible and annoying at others, but that's another story.)

'Seriously, Sar, you should have seen what just happened,' interrupted Donna, gearing up for a gossip. I didn't take it personally. Scandal is mother's milk to that girl. Twelve eyes fixed on her and she filled them in on the morning's events, with a little help from me – it was my story, after all.

'I've always said it,' said Ollie afterwards, shaking his head in disbelief. 'Girls are mental. No offence.'

'Ignore the Grace bitch, babes,' added Rich. 'You're worth a million of her. *And* she has BO.'

Cass gave him a look. 'She *once* had BO. And it was after PE. And you only heard that from someone else.'

'Trying to be supportive of our friend here?' squeaked Rich out of the corner of his mouth. Personally, I was surprised he'd even heard of Grace, let alone had information about her, but that's Rich for you. Dark horse an' all that.

'Don't worry about it,' I said airily. 'I am ignoring her. I don't give a shit what she – or any of that lot – think.'

'Good for you,' said Jack assertively. 'You're not a slag. You just like what you like.'

Everyone laughed. The last virgin in the group speaketh, although to be fair I couldn't have put it better myself.

Donna shoved the last bit of chocolate bar into her mouth. 'Anyway, listen . . .' She swallowed the mass of chocolatey peanut goo, and with it our Technicolor visual, thankfully. 'Marv's having a Christmas Eve thing at his house and he says I can bring a few friends. And . . .' She pulled down imaginary glasses and peered at me over them. 'Dylan's going to be there.'

Oh *man*. I so wanted to see him again. There was no point, but hey – I knew the score. He obviously didn't like me, so I'd just enjoy him as eye candy. Nothing more. (Right. Good luck with that, me.)

I shrugged and cracked my gum. 'OK. Count me in.'

Ha! See how they are fooled by my nonchalance. Apart from Donna, obvs, who gave me her patented heavy-lidded *yeah, right* look.

She opened it out to the floor. 'Anyone else fancy it?' The boys all said they'd come along, but my esteemed lady friends totally let the side down. And not for the first time, I might add. Cass and Sarah were not exactly party animals, unless the animal in question was a hamster or summink. A hamster who only ventures on to its little wheel thing on a Saturday night, and only then if it's finished its homework.

'I can't,' said Cass. 'I spend Christmas Eve with Adam, don't I?'

'Oh. Shame,' said Donna, furtively rolling her eyes at me and Jack, who happened to be sitting next to me.

'Ah, bum. I can't either,' added Sarah, sounding peeved (or as peeved as someone can who thinks 'bum' is a swear). 'We're going to my grandparents'.' She growled dramatically and dragged her hand down her face. 'I'd so rather be hanging out with you than watching bloody *Midsomer Murders* and eating tinned-peach flan.'

'Never mind, babes,' said Rich, who was flicking through Cass's *Grazia* magazine. 'We'll save you a mince pie.'

And on that bombshell, our personal tutor arrived. Paul was head of maths and liked to spout business bullshit: think outside the box, blue-sky thinking, etc. But he was harmless enough. You could set your watch by him. Every morning he rushed in, perched on the edge of his desk to take the register, read out any notices, then pissed off again. Some tutors liked to get involved – find out stuff about you, ask how things were at home, try to be your friend. I reckon Paul would've been hard pushed to pick any of us out in a line-up. Which suited me fine. So, yeah, as far as all that went, Paul was all right.

But this morning he had News.

'Okaaay, listen up, guys,' he said, his voice going just a leetle bit more Mockney, a teeny bit more Lord Sugar, as it always did when he was talking to us. I'd heard him talking to other teachers and sounding proper posh. Who knew, or indeed cared, which was the real Paul?

He hitched his trouser leg up so he could bend one knee over the other, revealing a Homer Simpson sock. Nice. A sudden image of novelty man-pants appeared in my head. I caught Donna's eye and she mimed retching. She'd so been thinking the same thing.

'A heads-up from the Principal, 'K ?' Paul continued. 'There's some fresh, pretty sexually explicit graffiti in the upper-school toilets, and message from above is that either it stops or heads will roll.' He fixed us with a penetrating stare. 'Not cool, people, yeah?'

And, with that, he gave us a mini salute and stomped out of the room. Hilarious.

Rich turned to us and spread his hands. 'Shall we?'

Of course we frickin' shall. We all trooped off to the upper-school toilets, the boys into the Boys', the girls into the Girls', but us girls were stopped short by Mr Cunningham, the caretaker, who was in the middle of painting over the offending stuff.

'Sorry,' he said. 'Give me a minute.'

Donna tried to peer through the wet paint, to no avail. 'What did it say?'

Mr C gave her a look. 'It wasn't very original, I'll tell you that much.'

Oh. Shame. We left him to it and went outside to wait for the boys, who turned up a minute later. Rich gave me a sideways smile. 'You OK, babes?'

'Uh, yeah, why shouldn't I be?' I said. The boys looked at each other.

'No reason. Just being my usual kind self,' said Rich airily. 'Come on, let's go.' He had started walking off down the corridor when something occurred to me. I was probably being paranoid, but something in the boys' faces . . . I dunno. They just looked shifty. I pulled the back of his coat.

'Hang on, did you see the graffiti?'

He furrowed his brow unconvincingly. 'What? Oh yeah. It was nothing exciting.'

I looked at Jack, who was physically incapable of lying. 'Jack. What did it say?'

He blushed and looked at his feet. 'Like Rich said. Nothing.'

'Ollie?' I folded my arms and turned to him. 'Are you going to have the balls?'

'Balls? What do you mean?' He tried to laugh in a *what's she going on about* way. That clinched it. Growling, I shoved open the door of the boys' toilets to see for myself, although I already had a pretty good idea what I was in for.

'Ash, don't,' called Rich, trying to drag me back. 'I'll tell you, OK?'

I shook him off. Written in black marker pen above the urinals was the block-caps legend: ASHLEY GREENE TAKES IT UP THE ARSE. Spinning slowly round 180 degrees, I saw some more above the sinks: ASHLEY GREENE IS A DIRTY HORE N WILL SHAG ANYONE ALL U HAVE TO DO IS ASK!!!

I swallowed, hating the words but hating the pity that was radiating off my friends just as much. I could sense them semi-circled behind me, giving each other concerned looks while they were all secretly not that surprised that the graffiti was about me. I closed my eyes briefly and took a breath. *You don't care what people think*, I reminded myself. *Get over it.*

'Nice,' I said lightly. 'Digging that crazy spelling.' I turned round and tried really hard, and almost successfully, to look them all in the eye. 'For the record, I don't take it up the arse . . . Wishful thinking there, I feel.'

'Ash –' started Donna.

'Don't,' I said quietly, trying to smile. 'It's fine. Let's go – we'll be late for next period.'

And I followed my friends out of the toilets, trying not to cry and wishing more than anything that I could beam myself to my bedroom and hibernate under my duvet until school was finished forever.

It was Donna's theatre studies coursework production after school that day. No way I'd miss it, but it wasn't exactly good timing. Sitting in a theatre auditorium does kind of make you a sitting duck for pointing and comments. At least I had the others around me as a kind of force field, although no one could do evils as well as Donna and she was up on stage.

She was even better than when she'd done the voiceovers for my documentary. Some of the others up there were so totally *acting*, but you believed Donna.

She did this one piece from *Cat on a Hot Tin Roof*. All she had was a wooden chair and a southern

American accent, but I swear to God you could practically smell the heat. She was there – you utterly believed it.

Donna was going to get an A in theatre studies, no worries, although her other subjects weren't such a shoe-in. She didn't really give a shit about them, to be honest. It was drama all the way. *jazz hands* She wanted to be an actor: stage and screen, sunglasses in the rain, red carpets, the lot. Actually, she didn't care about the fame and fortune bit, she just wanted acting to be her job. She knew it was a difficult business to get into – like, *duh* – and the careers adviser had told her often enough, but she was determined. Her parents were OK-ish with it. Her dad just wanted her to be happy and her mum kept telling her she should go for it and being all 'Go, girl!' *air punch* while at the same time suggesting that maybe she should get a 'proper' degree first to widen her options. But that wasn't going to happen. As far as Don was concerned, the only dilemma was whether to apply to do drama at uni or try to get an agent straight from school. She hadn't told her mum that part yet.

'Hey, Ash, look over there,' whispered Cass into my ear, snapping me out of my grim fascination with the awfulness of the current number, a lisping rendition of 'Where is Love?' from *Oliver* by a cutesie-pie, baby-voiced type called Heidi Minton.

There's something kind of sick about an eighteen-year-old pretending to be eight.

'What?' I frowned, following her gaze.

She growled with frustration. 'It's Dylan! Over there. One, two, three . . . fourth row from the front, bang in the middle.'

It was as well. He was sitting next to Marv, who was obviously there to support his cousin.

'Oh yeah,' I said casually, then pointedly turned my attention back to the stage. But I couldn't stop looking at him. Every now and then he'd turn and say something to Marv, but otherwise he faced forward. At one point Marv said something to him which made him laugh, showing his dimples. He was so beautiful. I longed for him. I'm not being melodramatic – that's how it felt. I could hardly bear to look away in case he left early, but at the same time there was no way I could talk to him. Not after Ollie's party.

After the show had finished and everyone had taken their bows – Donna getting way more whoops and cheers than the others, which made me kind of swell with pride – we all trooped outside to wait for her, my eyes skipping all over the place in case he was near. But he didn't appear. I didn't know whether to be relieved or gutted. On balance, I was both, with the emphasis on gutted. But that was probably more to do with what had happened before than with not seeing him again tonight. Every time I thought about bumping into him outside the loos at Ollie's party I felt sick.

'Hey, it's the star of the show!' sang Cass, as Donna appeared by our side, still wearing her stage make-up and smiling almost shyly. 'You were awesome, hon,' she went on, giving her a hug.

'You really were, babes,' I said. 'The best by miles.'

Donna blushed daintily as we all bigged her up, then held up her hands. 'All right, all right. I'm brilliant, I know. Let's move on, yeah?'

As we wandered out of school, she grabbed my arm. 'Did you see Dylan?'

'Yeah.'

'Did you talk to him?'

'No.'

She stopped in her tracks, her eyes bugging with disbelief. 'Why NOT? Ugh, I persuade Marv to bring him and what do I get in return? Frig all. Honestly, where are your BALLS?'

I shrugged. 'I didn't get the chance. He was sitting miles away.' Kind of true.

'Hmm.' She narrowed her eyes in suspicion.

'Anyway,' I said, changing the subject as we reached her bus stop. 'I'll see you tomorrow, yeah?'

She shook her head firmly. 'Nope, you're coming back to mine.'

'Who says?' I just wanted to get home and disappear up to my room.

'I do. I'm not going to leave you on your own, and I can't come to yours cos it's my turn to do tea.'

I slung my bag over my shoulder. 'OK, whatever. But we're not getting the bus.'

'You're welcome,' said Donna ironically. 'And we *are* getting the bus. Ian the Stalker never does my route.'

'Seriously, Don, I can't face him. Not today. Please?' I gave her puppy-dog eyes.

'Ugh, stop it. That's disturbing,' she said, but she started walking in the direction of home rather than the bus stop.

'Thanks, babes.'

'Hmph.'

I didn't mind going to Donna's. Hiding away isn't my style, even though having the whole school think I'm a slag made every fibre of my being want to do exactly that.

We picked up fish and chips on the way home and took them up to Donna's bedroom. Mick – her dad – didn't mind eating on his own in front of the telly, but only after he'd spent about ten years telling Donna how sorry he was that he'd had to work and miss her show while we hovered at the bottom of the stairs, chip grease congealing before our very eyes.

Mick was cool. I wouldn't have minded him for a dad, although I was fine without one.

'How's your mum?' I asked when we'd finally made it upstairs and I'd sat on the floor against Donna's bed and squirted mayonnaise over my chips (sooo much nicer than ketchup). I asked because I wanted to know, but also I wanted to start off on a subject that didn't have anything to do with (a) me and my new-found anti-status as School Slag, and (b) Dylan.

Don nodded vigorously while she finished her mouthful. 'Yeah, good. She's so well, Ash. It's rubbish that she's got to wait four and a half years till she's officially fine.'

Donna didn't mind talking about her mum's cancer. You just had to be straightforward. She couldn't stand furrowed-browed concern or exaggerated whispering as if the subject was too awful to speak of out loud. Anyway, Michelle had been in remission for six months, so no need for doom and gloom.

'D'you reckon you'll move back in with her, then?' I said.

She shrugged. 'Maybe. Not right now, though. She and Bryn have a good set-up, and me and Dad are fine here.'

I watched her nonchalantly tucking into her chips. 'And you're OK with that?' I asked.

She grinned at me. 'What, I'm missing out on a

mother's love?' She shook her head. 'It's all good. We get on better now than we did when I lived with her.'

Donna's parents got divorced when she was seven and her sister Jess was nine. Michelle had played away, but apparently the marriage had been pretty much dead for years anyway. Don and Jess had lived with Michelle and her boyfriend – now husband – Bryn till the breast-cancer diagnosis, then they'd moved in with Mick while Michelle had her chemo. At the time it had been really hard. Michelle's consultant told her it was for the best because the chemo would make her feel like shit and she needed to take it easy and not feel guilty about it. (And, to be honest, Michelle was pretty much a control freak. She probably wouldn't have handled not being in total charge at all times.) Then Donna and Jess felt bad because it was as if they were leaving their mum when she needed them most. But in the end it'd worked out fine. Donna got on well with Bryn, she got on OK with Michelle, she'd always been really close to Mick, her parents were civil to each other . . . As the girl said, it was all good. When Michelle had finished her treatment there seemed little point in uprooting everyone again, especially as Jess had gone to uni by this point, so the arrangement stayed as it was.

Donna screwed up her fish-and-chip paper and

chucked it in the direction of her bin, missing by miles. 'She's not too happy with me spending Christmas Eve at Marv's, though.'

'Cos you're supposed to be at hers for Christmas?' I guessed.

'Exactly. She thinks I'm spending too much time with that side of the family. It's like, I can't help it if all her family live in Birmingham.'

'She's going to let you go, though?' I said, suddenly worried about missing out on seeing Dylan again. (*Eye candy. He's just eye candy*, I reminded myself.)

Donna gave me a look. 'Yeah, don't worry. I promised I'd spend the whole of the rest of the Christmas holidays with her. Dunno why I should spend Christmas Eve with her anyway. Jess certainly won't.'

'You're lucky,' I said grimly. 'Sasha will have her perfect-daughter pinny on from the moment she gets home. It's not like she'd let me help even if I wanted to – she wouldn't want to risk letting her halo slip.' I had a go at chucking my paper in the bin, getting slightly closer than Donna did. 'Won't stop Mum singing her praises and making comments about how lazy, rude and generally shit I am, though,' I added, picking moodily at the stripy rag rug.

Donna grinned and jabbed her toes into my thigh. 'Right. Cos you'd just love to be in the kitchen, rustling up eggnog and shit.'

'Piss off,' I snorted. 'You don't even know what eggnog is.'

'Neither do you,' she shot back.

'Yeah, I do,' I said smugly. 'It's nog. Made from eggs.' Don produced a proper chortle and I smiled my first proper smile for ages. I'm not a natural beamer – no one could accuse me of being 'bubbly', thank God – but however shit my day had been, it was good to know I could still make my friends laugh. And Donna had the best laugh in the world. Full on throaty-filthy.

'Anyway,' said Donna when we'd finished chuckling. 'What's the plan for tomorrow?'

'Why, what's happening?' I had no idea what she was going on about.

She gave me a *duh* look. 'School? Following on from events of today, et cetera?'

I scowled. 'Oh, that. There is no plan. Carry on as normal.'

'Ash, come on . . .' She gave me what can only be described as a deeply patronizing look. 'You're only human. I know all that stuff today really hurt you. I just don't want you to be vulnerable.'

'I'm never fucking vulnerable, thanks very much. I don't do vulnerable.' I angrily studied Johnny Depp's lips in Donna's *Pirates of the Caribbean* poster (I know, but what can you do?) and counted to ten.

Donna totally recognized the signs. 'Look, forget I said anything,' she said quickly. 'Let's change the subject . . .' She smiled as she thought of something. 'I know, let's go for a drink on Sunday. I'll invite Marv and Dylan . . .' She paused meaningfully.

I frowned. 'No! I can't see him again. I'd die of embarrassment.'

'Oh, shut up,' she said scornfully. 'And I thought *I* was the drama queen. Come on, Ash. Pleeeease? In return for not getting the bus home today?' She fluttered her eyelashes.

'Why are you so desperate for me to see him again, anyway?' I said, scowling.

'Because you're my best friend, dickhead. I want to see you happy.'

I bit my lip, then banged my head down on her desk and growled.

Donna clapped her hands. 'Excellent! I'll text him now.' I watched as she did the deed and told myself he wouldn't want to come.

Donna hadn't had a reply by the time I left hers, which was fine. I wasn't any worse off than I'd been before she'd come up with the drink idea. I was still a bit gutted, mind.

At home I had a brief chat with Mum (sticking to safe subjects like her day at work and . . . well, just her day at work, really), then went to find Frankie. If anyone could make me feel better, it was my little sister.

She was sitting up in bed, reading. 'All right? Thought you'd be asleep,' I said. She looked up, blinking at the intrusion into her thoughts.

She held up a dog-eared copy of *More!* magazine. 'Emily brought this to school. It's got this thing where they draw a picture of a sex position and tell you how to do it.'

'I've heard tell of it,' I said drily. 'Going to give it a go, then?'

She turned heavy eyes on me. 'Very funny.' She idly turned the pages. 'Emily says she is, though. If one is a hug and ten is sex, she's got as far as nine and a half.'

'She tell you that, did she?'

Another scathing look from Francesca Greene. 'I believe her.'

I smiled at my sister. 'Course you do, babes . . . You going to let me in?' She shifted towards the wall side of the bed and pulled back the duvet.

'So, what number are you at, then, on this sex-scale thing?' I asked, getting in beside her.

Franks sniffed. 'About a five?'

I sat up and made boggle eyes at her. 'What?! Something you want to tell me, Francesca?'

She giggled. 'Not really. Just joking – I knew that'd get you going. Although there is someone I might fancy . . .' She hid her face under the duvet so only her eyes were showing.

'Oh yes, who's that then?' The thought of my little sister having a boyfriend was just too strange. I couldn't imagine it.

'Freddy Watson. He's in Year Nine.' She was still hiding her face, but I could tell by her eyes that she was smiling.

I giggled. 'Frankie and Freddy – love it!' She jabbed me with her elbow. 'Ow!' I rubbed my side. 'So what's he like?'

She grinned and bit her lip. 'I dunno.' She held her hands about twenty centimetres apart. 'He's about this much taller than me. He's got blond hair and really nice eyes. I like his hands. And he's sooo funny. Everybody thinks so.'

'And does *he* fancy *you*?'

'Emily reckons he does.' She paused. 'I think he might too. He says *I'm* funny.' Poor cow. Looked like she was going to have the funny-bird tag too.

'OK, here's what you do,' I said, as if I was any kind of expert. 'Don't play games, just be you. If he's got even the tiniest amount of good taste, you'll totally be in there. And, if he hasn't, you don't want him anyway.'

Franks pushed herself up and gave me a look of pure scorn. 'Right. Like you're not biased.'

I laughed. 'OK, I admit it, I think you're a bit amazing, but I also happen to know that I'm right.'

She thought about that one for a sec, then shrugged. 'Anyway, it's not like I want to *marry* him. Just a proper kiss with tongues would be good.' She looked kind of forlorn. 'I just wish I knew how to do it.'

'Don't worry about it, Franks,' I said. 'Take it from me, when it happens, you'll know what to do. It's like, I dunno, falling asleep or something. It comes naturally. One second you won't be kissing, then suddenly you will be, and you'll have no idea how you got there.'

'I hope you're right.'

'I am.' I held out my arm and she snuggled into my chest.

'Anyway, I've been worrying about you,' she said seriously. 'You should have texted that you were going to be back late.'

'What? Why?' I never let Mum know if I was going out after school unless I was going to be home later than ten. It was like an unspoken rule.

'Because of all that stuff about you taking it up the arse.'

Hearing my little sister say those words brought me up short. It was a jolt to the stomach, cold-sweat time. Seriously.

I kept my voice even, although I think I was phys- ically shaking. 'So even the lower school knows about it. Brilliant.'

'Do you?' she asked. 'Take it –'

I interrupted. 'No! Anyway, it's none of your busi- ness.'

'Actually, I think it becomes my business when Megan Cook and Varsha Varsani and that lot have a go at me because of it.' Her voice was quiet, but strong. I closed my eyes in despair. I felt sick.

'Shit, Franks, I'm really sorry. I'll tell you what hap- pened, if you want. But it definitely didn't involve . . . that.'

She rested her head on my chest. 'It's OK, you don't have to tell me anything. I'm just glad you're not lying all twisted and bloody after jumping off a multi- storey car park.'

I put my arm round her and gave her a squeeze. 'Course I'm not, doofus. I don't give a shit what a bunch of kids think or say. Or write.'

'Well, I think you're brilliant,' she said. 'And who- ever started the rumours is a total c-word.'

I bit my lip to stop myself crying. In fact, I didn't just want to cry, I wanted to sob, loud and hard. But I smiled and gave Franks a kiss. 'What would I do without you?'

She shrugged and smiled. 'Have a bigger bedroom?'

'There is that.'

Frankie leant over me to turn out her bedside light. 'Sleep here, if you want.' I wasn't about to argue. We snuggled down together, and within seconds she was snoring gently – she'd always been quick to drop off. But, although I was exhausted, I couldn't sleep. Getting a late-night text from Donna informing me that Dylan and Marv were up for meeting on Sunday didn't help – it just added a stomach-churning cocktail of hope, excitement and worry to the already pretty soupy mix of shame and fear that was doing loop-the-loops around my innards.

For a while I stared at the ceiling, wide-eyed and empty inside, but after half an hour or so I crept out of Frankie's room and into my own bed. Still I couldn't get comfortable. Even a couple of chapters from my *Woman's Book of Erotic Short Stories* didn't help. In the end I crept downstairs to see if crap telly could send me to sleep, which it did, although unfortunately while I was still on the sofa with nothing but my 'jamas and a couple of strategically placed cushions to keep me warm. I woke up, stiff and shivering, at four. Staggering up to bed, I slept fitfully till my alarm went off.

Swear to God, nearly drowning in a freezing October sea was nothing compared to dragging myself out of bed that morning. I'd rather have had a public bikini wax than go to school, but go to school I did. *Go, me.* I tried to give myself an inspiring pep talk on the way, but all I could manage was a half-hearted *yay* to the Christmas holidays. Only four days to go: what's the worst that could happen?

5

I got to school early enough to avoid seeing anyone and sat on my own in tutor, fiddling with my phone and ignoring everyone who came in. As far as I could make out, it was only Year Twelves doing the shit-stirring, but I wasn't taking any chances.

After a while – long enough for me to have added photos to every number in my Contacts list up to and including M – Sarah and Cass turned up, each giving me a hug before sitting down, which wasn't normal. It didn't exactly piss me off, but it was a bit annoying, as if I needed special handling.

'So, you ready for the screening?' asked Cass, who was sipping a grande vente blah-blah latte from her usual sandwich deli.

'Kind of. I've got to work on the film most of today.' All of my media studies group's documentary films were to be screened the next day to an audience of anyone who could be arsed to go. They were only ten minutes each, but still: not something you'd nec-essarily want to sit through unless you were directly involved. Or the *très* excellent friends of someone directly involved. I'd told everyone they didn't have to come, but they insisted they were up for it, gawd bless 'em. I couldn't wait to get into the editing suite and start cutting it all together, and not only because I'd be hidden away from the outside world.

'Oh my God,' said Sarah, covering her hand with her mouth. 'I didn't even ask you how the interview with the old lady went.'

I shrugged. I hadn't expected anyone to ask. 'It was good . . . You should have seen her house. It was like a Fifties museum.'

Cass wrinkled her nose. 'Did she give you tea with cat hairs in it?'

I gave her a look. 'Bit sexist, Cassandra. Not all old ladies are mental cat-fetishists. Actually, she was well on the ball. You'd never know she was about a hundred years old. She was *really* posh, though.'

Sarah leant forward, her chin on her hand. 'So was she all wise and thoughtful and full of, like, the secrets of life and death?'

I laughed. 'Kind of, but in another way really not. She wouldn't talk about whether she believed in heaven and stuff . . . I really liked her, though.'

'Oh, shame.' Sarah frowned. 'I always hope that by the time I'm really old I'll have, like, a deep understanding of all that stuff.'

Cass nodded. 'Me too. This can't be all there is.' She

gestured around her, as if the maths room was some kind of deep metaphor for life. Maybe it was. Couldn't see it myself.

'I know,' said Sarah. 'It seems so unfair that we all struggle along for eighty-odd years – if we're lucky – and then *pouff*: oblivion.'

'Exactly, but on the other hand the whole idea of heaven is a bit . . .'

'Fairy tale?' offered Sarah.

'Exactly.'

I felt the familiar black hole in my stomach. I was so not in the right frame of mind for this kind of conversation. 'Can we talk about something else?' I said. 'This is beginning to freak me out.'

'What's freaking you out?' asked Jack, as he pulled out a chair and joined us, swiftly followed by Rich, Ollie and Donna.

'Oh, you know. "Death and all its horrors" type thing.'

Jack grimaced. 'Right. Fair enough.'

'Full of the joys this morning, are we?' asked Rich, as he drained his can of drink and expertly lobbed it into the bin by Paul's desk.

'Couldn't be better,' I replied, giving him heavy eyes.

He looked slightly sheepish as he remembered the graffiti, blah blah. 'Oh yeah, course. Soz, babes.'

'You all right, though?' asked Ollie, just as Donna asked, 'How *are* you, though?'

I executed a perfect eye-roll. 'Fine. And, seriously, enough with the sympathy. It gets on my nerves.' I moodily stuffed a piece of gum into my mouth and chewed agitatedly. My friends made *ooh, hark at her* faces, but said nothing. It was like the rumours overshadowed everything else: some dirty looks and words painted on a toilet wall were realer than I was. Maybe they were.

'Anyway,' said Cass, smartly slapping her palms on the edge of the table as if to say *yup, changing the subject right here*. 'In other news, I've got an interview at Cambridge.' She tried to look easy-come-easy-go, but it was the worst effort ever. Her smile was wider than a wide thing.

'Oh my God, nice one, Cass!' said Sarah, over the general congrats and big-ups. Her smile was just a leetle fixed. I reckon she'd have loved to apply to Oxford or Cambridge, but her grades weren't good enough. Obviously I could have applied if I'd wanted to. Just decided against it. Not.

'Aw, fanks, everyone,' said Cass, grinning. 'I haven't decided if I'm going, though.'

'What are you talking about?' asked Jack, frowning.

'Well . . .' Cass hesitated.

'Oh, wait, I know,' said Donna, letting her forehead bang on to the table. 'It's cos of Adam, isn't it?'

Cass stuck her chin up like a cartoon defiant person. She'd obviously prepared herself for this line of questioning. 'Yes, well. Why would I choose to live hundreds of miles away from him?'

'Um . . . because it's an amazing opportunity? Because you'll love it? Because . . .' Donna hesitated. She wanted to say *because it'll get you away from that moron of a boyfriend*, but she held back. Prob for the best.

Cass interrupted. 'I can do law at Sussex. A law degree is a law degree – doesn't matter where I do it.'

Sarah looked at her disbelievingly. 'Really? You really think that having Cambridge on your CV won't carry just a *tiny* bit of weight?'

'I think if you're good, you're good,' said Cass loftily. 'And I fully intend to be brilliant.'

Huh: go Cass! I gave her a high-five. 'Respect to you, missus. Liking your style.'

She blinked in surprise. 'Thanks, Ash.'

'No probs. Don't go thinking I approve of your reasoning though' I said, wagging my finger (which, in retrospect, was both lame and annoying).

She shrugged. 'Didn't say I'd definitely decided not to go, did I?' she said. 'So get off your high horses, thanks very much.' And she leant back in her chair. Tick: point made.

Paul arrived soon after, and then it was first period. I couldn't be arsed going to French, but I went anyway.

It was so unfair that I wasn't in the same group as Ollie and Sarah – mine was OK, but there was no one in it who I'd call an actual friend. We got on fine during the class, and said 'hello' if we passed each other in the corridors, but that's as far as it went. I wasn't going to share my deepest secrets with them at a cosy sleepover any time soon, let's put it that way. Normally I'd have just bunked off and hung out in the canteen for an hour, but due to the rumour crapness I forced myself to go. Didn't want anyone thinking I was too scared to show up in class.

I had to pass a bunch of Year Twelves hanging outside the hall, but all they could offer was a feeble, 'Taken it up the arse recently?' I didn't know who'd said it, so I shot a *seriously, how old are you?* look in their general direction and continued on my merry way. The only other thing – that I noticed, anyway – was a couple of Year Ten girls with identikit bobs who had a frenzied whisper sesh about me as they walked past. Hilariously, I think I caught the word 'sodomy'. (By the way, what was people's problem with, y'know, the whole sodomy thing? Was it basically homophobia? Fear of the unknown? If you ask me, a hole's a hole, whether it's your mouth or your butt or whatever. Seriously, it was deeply weird how het up people were getting about it.)

You'll be devastated to learn that I can't tell you

what went on in French. We talked about industry, I think, but don't quote me on that. I spent the lesson writing a plan for my documentary, and straight afterwards I was back in the editing suite, where I stayed for the rest of the day. I wanted the film to be perfect and, anyway, I was sick of putting on a brave face. As I mixed Bridget's interview with still photos, Donna's stories and my own voiceover, I totally lost track of time in the quiet, windowless room. After I don't know how long, my teacher Matt knocked on the door.

'Ashley, you do know it's nearly five?'

I jumped, startled, and squinted at the bright light coming from the corridor outside. 'What?' I picked up my phone: 4:53. I rubbed my eyes, feeling disorientated and weird. I'd been in there for four hours! Get me, all Ms Conscientious. My shoulders ached from leaning into the computer and my eyes smarted from staring at the screen, but the buzz was amazing. I could have stayed there all night, but Matt chucked me out, saying he wanted to lock up and go home. Selfish. I suppose it gave me a reason to come into school tomorrow. It was a lonely business being a social pariah.

I'm not saying it's the same thing, but something happened the next morning that made me think about this girl Eloise who used to go to our school. I didn't really know her, but she had a kind of unfortunate gormless look as a result of the fact that she always, *always* had a cold. It must have been allergies or something, but her nose and top lip were forever red and chapped, and she talked all bunged up. It made you want to blow your own nose, you know? Anyway, for some reason someone started a rumour that she put dog food on her fanny . . . You can guess the rest. It was a really bloody vicious rumour and it just spread and spread. In the end, she took an overdose. She was found in time, rushed to hospital and had her stomach pumped, but she never came back to school.

So, yeah, what I was going through didn't even come close to that kind of victimization. But that morning it got just a bit harder to hold on to the idea that I was the lucky one.

I was walking down the road towards the crossroads where I turned left to go to school, listening to my music and thinking about the screening, when something whizzed out of nowhere and smacked me, hard, in the head. I shouted out, partly cos of the shock and partly cos it really hurt, and then screamed when something else hit me on my arm.

But it was when I felt something wet dripping down the side of my face that I really freaked out. At first I thought it was blood, although in retrospect it was too cold, but anyway. I was scared. When I saw and smelled that it was only egg, I spun round, yelling in the direction I thought it had come from. But I just heard laughter in the distance. I was walking by a block of flats, so it could have come from anywhere. Had they waited for me? Did they hate me so much that they lay in wait for the joy of seeing me with yolk dripping off my hair? It was both really fucking pitiful and really fucking horrible.

I couldn't exactly go to school now, looking like this, so I turned round and walked home as quickly as I could. I couldn't stop shaking. As I turned into our street I prayed that Mum would have already gone to work. It was her admin day, so the shop was closed – she didn't have to be in at any particular time. Her car was missing and I knew as soon as I walked into the house that it was empty, but I called out anyway. Nothing. Which was something. Mum would've been pissed off cos she'd assume I'd been messing about, then disbelieving when I started telling her what happened, then all tearful and dramatic. Couldn't be arsed with any of it.

So I showered and put on clean clothes, then buried my eggy outfit deep in the laundry basket.

Downstairs, I stood in the kitchen for a bit, listening to the quiet of home on a school day and wondering what to do. My screening wasn't till four, but I didn't want to give anyone the satisfaction of staying away till then. But at the same time I so, *so* wanted to stay away. I wanted to lie on the sofa in my PJs, eating biscuits and watching DVDs. The clincher was remembering that I hadn't had time to watch my film all the way through before Matt had chucked me out of the editing suite. What if it needed tweaking? What if it was actually rubbish? I had to go in.

I ran though. All the way. I was sweating and panting like a dog when I arrived, but I'd escaped the Attack of the Egg Products. Walking into school with my head up, but my eyes unfocused so I wouldn't be able to see anyone staring at me or talking about me, I accidentally blanked Donna. Yes, in a school of a thousand-plus, I bump into Donna. The words 'sod's' and 'law' spring to mind.

'Oi, Ashley!' She glared at me, hands on hips.

'Sorry, babes. Didn't see you,' I said, panting.

'Hang on, why are you out of breath?' she said with a frown.

'I ran.' I pretended I was too knackered to say anything more.

'No shit.' She gave me one last quizzical look.

'What?' I said, forcing out a smile.

She paused for a split second. 'Nothing . . . I'll see you lunchtime, yeah?'

I nodded and staggered off to the editing suite. Making a mental note to text Don to tell her I was working through lunch, I settled down in front of the computer, everything else already fading into the background.

I'd finished the film by lunchtime, but I didn't go to meet the others. I polished it a bit and then, after showing my face at the beginning of media studies, I spent the rest of the ninety minutes generally making it so shit-hot they'd probably have to invent a new Oscar category for it. Joke. I was really proud of it, though. If it turned out that no film school wanted me, at least I'd know that I'd given it my best shot. (Who was I kidding? I'd be gutted.)

I made two DVDs of the film, had one last read of my write-up, then printed it out, put it together with one of the DVDs into a plastic sleeve, and closed down the computer. Blinking as I went back into the classroom, I handed my coursework to Matt.

'Well done,' he said, smiling. 'I've been looking forward to seeing this one . . . Have you got anyone coming to the screening tonight?'

I shrugged. 'Friends. My mum's working, so . . .' (She'd got a last-minute out-of-hours appointment from a massively wadded daughter of a lord or some such. 'I'm so sorry I'll miss your screening, Ash. You don't mind, do you?' she'd said. What was I going to reply? 'Yes, actually, I do mind'? No way, man.)

He nodded. 'Well, enjoy it.' He waved the plastic sleeve at me in a kind of *atta girl, go get 'em* style. Didn't really know how to respond to that, so I just said thanks and sat down at a table to spend the last five minutes of the lesson twiddling my thumbs and feeling nervous.

One of those big canvassy screens had been set up in the theatre, and in front of it on the stage was a lectern where each of us was supposed to introduce our films. Personally, I'd rather have, ahem, let the film speak for itself, but Matt had insisted. It was for the parents in the audience, apparently. I'd gently reminded him that, sob, I wasn't going to have a parent in the audience, but he'd just given me an arch look and said nothing. Backstage, we all stood hugging ourselves and talking vaguely hysterically. Nothing like shared terror to turn a bunch of people into instant best buds.

'Right, everyone,' said Matt, rubbing his hands together. 'Here we go.' He pointed at a piece of paper that he'd taped to the wall. 'This is the running order . . . Ashley, you're first. I'm going to do a brief introduction, then, just as we discussed, you walk on to the stage, wait for your applause to die down, say a few words, walk offstage, and the film will begin.'

Great. I tried to breathe more slowly. My stomach had turned to liquid – I was going to soil myself in front of the whole school. At least it would get people off the slag thing, I thought, a bubble of hysterical laughter forming inside me. Closing my eyes and doing a big ol' out-breath to stop me actually passing out with fear, I stood in the wings and watched Matt do his stuff. After a couple of minutes of general spiel, he said: 'And so I give you our first film: *Towards the Light* by Ashley Greene.' Then, to a mixture of polite applause and a pocket of frenzied cheering from a small section of the audience (I'd recognize Donna's wolf-whistle anywhere), I walked on to the stage.

Standing at the lectern, I cleared my throat and took a second to compose myself, just as the results of Googling 'public speaking' had told me to. Fixing my eyes on the back of the room, I said, 'A couple of months ago I got into trouble in the sea and nearly drowned.' I paused. You could still here the echo of my voice in the silence of the auditorium.

'While I didn't have a near-death experience, it got me thinking. What exactly is a near-death experience? Why do people have them? And are they proof of life after death? I hope my film, *Towards the Light*, will at least begin to answer these questions. Thank you.'

To further applause I walked offstage, but hovered in the wings to watch.

The opening shot was a wide expanse of sky, which panned down to a busy high street (Brighton the previous Sunday, to be precise). 'It is estimated that as many as a third of people who, whether through illness or accident, come close to death have a near-death experience,' went my voiceover.

And so it continued. The bits with Bridget in were bloody great. The expression on her face and the look in her eyes as she talked about what she'd been through . . . It was properly moving. Donna's voice-overs were really good too, especially against the photos and stills I'd used to illustrate the stories she was narrating.

When it had finished there was a good bit of applause from the audience. It wasn't exactly a rapturous standing ovation, but I hadn't expected it to be. I had to bite my lip to stop myself crying, though. Not being big-headed or anything, but I could hardly believe the film was mine. *I made that*, I kept thinking.

As the next person went on to do their introduction, the others congratulated me, spouting all the usual rubbish that people come up with at times like these. 'Oh my God, it's sooo much better than mine.' All that crap. But, actually, I watched the other films and maybe I wasn't the best person to judge, but they *weren't* as good as mine.

Afterwards Matt gathered us together backstage and passed round a box of Heroes. 'It's not exactly Champagne, but the sentiment's there,' he said. He was beaming from ear to ear like *he'd* made the films. 'Seriously, guys. Really brilliant work. I'm proud of you.'

I can't even describe what an amazing feeling it was. I was more certain than ever that I wanted to keep doing this. And that I *could* keep doing this, if only some stranger in a university admissions department would let me.

As I was about to leave the stage to find my friends, Matt stopped me. 'Ashley, have you got a sec?'

Uh-oh. I shrugged and nodded.

'Your documentary is excellent. Really,' he said, smiling.

I grinned. 'Thanks, Matt. I loved making it.' It just came out. So much for keeping my cards close to my chest.

He nodded. 'I could tell . . . Listen, have you thought about what you want to do next year?'

I hesitated. 'Er . . .'

'Because I think you should seriously consider applying to do film. If you want to, of course.' He looked at me expectantly.

'Well, the thought had occurred to me,' I said cagily, but Matt clapped his hands together as if I'd just told him the applications were in the post.

'Great. I'm more than happy to write you a reference, so just ask, OK?'

I nodded. 'OK. Thanks.'

He patted my upper arm, said, 'Really great work. Well done,' and strode off, leaving me grinning inanely into space. I clenched my fists and did a little 'wheeeee' of joy, then skipped down the stairs off the stage to meet the others.

'Hey, it's Ashley Hitchcock!' crowed Ollie, throwing his arms round me in a bear hug as I finally found everyone except Donna by the stage door.

'Brilliant film, Ash,' said Sarah, smiling. 'I'm seriously impressed.'

'God, me too,' said Cass. 'You're properly talented, aren't you?'

'Aw, shuddup,' I protested, going red.

'Let me to her, let me to her,' shouted Donna, appearing from nowhere and fighting her way through the group. She grabbed me in a hug and thumped my back in what I guessed was supposed to be a congratulatory and supportive manner, but actually left me feeling pummelled. 'Shit, babes. You're a star. A STAR, I TELL YOU!' Pushing me away, she held me at arm's length and regarded *moi*. 'So proud of you, bitch.' She shook her head, grinning and biting her lip at the same time. She really did look proud. Aw, my friends!

'Thanks, everyone,' I said, meaning it. 'I heart you all.'

Egg on my face this morning, but not this evening. Eat that, poxy rumour-mongers. Tra la laaaa!

I went to bed on a high, but woke up as low as ever. The fact that my documentary hadn't sucked was not some kind of talisman against all the crap at school, however happy I'd felt in the moment. And now I'd finished the film I didn't even have that to focus on. It was just me versus false rumours. No contest. I still ran to school to avoid eggage, I still walked with my head down to avoid eye contact and there was still the soul-destroying, energy-sapping drip-drip of whispered asides, mean looks and bitchy comments. At least there was no more graffiti, or none that I knew of.

(Don't call it bullying, by the way. I hate that word and, anyway, it's only bullying if you let it be, IMO. What was happening to me was nothing but a tiny-brained, puke-eating fly, buzzing around my head annoyingly. I could have splatted it, but it was more efficient and less knackering just to let it buzz till it died of exhaustion. Or till term ended. Whichever came sooner.)

Walking into the canteen at lunchtime was like being mugged by a manically laughing Santa. The servers were wearing tinsel deely-boppers and dishing up turkey with all the trimmings while crappy Christmas music played tinnily over the PA system. The noise of people being joyful was deafening.

I winced and turned to Donna to ask if we could go somewhere else, but she was only semi-ironically getting on down to 'Christmas Wrapping' by The Waitresses, which is admittedly an excellent Christmas song – if there is such a thing – and the only one I liked apart from 'O Come All Ye Faithful' (got to love that bit in the last verse when the harmonies go all high and climaxy).

'Nice moves, lady,' I said, raising an eyebrow. She closed her eyes, bit her bottom lip and started jabbing at me with pointy funk fingers. 'OK, now you're just embarrassing yourself,' I said, laughing. Which was pretty much like saying, *Please. Be more outrageous. Not enough people are staring at you*. When she began doing the twist, I stuck my nose in the air, sighed massively, and ostentatiously walked off. Someone at a nearby table called out something, I don't know what, but it was directed at me and it made the rest of the table laugh like robot lackeys. Whatever it was, I'm sure it was *hilarious*. But it did kind of put a dampener on the little root of good mood that Donna had planted, so by the time I got to our table I was back in Morose-ville, population: me.

'All right, smiler?' asked Ollie, grinning at me round a mouthful of roast potato.

'Brilliant, thanks,' I said, a *tad* ironically. 'Nice gravy, by the way. Love the way you've got it dripping out of your actual mouth.' Ol licked it away and rolled his eyes saucily (no pun intended). So I rolled mine back. Not saucily.

'Are you coming to the pub later?' asked Jack, who was tucking into his Christmas dinner like he hadn't eaten in a week.

I wrinkled my nose. 'Dunno. Where are we going?'

'Hobbit.'

'I'm not really in the mood,' I said, stealing a chip off Rich's plate.

He slapped my hand away. 'First, get your own. And second, shut up. You've got to come out. It's the end of term! It's Christmas!' He stuck his bottom lip out. 'Go on, Ash. Don't be a party pooper.'

I was officially never going to have a go at Sarah and Cass for not coming out ever again. It was really annoying.

'I'm not being a party pooper,' I said through gritted teeth. 'I just don't want to come out. OK?' I glared at him meaningfully and light finally dawned. He winced and gave me a *whoops, sorry* look.

'Oh, don't worry about all that,' said Cass, putting her hand over mine. I resisted the urge to flinch. 'You'll be with us.'

'Thanks, but I don't think that will stop anyone, no offence,' I said. 'If someone wants to have a go, they'll have a go, and I just can't be arsed to deal with it. You'll have more fun without me.'

Ollie shook his head and sucked air through his teeth. 'It's a sad day when Ashley Greene doesn't come out to celebrate the end of term. We'll miss you, babes.'

Donna finally arrived at the table, putting down her tray with a clatter. 'Miss you? Why, where are you going?'

'Nowhere.' I couldn't believe I had to go through all this again. 'I'm not coming out tonight.'

'Oh yeah. I didn't think you would, to be honest.' She shot me a quick smile, which I returned.

Suddenly my phone jumped, whirring loudly against the table as a text arrived. 'No name,' said Sarah, looking at the display. 'Ooh, who's texting you?'

'It'll be Ian the Stalker,' I said, picking up the phone. 'I've never saved his number.' For some reason he'd upped his game this week, texting me every day, some to suggest a time and place to meet up, others just to ask how I was.

I read the latest out loud.

Hey ashley, actually
earlier wd be better on
Sunday. 3 good 4 me.
Lemme know!!!!

'Oh my God, you're not actually going to meet him?' asked Cass, looking at me incredulously.

'No!' I gave her a *duh* look. 'In his last text he suggested meeting on Sunday at four.'

'He's optimistic, isn't he?' said Ollie. 'Have you even replied to any of his texts?'

I shook my head. 'Or to his Facebook posts.'

'It's kind of sad, really,' said Sarah. 'He's so pathetic.'

'I know . . . He never asks why I never reply or sounds even remotely angry.'

'Maybe you need to tell him you're not interested,' she added.

'Maybe he should have got the message by now,' I said, deleting the text.

'Yeah, but he's probably thinking no news is good news,' said Jack. '"You might need to be cruel to be kind" type thing.' He cleared his throat. 'You did . . . do stuff with him, after all. Maybe you can't blame him for hoping.'

I thought about that one. 'Yeah, I'd go for that if he was, like, thirteen years old. But he's a grown man . . .' I tailed off. Jack might have a point, but with everything that was going on at the moment I only had the head space to delete the messages and forget about them.

'Anyway,' said Donna, 'I'm going up for more parsnips. Anyone want anything?'

School ended early, with a crushing sense of anti-climax. The clock ticked past two and term was over. It was the moment I'd been looking forward to all week, but I felt nothing apart from exhaustion. Without saying goodbye to anyone, I left the building. I was home by half two. Probably earlier, what with having to run to avoid low-flying eggs and every-thing. Without really forming the idea in my head, I went straight up to my room and dialled Bridget's number, but cancelled before I'd reached the end. I didn't know what I wanted to say to her, other than to ask her to make it all OK, and that was just stupid. What could she do? Say wise words down the phone like some poxy premium-rate advice line? So instead I got into bed, fell asleep almost immediately and slept till nine the following morning.

When I woke up, the last week already seemed in the past. History. A tiny footnote in the story of my life. Not even that. I told myself that by the time school started again in January, the shit-rakers would have moved on to something else. But, whatever, I wasn't going to devote even one brain cell to thinking about it. The whole thing could piss off. It was time to move on – starting with meeting Dylan and Marv at the pub tomorrow.

6

I spent a stupid amount of time working out what to wear to the pub. Everything I tried on looked wrong: either boring or try-hard. I even resorted to looking through Frankie's wardrobe for inspiration, and she owned both a JLS T-shirt and jogging bottoms with 'Girl' written across the bum. But in the end I went for a black (*naturellement*) laddered jumper dress I'd bought in the sales ages ago and forgotten I even owned, which I wore with thick black tights and my trusty hobnail boots. My biker jacket finished the look. I practically whimpered with relief when I stood in front of the mirror. I looked pretty good, even if I do say so myself, blah blah. After quickly pinning my hair into a messy topknot and touching up my eyeliner, I was ready. And feeling slightly sick with dread and excitement. I couldn't wait to see Dylan again – the fact he'd even said yes to meeting up was a good sign, right? – but at the same time, oh GOD, the humiliation of seeing him after what had happened at Ollie's party. As I walked to meet the three of them I practised what I was going to say. If nobody mentioned it, neither would

I. If someone did mention it (and Donna had crossed-her-heart-and-hoped-to-die that she wouldn't), I was going to try groaning, putting my head in my hands and saying something like, 'Oh God, I'm so embarrassed. Let's not even go there,' which I thought had the right mix of self-deprecation and sorry-ness.

But when I got to the pub, Dylan wasn't there.

'All right, everyone?' I said, sooper brightly. 'Dylan not here yet?'

Donna shot me a sympathetic look. 'He's not coming, babes.'

Marv held up his phone. 'He just texted me. He's got to babysit his step-sibs.'

'Oh. Right.' Trying desperately hard to look as if that was a shame but, y'know, no biggie, I sat down, then immediately stood up again when I realized I hadn't got myself a drink yet. 'What are you having?' I asked, my voice wobbly. I was stupidly close to actually crying. Dylan didn't want to see me or he'd have come. Simple as that.

'I'll come with you,' said Donna, jumping up. She looked at Marv. 'Same again?' He nodded and she took my arm.

'I know what you're thinking, and don't,' she hissed into my ear as she dragged me to the bar. 'If he didn't have to babysit, he'd be here.'

'Oh yeah, totally,' I said sarcastically. 'He couldn't wait to see me.'

'Don't be a tit, babes,' said Donna reasonably. 'It doesn't suit you.' She waved her hand to attract the attention of the barman. 'Three Becks, please.'

'Hmmph.' I paused, scratching at the wood of the bar with my fingernail. 'Actually, babes –'

But she interrupted. 'No way. Don't even think about leaving. We can still have a good night. You'll be fine after a few drinks.' She leant across the bar. 'Actually, mate?' The barman looked round. 'I'll have two Jaegerbombs as well.'

He frowned at her. 'You got ID?'

She rolled her eyes, pulled her fake student card out of her wallet and held it up for him to see. 'OK?' Without even looking at it, he nodded and reached for the Jaeger.

'I hate Jaeger. It tastes of Benylin,' I moaned.

'Shows it's good for you, then,' said Donna. 'Now get that down you.' She handed me a glass, picked up the other and we both downed them in one. I pulled a face, but the boozy burn was good. Don was right. There was no point getting all vortex of despairy about Dylan. I'd known he wasn't inter-ested before tonight, so really nothing had changed. And if I still felt gutted about it – which, let's face it, I did – I was just going to ignore it via the medium of alcohol. A healthy attitude, I think you'll agree.

'Come on, then,' I said, hooking my free arm through Donna's. 'Let's rock this crazy joint.' She shook her head in despair at my extreme geekitude, and we went back to join Marv, where we spent the next couple of hours drinking, talking and occasionally laughing. It wasn't the best night of my life, but it wasn't the worst either. Which, considering the circumstances, wasn't bad going.

I had slightly higher hopes for the first official festive event of the season: the Great Gift Exchange, in which we ate, drank and exchanged gifts. For the last couple of years we'd done Secret Santa – each of us spending £5 max on only buying one person a present, rather than all buying something for everyone. Good thing too. I couldn't afford to give six decent presents, and I hated receiving any kind of present in front of an audience. Too much pressure.

Anyway, Sarah had booked the restaurant; the rest of us just had to turn up. Sweet. Although it has to be said there was a leetle bit of heart-sinkage when we arrived to find the place bursting at the seams with screechy office parties. Honest to God, I'd never seen so much artificially straightened hair and exposed boob crack in my life. And that was just the men. Ha ha. But Sarah had a voucher for half-price mains, so we were willing to put up with it. And at least it meant we could be loud too, if we wanted. Nothing worse (well, there is, but you know what I mean) than sitting near po-faced oldies who like to look over and shake their heads despairingly at the youth of today. So being surrounded by over-dressed adults getting pissed up was not the worst that could happen. And, anyway, it was Christmas. Ho ho ho and a bucket of festive cheer, etc.

'Right,' said Cass, settling herself down and opening out her napkin with a practised hand-flick. 'We'll order and *then* we'll do presents. Otherwise we'll never get round to ordering and we'll all get too drunk.'

'Can't have that,' said Rich with a smile, and he flagged down a waiter to bring us house wine and tap water (not together, you understand – that would be like the world's rubbishest cocktail), before asking him to come back in two minutes for our food order. Rich could be just as efficient as Cass when he wanted to be, which wasn't often, to be fair.

'C'mon, look lively, people,' said Ollie, rubbing his hands together. 'Let's order quickly. I can't bear the bloody excitement.' He grinned around at us. He wasn't even joking. I'd picked Ollie out of the hat this year, and I'd spent my £5 maximum on a £3 book of quotations I'd come across in one of those cheap bookshops. I found myself really hoping I didn't disappoint him. Stoopid, really. It was only bloody Secret Santa. I wondered who'd picked me. Last year Cass had got me a pair of neon pink towelling socks, which I'd genuinely loved. What were the chances of getting two good presents in a row? I was crap at fake delight.

So we all ordered quickly, and Cass reached under her chair to bring out the bag of presents. I looked around the table. Everyone had these hilarious expectant *don't really care but ooh really do care* half-smiles on their faces. I say 'hilarious'; actually, they made me feel a tiny bit dead inside. I'd have been happier not to do the gift thing at all, but I knew I was on my own with that one. It's not nice being the Scroogey one. At that moment, I felt for the misunderstood Dickensian bastard.

Cass handed round the gifts. The wrapping totally gave away who they were from. Like, the present for Sarah was wrapped in brown paper with MERRY XMAS! scrawled all over it in blue Biro. My guess was on Ollie, although the undisguised apprehension on his face was also a bit of a giveaway. Donna's present was wrapped in thin, crappy, robins 'n' foliage paper like you get from newsagents – and was from Jack, I reckoned. Jack's was perfectly wrapped in sparkling white paper tied round with an enormous blue and silver bow. From Cass, without a doubt. Rich's gift was done up in Hello Kitty paper, which had Donna written all over it (not literally, obvs). And I'd wrapped Ollie's present in a page ripped from *Kerrang!* magazine, which I thought was a *très* creative and yet eco-friendly solution to the excess of festive wrapping. And looked *très bon* to boot.

My present was last out of the bag. It was a long, thin box wrapped in black paper with purple ribbon round it. Process of elimination told me it was from Sarah, but I'd have known anyway: neat, tasteful and with obvious thought into what I'd actually like, wrapping-wise.

Cass looked around with satisfaction at us all sitting expectantly with our gifts neatly on the table in front of us.

'Can we start, then?' asked Donna.

'Course we can,' said Ollie, and he ripped into the paper, everyone else taking his lead. I pretended to be studying the wrapping on mine while watching him out of the corner of my eye. He took out the book of quotations and read the blurb on the back, his expression neutral. My heart was about to sink when he nudged my foot with his and held up the book. 'From you?'

I shrugged. 'Yeah.'

He grinned. 'Nice one. Seriously.'

I shrugged again. 'Cool.' (Taking compliments wasn't my strong point.)

I had a quick look around the table. Opposite me, Sarah was holding a pale wooden picture frame and staring intently at whatever was in it, a massive smile spreading across her chops.

'Hey, Sar, what is it?' I asked.

She turned it round. Ollie had framed a page from a book. 'It's from *Jane Eyre*,' she said.

'God, that's a great present!' It was perfect for Sarah. Go, Ollie.

'Aren't you going to open yours?' she asked.

'Oh yeah. Course.' I ripped into it, tension tightening my chest. If there was such a thing as *getting-presentsaphobia*, I had it. Or at least a phobia of opening a present in front of the person who gave it to me. I prepared to adopt a rictus grin and tore the paper off, revealing a clear plastic box. It had a kid's watch inside, black with thin silvery spiders picked out all over it and a glow-in-the-dark face. I relaxed, suddenly realizing my shoulders had been hunched like I was flinching from a punch in the face. I leant across the table and gave Sarah a hug. 'I love it, babes!'

She blushed and grinned. 'How'd you know it was from me?'

'What, you want me to big up someone else?' I took the watch out and wrapped it round my wrist. It just fitted. And no way it cost under a fiver – not that I was going to make a stand.

Rich interrupted my arm admiration. 'OK, show-and-tell time.' He held up a water pistol that, apart from being obviously made of plastic, looked so real I was surprised it was legal. 'Everyone should have a replica gun to play with in the bath, am I right?' He did the point-and-click at Donna. 'Nice one, lady.'

Cass had a mini desk dustpan and brush from Rich; Donna got shower gel (a bit of a rubbish present compared to the others – Jack had never been great at the Secret Santa thing); and, finally, Jack had been given a Brighton and Hove Albion pen and pencil set. Kind of obvious, but as it was clearly from Cass he gazed upon it as if it had been fashioned from, like, Venus dust and elf gold.

And then, as if by magic (or, y'know, by waiter), the food arrived, and presents were put aside so we could get on with the serious business of stuffing our faces. My spaghetti and meatballs was *très* tasty, even if it did leave me surrounded by orange splatter. I'm sure I've heard somewhere that you need to slurp spaghetti to get the full flavour. Something to do with oxygen? I dunno. Anyway, slurping's fun.

'So what's everyone doing between now and the big day?' asked Rich, a gloopy triangle of pizza dangling from his hand. 'Anyone want to do my Christmas shopping for me?'

'No, you're all right,' said Donna. 'I've still got to do mine.'

Cass shook her head in disbelief. 'I've had all my presents bought and wrapped for weeks.'

Sarah interrupted. 'Tell them about the spreadsheet.'

Rich shook his head in sorrow. 'Cass, babes. Tell me it's not true.'

'Oh, pooh. *Everyone* has a presents spreadsheet,' said Cass snootily, but she was smiling.

'She's right,' said Ollie, nodding. 'If by "spreadsheet" you mean "vague list in my head".'

'I've got to work,' I said, answering Rich's first question. 'I better get some frickin' am*az*ing presents this year for all the free labour my mum gets from me.'

'Aw, hon, you're working all week?' Sarah creased her brow in sympathy.

'No,' I admitted. 'I'm taking Frankie shopping tomorrow.'

I was really looking forward to me and my sister's annual trip. Mum always gave us money to have lunch in this bakery-slash-cafe that had been our special-treats venue since I was tiny, and then we'd go to this amazing ice-cream shoppe (that's how they spell it) on the seafront for hot-chocolate floats. Which sounds disgusting but so isn't. And somewhere along the line we'd buy Mum's and Sasha's presents, and choose something for each other. Franks had been talking about it for weeks. I don't do festive, but I came pretty close when I took her Christmas shopping. Lucky, really, since spending most of the week before Christmas sucking up to rich bitches and their even bitchier bride-to-be daughters in Mum's shop was pretty much guaranteed to make me want to stab someone. If and when I ever get married, I swear I'm giving myself a fifty-quid budget. Spending, like, three grand on a dress you're only going to wear once is obscene, I don't care what anybody says. Although, obviously, the more my mum sold, the better. Each stupidly expensive dress that left the premises took me one step closer to actually getting paid for my efforts.

I was broken out of my musings by Donna clicking her fingers in front of my face. 'Oi, Ashley!'

I batted her hand away. 'What?'

'Do. You. Want. Pudding?'

'All right, all right.' I scowled. 'No need to talk to me like I'm educationally subnormal.'

Don gave me an *if the cap fits* look. I gave her a *ha ha most amusing* look and had a quick peruse of the dessert menu. 'What's everyone having?'

'Chocolate fudge cake, mainly.'

I put my menu back down. 'I'll have the cheese-cake, then.'

I caught Sarah and Cass smirking and rolling their eyes at each other. It pleased them to mock me for wanting to be different. Whatever. Just cos they were Mrs and Mrs Conventionality.

Looking around the table, I realized that everyone was way drunker than me. I checked my new watch: 9.30. I grabbed the bottle of red and filled my glass, and before I knew it nearly three hours had passed and we'd been turfed out of the empty restaurant. We stood for a minute in the freezing rain, giggling drunkenly and hugging each other goodbye. In the good old days before the Ian Incident I'd have got the bus, but now, despite the fact I was freezing my arse off in the middle of town in the pissing rain without an umbrella, there was no option but to put my head down and walk home.

I'd been walking for about five minutes, and was already soaked to the skin, when a car pulled up alongside me. Obviously I was wary. It was midnight and I was on my own: *Crimewatch*-tastic. But then a guy stuck his head out of the window and even in the dark I recognized him, although that was all. I didn't *know* him, know him. He was just a dude I used to see at the Hobbit, and I thought I'd seen him in a club once or twice.

'Do you want a lift somewhere?' He smiled, his face open. He didn't look like a psycho rapist, although presumably psycho rapists don't wear a badge advertising their psycho-rapist credentials. It was tempting, what with the prevailing weather conditions, but I shook my head and said, 'No, you're all right, thanks.'

'You sure?' he said, looking surprised. 'It's not a problem. To be honest, you'd be doing me a favour. I've got a new baby at home and my girlfriend's just texted to say he's screaming the place down.' He smiled sheepishly. 'I'd be glad of an excuse to stay away for a bit longer.'

I bit my lip and shivered as rain dripped down the back of my neck. I was about to give in, when he got out of the car and opened the passenger door.

'In you get.' He laughed a strange, nervous laugh. 'Haven't got all day!' He swallowed, his Adam's apple bobbing up and down, and started drumming the side of the door impatiently.

'No. I'm fine,' I said firmly, then turned and started hurrying away. I heard the car door slam and then fast footsteps behind me. Shit shit shit. Adrenalin rushed through me, making my fingers tingle like pins and needles, and I was about to start sprinting when I heard my name. Spinning round, I saw Cass and Sarah with their coats over their heads, walking briskly towards me. The man saw them too. He got back in his car and sped off, his tyres skidding slightly on the wet road.

'Who was that?' asked Cass, squinting after the retreating car.

I leant against a lamp post to get myself together. My heart was thumping like a mentalist. 'I don't know,' I said. 'Some freak who wouldn't take no for an answer.'

'Oh my God,' said Sarah, looking shocked. 'Are you OK? Do you think you should tell the police?'

I shook my head. 'No, nothing happened. He was just weird . . . Anyway, what are you doing here?'

'Missed our bus,' said Cass. 'We were going to share a cab. Do you want in? My treat.'

'I'm up for that.' I closed my eyes and breathed out slowly. It felt like I couldn't get enough air into my lungs. Sarah put her arm through mine. 'You're OK,' she said, nudging me with her side.

'Yeah, course,' I said lightly, although really I was pathetically grateful not to be on my own. I'd so nearly got in the car with him. I shivered as I thought about what could have happened.

I got home without incident and, exhausted by my close encounter with freako man, slept like the dead until Frankie pulled up my blind with a rattling flourish, singing, 'Oh, what a beautiful morning!' at full-throated, opera-diva volume. I huffed and grumped, but secretly (very secretly) I was as excited about today as she was.

'I've brought you a cup of tea,' said Frankie, pointing at the mug on my bedside table. 'Drink it quick.'

'All right, babes. Give me a sec.' I rubbed my fore-head. 'Go and get us a Nurofen, will you?'

Her brow creased in disappointment. 'Oh, Aaaash,' she whined. 'Don't be hungover today.'

'I'm fine.' I smiled and slurped my tea noisily. 'See?'

She raised an eyebrow (learnt from the master). 'Hmm.'

I checked the time. 'Look, I'll be ready by ten. I promise. I don't need breakfast or anything.'

'Yes you do. I'll make you some toast while you're in the shower.'

I smirked. 'OK, Mum.'

'It's not funny,' said Franks seriously. 'Emily read in a magazine that if you don't eat breakfast you'll get fat.'

'Emily reads too many magazines.' I stuck my foot out from under the duvet and gave her a kick. 'Now piss off and let me get dressed in peace.'

'OK,' said Franks reasonably. 'Breakfast will be on the table in ten minutes.' She gave me a warning look. 'You know how much you hate cold toast.'

'Whatever.' I sighed and stared at her until she left

the room. After a couple of minutes of enjoying my cosy bed and the good-day potential, I got up.

Don't hate me, but since meeting Dylan I got dressed with him in mind. Every. Single. Day. Deluded and sad, but there it was. I couldn't help myself. Before Dylan, I often left the house without make-up on. Now, I never would. And, yes, it's what's on the inside that counts. But he had to get past the outside before he could get to the inside, didn't he? And he was beautiful; I wasn't. I needed all the help I could get. It also made getting dressed in the morning kind of exciting, as if the more effort I made the more likely I was to bump into him. Was I going mental? Possibly. Anyway, that morning I chose leggings, a sheer black shirt and a big chunky knit cardi to cover my modesty (ha). See? Not over the top, just carefully considered.

Within an hour we were on our way to town, with Frankie merrily skipping along beside me. The word 'unabashed' could have been invented for the kid. I kept expecting her to get all awkward and embarrassed, like I'd done when I was twelve, but so far it hadn't happened. It was kind of refreshing, but at the same time I worried for her. Naive might be a good look when you're twelve and small for your age. But at fourteen? Not so much. Anyway, I kept my mouth shut and let her get on with it. Having a crush on that

Freddy dude meant she was at least on the road to the shit that is puberty, poor cow. She was obviously just a late starter – she didn't even have periods yet.

'Can we go to the ice-cream shoppe first?' She pronounced it 'shoppy'. 'Pleeease? They always run out of white chocolate and raspberry flavour by the afternoon.'

I gave her a look. 'Not in the middle of winter they don't. But, yeah, all right.'

She gave a whoop and we strolled to the seafront.

'So, how's it going with Freddy?' I asked casually.

She paused. 'I think it might be going OK, actually. He's asked to be my friend on Facebook.'

'Result.'

'He makes me feel . . . I dunno. Sort of *me*, but more so. Do you know what I mean?'

I smiled. 'Totally. Like all the best things about you are better, and the worst things are hidden.'

She squeezed my arm. 'Exactly.' She paused again, then said, 'He's got lovely teeth and when he smiles at me my fingertips tingle.' She was biting her lip, smiling to herself.

'Go for it, babes,' I said. 'Facebook him and ask if he wants to go to the cinema or something.'

'What, like a date?' She said it as if only total cretins went on dates. 'Nobody does that any more.'

'Well, what do you do, then?' I asked. I was only six

years older than her: things couldn't have changed that much.

'I dunno. "Meet by a bus stop and sit around drinking cider from a lemonade bottle and snogging each other" type thing.'

I relaxed. Things hadn't changed at all. 'Fair enough. But if you really like him maybe you don't want to just snog him by a bus stop.'

'Maybe.' And that was that. She changed the subject. I didn't push it. She was clever enough to sort it out for herself, although part of me was tempted to break into Frankie's Facebook, find this Freddy and gently inform him that if he made my sister sad I'd break his legs.

We carried on mooching, yapping about this and that and stopping every now and then to look in shop windows. I was bracing myself for her to ask again about the graffiti, but she didn't.

'One of those, thanks,' I said to the man behind the counter in the ice-cream place, pointing at Frankie's white chocolate and raspberry. 'And a hot-chocolate float.'

'Oooh . . .' Franks bit her lip and looked at me pleadingly.

'Oh, for f—' I looked at the man. 'Scrap the ice cream. Two hot-chocolate floats, please.'

'Sorry, Ash. I'd forgotten about those.'

I shook my head. 'Right. Cos we only have them every single year.' Frankie giggled and we chose a table by the window. Like all the others, it had a kitschy red-and-white gingham tablecloth and a hand-written menu card on it.

Franks groaned as she licked whipped cream off her spoon. 'Oh God, orgasm . . .'

I smirked. 'Really?'

'Shuddup.' She smiled, but she'd gone bright red. I felt a bit bad. For all I knew, Frankie was providing herself with five a night, although I guessed not, if the taste of whipped cream was her ecstasy barometer. I changed the subject. 'So, what shall we get for Mum and Sasha?'

Frankie reached into her coat pocket. 'I got them to write a list each.' I was impressed – I'd never thought to do that. Disappointing Daughter strikes again. She smoothed them out on the table. Mum had asked for some posh anti-ageing cream, a silk scarf, earrings and, weirdly, an iTunes voucher. Sasha had requested a gardening-centre voucher, pricey olive oil, new pyjamas and a donation to the charity of our choice. I scowled. 'Donation to charity? Give me an effing break.'

'It's a really nice thought,' protested Frankie.

'Yeah, no, you're right,' I said, sighing and leaning

back in my chair. 'It's just . . . she gets on my tits, that's all . . . And what's with Mum asking for an iTunes voucher? She hasn't got an iPod.' Franks smiled. 'Sasha's getting her one.'

'Of course she is.'

I sat up again, suddenly businesslike. 'Right, then. We'll get Sash some PJs from Oxfam and kill two birds with one stone. And maybe we can get Mum some earrings at the same time.'

Franks looked doubtful. 'I think Sasha was thinking more of, like, silk M&S ones.'

'Either she wants to give to charity or she doesn't,' I huffed.

'Really?' Frankie frowned with concern for our dear sister.

I sighed impatiently. 'Oh, look, we'll get a couple of goats on her behalf from Oxfam and then pop to her beloved effing Waitrose for the fancy olive oil, OK?'

She smiled and put the lists back in her pocket. 'OK. Good idea.'

Later on, after we'd bought the presents and were wandering around Debenhams, Frankie suddenly pinched my arm. 'OW! What the –?' I said.

'There's a boy in Lingerie looking at you,' she hissed. I squinted over and, yes, there among the bras and pants was a boy. But not just any boy. My heart leapt then immediately sank, leaving me in very real danger of fainting clean away. I wasn't prepared for this. I was frantically trying to work out how to handle talking to Dylan for the first time since Ollie's party, when he started loping towards us, smiling easily.

Frankie gasped. 'Who is *that*?' I had just enough time to shush her before he reached us and bent down to kiss my cheek.

'Ashley! Really good to see you,' he said. He actually looked like he meant it. 'And you have to be Ashley's sister,' he continued, turning his dark eyes on Frankie. 'You've got the same smile.'

She actually sighed aloud, the crazy mare. 'I really am,' she breathed. 'But who are *you*?'

Huh. Maybe she wasn't such a slow starter after all.

He laughed and stuck out his hand for Frankie to shake. 'I'm Dylan, a friend of Ashley's. Nice to meet you.'

While Frankie succumbed to a quick simper – and I'd never seen her do *that* before – I took control of the situation.

'Good to see you too, Dylan,' I said, smiling. 'This is Frankie.' I raised an eyebrow at Franks and she gave me one right back. Fair enough. I didn't know why I hadn't told her about him although, honestly, what was there to tell? 'I fancy someone who doesn't

148

fancy me?' Whoa, big news. And maybe it had just become too tied up with Ollie's party, and that Billy arsehole, and the graffiti business. Although to look at him now, all smiling and relaxed, it was as if Ollie's party had never happened.

'It looks like you've had better luck than I have,' he said, nodding at our bags. 'I'm supposed to be getting my mum's present, but so far I've drawn a big, fat blank.'

'Oh, bummer,' I said. 'What kind of thing does she want?'

He drew a breath as if about to reel off a list of items, then exhaled loudly. 'No idea . . . I usually get her Body Shop stuff, but she subtly hinted that this year it might be a good idea to ring the changes.'

I smiled. 'Ouch.' He smiled back, his eyes meeting mine. I don't have a problem with eye contact, but his did something to me, turning my insides into knots of . . . well, desire, I suppose. I cleared my throat while at the same time trying to clear out any ideas that he might ever have any kind of feelings for me. But, AGH! Those eyes! We're talking limpid pools, people. Bottomless, limpid pools of intelligence and humour and an underlying seam of good-in-beditude. I caught Frankie smirking out of the corner of my eye and snapped myself out of it. She was right: I was embarrassing myself.

'Right, well. We'd better give you a hand then,' I said briskly. 'Seeing as we're girls and everything . . . So, what kind of person is your mum? Is she, like, a Carol Vorderman foxy type, or a sensible but nice Fern Brittony type, or a MILFy . . .' I searched my brain for a sexy mum figure.

'A MILFy Fiona Brucey type?' offered Frankie.

'Exactly,' I said. We turned our collective gaze on Dylan, and he started properly laughing.

'I'm sorry,' he said, his dimples more pronounced than ever. 'But you both raise your right eyebrow in exactly the same way. Do you *practise* that?'

I smiled. 'Of course.'

He laughed again and rubbed under his eye with a fingertip. 'Anyway, to answer your question . . . God, I don't know. I've never thought about her like that . . .' He considered for a moment. 'Disregarding the very idea of my mother being a MILF, which obviously disturbs me to my very core . . .'

I nodded earnestly. 'Obviously.'

He paused. 'Well . . . I guess she is kind of like Fiona Bruce. She's sort of businesslike and stylish, maybe. Oh, I dunno. She's just my mum, y'know?'

'No, that's good. Definitely gives us something to work with. Right, Franks?' She turned her enormous eyes on me and nodded, mutely. Okaaay. Looked like I'd lost Frankie to some kind of lust reverie. Nice.

I narrowed my eyes and looked around. 'OK, how about these?' I asked, moving towards a display of leather gloves. 'Maybe some turquoise ones, or even bright pink.' I put on a lady-who-sprays-you-with-perfume-in-department-stores voice. 'They're useful, classy, but with a slight edge.' I sucked in my cheeks campily.

'Actually, that's a really good idea,' said Dylan, rubbing the glove between finger and thumb (lucky glove). 'I reckon she'd love these.' He turned to me and beamed. 'You're amazing!'

I shrugged. 'Try my best.'

'God, I can't believe I've found her a present,' said Dylan, choosing a turquoise pair. 'Are you two free for a coffee to celebrate?'

I looked at Frankie, who nodded frantically. 'Looks like we are,' I said, smiling and hiding the fact that inside I was nodding just as frantically – and dancing down the street, clapping my hands and laughing hysterically to boot.

Get a grip, I told myself. *It doesn't mean anything except he's thirsty and/or needs caffeine.*

He held the gloves up. 'You go and grab a table. I'll pay for these and see you there.'

'And just who exactly was that, may I ask?' demanded Frankie as we joined the escalator up to the cafe floor.

'Oh, I'm sorry,' I said, turning round. 'Did you not catch his name?'

She narrowed her eyes. 'Amusing.'

I laughed. 'Come on, Franks. It's just Dylan. A friend. End of.'

She pursed her lips meaningfully. 'It looked more like "beginning of" if you ask me.'

'Well, it isn't.' I turned to face forward again, but that didn't stop her. She trotted beside me as I got off the escalator and started marching towards the cafe.

She put her hand on my arm. 'Come on, Ash. You fancy him, don't you?'

I shook her off, suddenly irritated. 'So what if I do? He doesn't fancy me back, so . . .'

Frankie stopped in her tracks and I turned back impatiently.

'He so does! He said you were amazing.'

I raised my eyes heavenward. 'Right. For finding a present for his mum. Don't be naive, Franks . . . Anyway, *you* obviously took a shine to him.'

'Yeah, he's really nice.' She smirked. 'Perfect for you.'

'Oh, piss off.'

She giggled and I smiled. 'Come on, bitch-face. Let's find a table before he catches us up.'

By the time he arrived, we were drinking tea and debating what Toby would get Sasha for Christmas this year. Last year it had been a foot spa and a neck-lace, and the year before that a kitten. Frankie had just suggested a dildo, giggling slightly hysterically with the naughtiness of it all (I didn't even know she knew about dildos – I guessed her mag-reading friend Emily was the source of this new info), when Dylan appeared at our table.

'You have way more interesting conversations with your sister than my step-brother does with me,' he said, grinning at Franks, who looked mortified. Hilarious.

'How old's your step-brother?' I asked.

'Twelve. And my step-sister's ten.'

'I'm twelve,' piped up Frankie.

'I thought you'd be about that,' said Dylan, smiling. 'Although you're much more mature than Riley.'

I caught his eye. He knew all the lines. He offered me a rather lovely little closed-mouth secret smile. If I hadn't known better I'd have thought we were sharing a moment.

For the next twenty minutes we chatted about nothing in particular: which cafe did the best coffee, whether you should be able to get mince pies all year round, when we worked out that Father Christmas wasn't real – and when we admitted it to our parents. Like, if you were listening in you'd think we were the dullest people on earth. But it was relaxed and easy. I hate chit-chat, but somehow he made it seem like boring things were just interesting things waiting to be discovered. He had a kind of fascinated-by-the-small-stuff vibe. I liked that. And he was brilliant with Frankie. In short and to sum up, I fancied him so much I could have cried with the frustration of not being able to have him.

He drained his coffee. 'I'd better go. Really good to see you, Ash.' (He called me Ash!) 'And lovely to meet you, Frankie.' He kissed us both on the cheek. He looked at me. 'See you Christmas Eve?'

I nodded. 'Yep.'

'Great. Till then, then.' And he loped languidly away from us, the hand in his bum pocket dragging them down to reveal a hint of faded black boxers.

'Oh my God, you should totally marry him,' breathed Frankie as we both gazed after him.

Well, I wouldn't go that far.

When we finally got home I paused outside the front door. 'Don't mention Dylan to Mum, OK?' I said. 'She'll ask too many questions and I can't be arsed.'

She shrugged. 'All right. Dunno why not, though.'

I gave her an extreme-patience face. 'I just told you why not.'

She rolled her eyes and we went into the house. I was knackered. After chucking my bags into the bottom of my wardrobe, I went into the bathroom, turned on the taps and added a glug of oil (I don't do bubble baths – they make my skin feel like it's too small for my body), then stripped off and waited, shivering, for the water to reach wallowing level. By the time the bath was full I was proper freezing and fully able to appreciate the joy of sinking into almost unbearably hot water. *Et voilà*, the perfect way to run a bath. (You're welcome.)

As I soaked, my brow beading with sweat and my body rocking the attractive hot bath two-tone red-and-white look, I thought about Dylan. Seeing him today was like a present I could open again and again just by thinking about it. But no matter how much I tried to push it down where it came from with a palm to the face, the thought *Maybe he really does like me* kept popping up. Stupid, destructive, pointless, doomed thought that it was. Seriously, my brain needed to get a grip.

But he'd been so friendly, and so brilliant with Frankie . . . And he'd said I was amazing! Yes, because of my excellent present-choosing skills and not my scintillating repartee and/or hot bod, but still. 'Amazing' had to be good, whichever way you looked at it. Oh God, and Frankie had really liked him too. Seal of approval, right there.

I hoped she would keep quiet about him, like I'd asked. The more people knew that I fancied him, the less likely it was to happen. Boy Maths 101. And I could really, really do without Mum and Sasha knowing about it, and then being all sympathetic and making bottom-lip-out and wide eyes at each other over my head when I had to tell them there was nothing doing. Ugh, the thought made my toes itch.

Putting all that out of my mind, I closed my eyes and conjured up a storyboard of Dylan and me, a secret cupboard, and people obliviously walking past as we did steamy romance within. Boy Fantasy 101.

7

My alarm went off at seven the next morning, rudely waking me in the middle of another Dylan scenario, this time involving sex in a Jacuzzi (I'd never even been in a Jacuzzi, but if it was anything like my dream, I was a big fan). I could hear Mum faffing in the kitchen, so I hauled my sorry carcass out of bed and went straight into the bathroom. I showered, then put on the black skirt suit my mum insisted I wore for work, complete with thin black tights and black court shoes. I dried my hair and brushed it back into a low ponytail, then finally circled my eyes with the thickest line of eyeliner my mother would allow, i.e. so skinny it made Victoria Beckham look a bit of a porker. And, *voilà*, I was all ready to vomit over myself. I hated this outfit. Like, I can't even put into words how much I hated it. But, however much I felt like telling Mum where to stick her unpaid slavery, I knew I wouldn't pack it in. Helping her out in the shop was the only thing saving me from the daughter dumper and, frankly, I wouldn't give Sasha the satisfaction.

'Ashley, are you up?' Mum called from the bottom of the stairs just as I was coming out of my room. 'Oh, you are. There's a cup of tea for you down here.'

'Cheers.' I plodded down the stairs with heavy, flat feet (a tiny victory – there was a certain pleasure in seeing Mum's face twitch with the effort of not letting it irritate her) and followed her into the kitchen.

'Is it busy today?' I asked as I poured Crunchy Nut Cornflakes into a bowl.

She shook her head. 'Not really. Just a couple of appointments.' Mum's was the kind of boutique where you couldn't just walk in off the street. You had to make an appointment so you could get her un-divided attention. Personally, I thought it was stupid. We were always turning people away who could be browsing while we were dealing with a customer. But what did I know? I was just the unpaid help.

'Any chance of leaving early this afternoon then?' I shovelled breakfast into my mouth. Seriously, I could live on cereal.

'Hmm. Maybe.' Mum bustled around getting her bag together and taking occasional bites from a piece of toast. 'I think this afternoon's lady is quite wealthy, so . . .' She didn't need to finish. The richer the customer, the more disgustingly we sucked up to them. I supposed it made sense, in a sick kind of way.

'All right, poo-heads?' Frankie appeared in the doorway, looking sleepy in rumpled pyjamas. She squinted at Mum. 'How long have I got?'

Mum looked at her watch. 'Ten minutes. Go and get dressed. I'll make your toast.'

Franks sloped off upstairs. In the school holidays she went to Emily's house while Mum and I were at the shop. Emily's parents had got married a couple of years back, but in a ridiculous twist of fate they'd both lost their jobs, like, two weeks before the wedding, so Mum had given Em's mum a dress for free. It was a display model – off the peg, no alterations, but still. It was a nice gesture. *Et voilà*: free childcare for life. Mum wouldn't need it for that much longer, though, since Franks would soon be old enough to stay in the house on her own.

We were at the shop by half eight. I busied myself drinking tea and staring into space while Mum got the float out of the safe, sorted the coins and notes into the till, refreshed the water in the huge vases of flowers and made sure there was enough Tesco Finest biscuits in the cupboard and cheap fizz in the fridge for the customers' 'complimentary refreshments'.

She paused in her busy bee-ness to give me a quick once-over. 'Your hair could do with a brush, love,' she said. 'You're getting a bit flyaway. There's hairspray in my bag.' I didn't move. 'Please, Ash.' She stared me out and, scowling, I dragged myself into the loo to contribute to the destruction of the ozone layer.

When I reappeared five minutes later the first customer had arrived. Mum smiled in my direction. 'Ah, Ashley. This is Charlotte Simpson, our bride-to-be.' She broke off for a bit of a simper in Charlotte's direction. 'And this is her mother, Mrs Simpson, and her sister, Grace.'

The sister was examining a display case of fascinators and turned round when she heard her name. *Shit*. It was Grace Simpson. As in Grace Simpson of the nail acrylics and boyfriend who I shagged? She shot me daggers and in an instant I decided the only way forward was to brazen it out.

'Hiiii! Lovely to meet you, Charlotte. When's the big day?' (That's how I have to talk in Mum's shop. Annoying, *non*?)

Grace's sister, who was pretty in a mousey kind of way, beamed. 'Next September.'

I gasped heroically as I caught sight of her engagement ring. 'Ooh, let me see?' I lifted up her hand and pretended to practically orgasm with joy at the gorgeousness of the entirely boring, albeit massive, solitaire diamond she was wearing. 'Oh. My. Gosh. It is *beautiful*.' I bit my lip and shook my head as if I was gutted that I wasn't her right now, and she giggled.

'It *is* lovely, isn't it? Alan – my fiancé . . .' She giggled again. 'He chose it all by himself.'

Mrs Simpson interrupted. 'He works up in London, in the City, so . . .' Wow. Nice crowbarring in of future son-in-law's credentials there, Mrs S.

Mum sighed. 'Oh, that's great. You must be very proud.' Mrs Simpson smiled modestly and nodded.

Are you beginning to see why I hate my job?

Mum rubbed her hands together. 'Right, then.' She turned to Charlotte. 'Do you have any thoughts about what kind of thing you're looking for in your dress?'

While they were discussing bodices and lace and veils and all that crap, I stole a quick sideways glance at Grace. She'd plonked herself on a chair and was staring at her feet.

'Grace!' Mrs Simpson spoke sharply. 'Come and help your sister choose a dress.' She lowered her voice a bit. 'It might be your only chance to be this close to a wedding dress, seeing as you've let yet *another* boyfriend slip through your fingers.' She pulled in her chin and pursed her lips meaningfully. Whoa, what a bitch. Grace sighed massively and stood, shoulders stooped, beside her sister.

It was only then that the significance hit me. She must have 'lost' her boyfriend because she'd chucked him after finding out he'd been unfaithful. With me. I was suddenly in the bizarre position of admiring Grace. It was pretty brave to respect yourself enough to chuck your boyfriend for being unfaithful when you've got a mother who's already putting partner pressure on and a big sister who's engaged to a banker. There was also another strange feeling. Empathy. When it came to failing to live up to a perfect older sister, I was the expert.

'So, who'd like a Buck's Fizz?' I said. 'Might as well start as we mean to go on, eh?' And I tinkled away merrily.

'Oh, go on then. Why not?' said Mrs Simpson, with the air of someone who thinks alcohol before seven p.m. is totally living on the edge.

'Grace, could I ask you to give me a hand?' I said. Mum frowned at me: this wasn't in the script. Grace looked up, surprised. I stared her out. She took the challenge and followed me into the kitchen area at the back of the shop.

As soon as we were out of sight, I hissed. 'Listen, before you say anything I would never in a million years have touched your ex if I'd known he was with you. It's a cast-iron rule with me. Whatever I do, I only do it if I'm sure no one will get hurt. Honestly.' I swallowed, and put the images of Ian the Stalker and Sam – the boy who still hated me because I hadn't believed him when he told me he liked me – out of my head. I looked Grace in the eye. 'I'm sorry it ever happened. Believe me.'

She kind of smiled to herself and nodded wryly. The gossip and graffiti and shit had done their job. 'All right. Whatever.'

I nodded, poured fizz and OJ into two glasses and handed them to her. After pouring another one and arranging biscuits on a plate, I gestured to her to lead the way and followed her back to the shop floor, where her mum was gasping at the sight of her sister wearing a bright white monstrosity covered in flounces. I set about *oohing* and *aahing* in all the right places while completely ignoring Grace. It wasn't as if I was about to be friends with the girl, not after what she had done to me. But at least I could be fairly sure there'd be no more of it when we got back to school after Christmas.

Her sister didn't even buy a dress in the end. They wanted to 'research all avenues'. Mum's smile vanished as soon as the door closed, its bell still tinkling. She flopped in one of the expensively upholstered chairs and sighed. 'Another one bites the dust.'

'They might come back,' I said.

Mum gave me a *yeah, right* look and checked her watch. 'The next appointment's not till four . . . Let's get an early lunch. My treat.'

I should bleeding well think so, I thought, but I smiled gamely and fetched our coats.

'Shame about the Simpsons,' commented Mum as we sat down in Pret with our sandwiches. 'They seemed all right. That Grace looked about your age.'

I nodded vaguely. 'Yeah.'

'I felt a bit sorry for her, actually,' she mused. 'It must be hard when you've got an older sister like Charlotte and a mother who puts all that boyfriend pressure on.' She took a bite out of her egg and cress, delicately pushing stray strands of greenery back into her mouth with a done-at-home French-manicured finger. 'At least you can be sure I'd never do that to you girls.'

I kind of laughed. 'Yep, we can be sure of that.'

She smiled. 'Not the best advert for blissful union, am I?'

'Guess not.'

'Although . . .' She shrugged coquettishly. 'There's still time. I'm sure Mr Right is out there for me somewhere.'

Yes, my mother really does think there's a Mr Right for every girl (and, yes, she really does refer to women as girls). The fact that my dad scarpered was not because he was a waster, but because he wasn't Mr Right. Not his fault, see.

I finished my sandwich and cupped my hands round my tea. 'So, just out of interest . . . Do you think Toby is Sasha's Mr Right?'

She beamed as if I'd just given her proof that heaven exists. 'Oh, yes. Those two have it all sewn up, don't you think?'

I stuck out my bottom lip. 'Maybe. Who can say?'

'Well, obviously we can't know for sure,' Mum said, at the same time dismissing the idea with a wave of her hand. 'I'm quietly confident. They're a lovely couple.'

WTF does that even mean? Lovely couple. Does it mean they're better together than they are as individuals? Bit of a sicko idea if you ask me, like your personalities become morphed and you're no longer your own person. No thanks. I watched Mum wiping her mouth with her napkin and shifting in her seat, and I just knew what was coming.

'Before you ask,' I said, putting up my hand to stop her, 'the answer is *no*. I don't have any boy action to tell you about.'

She smiled indulgently, her head on one side. 'My Ashley: always a secretive soul. I don't know where you get it from.' I raised my eyes heavenward in long-suffering stylee. It wasn't the first time she'd said that.

*

This seems as good a point as any for a few words about the man who provided half my genes. After years of disappearing for a few months then reappearing out of the blue, all loving and contrite, our dad finally cleared off for good when Frankie was a few days old, charmingly informing Mum that 'Milky tits have never been my thing, babe.'

I didn't miss him. He was never around long enough for me to form any kind of bond with him and, apart from the odd riotous game involving throwing us up in the air until we screamed with actual terror, he never really paid us any attention. I do know that he had a knee-weakening effect on pretty much any woman who met him. He was good-looking, charming, laid-back – and a total arsehole. For all I know, I've got hundreds of half-siblings all over the world. I wouldn't be surprised. As Mum puts it, she was just completely in love with him and had been ever since the moment he'd caught her eye in a pub. Every time he came back, he promised that this time it was for good, and Mum – the dumbo – believed him.

In fact, it took a good few years for her to accept that this time he wasn't ever coming back. She'd had a few boyfriends since then, but only Bob the butcher lasted for any time. In a way it was my dad's fault that Bob didn't last. Mum had loved my dad too much: no other man could measure up. Mental, *non*?

Anyway. There you go. I had no idea where he was now and, as far as I knew, Mum didn't either. He'd disowned his family, so I never knew my grandparents or any aunts and uncles that might have been knocking around, and there was probably no chance of us ever finding out. Suited me fine. Mum might be irritating, with a blind passion for my darling big sister, but she'd done OK bringing us up. Well, in bringing Sasha and Franks up, anyway – I was obviously a bit of a blot on her parenting copybook. *C'est la vie*, people, *c'est la vie*.

'Anyway,' said Mum, interrupting my thoughts, 'I wanted to talk to you about your Christmas present.'

That perked me up. 'Oh?'

'Yes. Sasha suggested I might buy you a course of aerobics classes. What do you think?' She smiled at me expectantly.

I sighed. 'Mum, when have you ever known me do anything like that?' The very idea of spending an hour sweating to crappy dance music with a bunch of try-hards in leggings made me want to shoot myself.

'Well, I think that was partly Sash's point,' she continued. 'She thought maybe regular exercise would do you good. Brighten your complexion, lighten your mood. That kind of thing . . .'

Fucking Sasha. 'My mood is fine, as is my bloody "complexion".' I gave it some finger quotes, then put my head in my hands in frustration. 'God, Mum, can you honestly not see what a totally shit idea that is?'

I couldn't see her face, but she sounded stung. 'Fine, then. All you had to say was "no thanks".' We ate in silence for a moment, then she said: 'What *do* you want, then?'

I shrugged. 'Money?'

'Fine.'

I watched Mum angrily spooning up her fruit salad. She'd be thinking I should apologize, but honestly. *She* should have been apologizing to *me* for suggesting such an offensively inappropriate present in the first place.

'Actually, I had an idea for what you could get for Sasha,' I said slyly. *Two could play at this game, sister mine.* I quickly searched my mind for a present my perfectly groomed, clever, clean-living sister would hate. 'I was thinking she'd love a paintball session for her and Toby.'

Mum frowned. 'Oh, I don't think so, Ashley. You know Sash hates masculine competitive sports.'

Great. So she can forget my life-long aversion to group exercise but remember something as niche as

Sasha not liking masculine competitive freaking sport. I rest my case. Shrugging, I finished my sandwich in silence, quickly texting Donna under the table.

> Am about to kill my
> mother. Pls tell me ur free
> 2nite??

She texted back to say yes, and we arranged a time and place. TFFT.

The afternoon's bridezilla ended up buying five grand's worth of wedding kit, including dress, veil and bridesmaids' dresses, so Mum finished the day on a high and I ended up with my £50 'commission'. Result.

I met up with Donna later that night with twenty of it burning a hole in my pocket. Rather than wasting our money on pub prices, we bought a bottle in an offy and then met in the play area near her house. We had a thing for the see-saw at the moment. We'd spend hours on it, putting the world to rights. The slow, regular up-and-down was weirdly satisfying. (And not in a sexual way, before you put two and two together and make an orgy. A slab of cold metal between my thighs doesn't do it for me, strangely.)

Don and I had been on the see-saw for about ten

minutes when a familiar voice sounded from the other side of the low playground wall. 'All right, kids?' Ollie. He deftly vaulted over the bricks to join us.

'What are you doing here?' asked Donna, still *sawing* to my *see*.

'Just doing a delivery job for my mum. Some charity leaflets to some charity lady's house.' He shrugged – didn't know, didn't care – then gave us the patented Ollie cheeky smile. 'I didn't know you liked after-dark swinging.'

I rolled my eyes. 'Funny . . . Actually, we like after-dark *see-sawing*?' I stared meaningfully at said piece of equipment.

He leered. 'Ooh, dirty.'

'Ollie, have you not been getting enough recently?' asked Donna. 'You seem even more sex-obsessed than usual.'

He shrugged again. 'Same as always, I'd say. On both counts.'

(BTW, the fact hadn't escaped me that Ollie didn't get the graffiti-and-gossip treatment, even though he was as much into commitment-free shagging as I was. Amazing what having a penis can do for you in this world.)

I rested my feet on the floor, leaving Donna hanging in mid-air, and offered Ollie the bottle of wine we'd bought from the offy. 'Want some?'

He shook his head. 'I'd better get back. I'm supposed to be meeting someone . . .' He checked his watch. 'Exactly two minutes ago.' And, with that, he gave us an open-palm wave and vaulted back over the wall, leaving behind the carrier bag he'd been holding. By the time I'd clambered off the see-saw, checked the bag, seen it had his wallet in it and shouted after him, he was gone.

Donna appeared by my side. 'Let's have a look through it, then.' I was already opening it, but there was nothing exciting. It was practically empty: just a bank card, twenty quid and a condom. 'Uh-oh,' said Donna, holding it up. 'Hope whoever he's meeting tonight comes prepared . . . What do you think we should do?'

I clicked on his name in my phone's Contacts. 'I'll ask him.' But it went straight to answerphone, so I left a message telling him to get back here pronto.

'Actually, I'm freezing. Can we go back to mine?' said Donna, hugging herself.

I shivered. She had a point. Sitting on a see-saw doesn't exactly get the blood flowing. 'Suits me.' I texted Ollie to tell him we'd gone to Donna's and if we didn't see him tonight I'd drop his wallet off on my way to Mum's shop in the morning, and away we trotted.

*

The next day, I completely forgot about Ollie's wallet until I got back from work in the evening and saw it on the table. I was surprised he hadn't texted me. I certainly wouldn't be that careless about twenty quid. But anyway. I wanted a bath and a night of mindless telly, not to go back out into the cold, but a promise is a promise 'n' all that. I grabbed an apple from the kitchen and munched it as I speed-walked the ten-minute journey to Ollie's.

'Oh, nice one, thanks,' he said, as I handed over his wallet. He opened the door wider. 'You coming in?' I started to shake my head, but he said, 'Go on, have a beer with me.'

Well, when he put it like that. I followed him into the warmth of his house. 'Something smells amazing,' I said, sniffing the air.

'It's bread.' He opened the oven door a smidgen, releasing a fragrant gust of hot air, and peered in. 'It'll be ready soon.'

I took the beer he offered me. 'Full of surprises, aren't you, Olligogs?'

'Oh yeah. Man of mystery, me.' He sat down at the kitchen table and I joined him. I was glad I'd come out.

'How was your date last night?' I asked.

'Yeah, all right. She's cool, but we didn't really fancy each other.' I started to say something, but he interrupted. 'No, we didn't. She wasn't up for it.'

'Bummer.'

He took a swig of beer. 'Nah, it's all good. We had a laugh.'

I stroked my chin. 'Could it be that your feelings for someone else are stopping you, hmm?'

'No, course not,' he said amiably. 'So how was work?'

Right. Change of subject it was, then.

'It was all right,' I said. 'We sold one dress, so it wasn't a total waste of time.' I started picking the label off my beer, then stopped when I remembered that someone had once told me it's a sign of sexual frustration. Then started again because, even if it was a sign that I was a psychotic axe murderer, I still couldn't give a shit.

'Are you still doing it for free?' he asked.

I pretended to look shocked. 'No! I am doing it for the love and respect of my mother and to flip the bird at my older sister. Riches indeed, innit.' I rubbed my eye. 'And my mum bungs me fifty quid every time she gets a sale.'

Ollie got up to check the bread again. 'What is it with you and your sister, anyway?'

I watched as he opened the oven, reeling back from the sudden blast of heat. 'I feel funny moaning about Sasha to you, Ols.'

He looked surprised. 'Why?'

'Well, cos of your twin dying and that. You haven't got any brothers or sisters.' I drank from my beer to avoid looking at him, in case he was upset. Ollie's twin brother had died less than a day after they were born, and his parents never managed to have any more kids.

'Don't be stupid, I can't miss something I've never had,' he said, kind of scornfully for him. He put the bread on the side and came back to the table. 'Though bless you for worrying, obviously.'

'You're welcome.' We clinked bottles.

'So. Your sister . . .' he said.

I sighed. 'Oh. It's hard to explain. She's just kind of perfect, or at least my mum thinks she is.'

'Perfect how?'

I shrugged. 'Kind, clever, thoughtful . . .'

Ollie creased his forehead. 'You're all those things, Ash.'

I shot him a grateful-yet-sceptical look. 'Thanks, but I think my mother would beg to differ. Sasha always had glowing school reports, she and Mum agree on pretty much everything, she never slept around, she went to university and got her degree, and now she's bought a house in Kent with Toby, her Mr Perfect boyfriend, earns good money in her good job and visits Mum regularly to give her a break by rustling up "healthy, balanced meals".' I hunched my shoulders. 'Me and Mum don't agree on anything, I don't get glowing reports, I'm crap at cooking . . .' I tailed off.

'Hmm, yeah. I see where this is going,' said Ollie, nodding. He sniffed and stretched his hands behind his head. 'No offence, but your sister sounds kind of boring.'

I snorted. 'None taken.'

Ollie looked at me. 'Do you wish you were more like her?'

'No!' I shuddered and he laughed.

'What are you moaning about, then?'

I searched for the right words. 'She just makes me feel small and . . . I dunno. A bit dirty, maybe. Useless. Like everything I do is kind of small and selfish, and maybe a bit stupid.' I'd never said this to anyone before, even Donna, who got on fine with her older sister.

Ollie exhaled. 'Whew. I can see why you might have an issue with her.'

I huffed dismissively. 'Yeah, well. Whatever. It's not like I live my whole life in her shadow. She's just annoying, is all.'

'Well, for what it's worth, I don't think you're any of those things. I think you're cool.' He beamed at me.

'Cheers, Ols. I think you're cool too.'

I drained my drink and put Sasha out of my mind. I focused on Christmas Eve. Only two days till I'd see Dylan again. Since the other day when he'd been so friendly in Debenhams a little tremor of hope had been fluttering inside me, and I couldn't stop it. No matter how hard I tried.

8

Me and Frankie were making mince pies. Idyllic festive scene, *non*? Franks had just fancied it. She was in Tesco buying whatever and they had an offer on mincemeat, so she bought a mahoosive jar of the stuff and came home brandishing it like she was about to brain someone. 'Let's make mince pies!' she'd said, all breathless and excited as if our life had suddenly turned all old-school Disney kids' movie: 'laughing and chucking flour at each other to uplifting pop soundtrack' type thing. Anyway, I was up for some baking. I used to enjoy doing a bit of stirring and spoon-licking with Mum before Frankie came along. So here we were, hair tied back all profesh-like and Frankie wearing a tea towel as an apron. We'd found a recipe in one of Mum's books and an ancient cupcake tin in the saucepan cupboard, and we were ready to go. Franks ran her finger down the list of ingredients. 'OK, we need flour, butter, sugar, salt, an egg and icing sugar.'

I opened the fridge. 'No eggs.' I watched Frankie reading the recipe, her eyes darting across the lines as she bit her lip with concentration.

'Oh, it's OK. It's just for brushing the tops of the pies to give them "that lovely golden sheen",' she quoted. 'We can do without that, right?'

I shrugged. 'Guess so. OK, what's first?' Frankie read out the recipe and we weighed and sifted and all that business. It was weirdly relaxing.

After cutting out discs of pastry using the bottom of a glass, and wedging them more or less evenly into the dips in the cake tin, Frankie did the ceremonial opening of the mincemeat jar.

'Why do they call it mincemeat anyway?' she said, closing her eyes and inhaling deeply. 'God, I love that smell.' She offered me the jar and I had a quick sniff.

'Yeah, nice,' I said. 'And I dunno. Google it.'

She gave me a defiant look. 'I might just do that.'

I raised an eyebrow. 'Crazy-ass mofo.'

'Totally.' She glanced at the oven, frowned, then started scooping out browny-orangey-fruity gloop and splodging each spoonful into a pastry case as if she was going for some sort of speed record. I made a grab for the jar. 'Let's have a go.'

'In a minute,' she said, snatching it back. 'I'm doing six and you're doing six.' She continued doing the scoop-and-drop thing. She was getting mincemeat everywhere.

'Take it easy, Franks,' I said. 'That's going to be a

pig to clear up.' It wasn't like her. She was usually totally fastidious. She took about six months to clean her teeth, for example, insisting on brushing each one separately. Which is arguably more OCD than fastidious, but you know what I mean.

'Sorry,' she said without looking at me. 'I'm in a bit of a hurry.'

'What do you mean? Where are you going?' I asked, running my finger along the worktop and then sucking off the collected mincemeat.

She cleared her throat. 'I'm meeting Emily at the cinema at four.'

I checked the time on the oven. 'It's not even three.'

'Yeah, well. I need to get ready, don't I?' she said almost irritably as she finished her six pies, handed me the mincemeat, then started cutting out more pastry to make lids.

'What do you need to do?' I asked, genuinely confused. 'You're going to be sitting in the dark for two hours.'

She shrugged. 'I just want to look nice, OK?' She put the last lid on. 'Anyway. You're all right to finish up here, yeah?' And without waiting for an answer she pulled the corner of the tea towel out of the neck of her jumper and disappeared upstairs.

'Of course, no problem. I'll do all the tidying up,' I

said grumpily. So much for sisters spending quality baking time together. It had been her frigging idea. I considered going after her, but left her to it. Maybe she was premenstrual at last.

Usually the pressure of forced festive happiness builds and builds until by Christmas Eve I'm morose with a side order of moody, but not this one. This one had potential. And me and Rich were in Donna's bedroom at her mum's house, where we were all getting ready together. Rich would normally have gone to the party with Jack, but I'd persuaded him to join us instead. Call me a pessimist, but while tonight was exciting it also had massive potential for going tits up. I wanted to make the most of the good bits, and that meant getting ready with my two bezzies while drinking more Baileys pilfered from Rich's parents' booze cabinet.

Rich lounged on Donna's bed, swigging from his hip flask and passing judgement on our outfits like effing Cleopatra in Topman slacks (Rich liked a good slack, especially if it had razor-sharp creases down the front).

I'd gone for a black 90s bustier I'd found in Oxfam, a black leather skirt and my Doc Martens.

'Do me up,' I asked Donna, turning round so she could tie the laces at the back.

'Phwoar,' leered Rich. 'It's like Victorian lezzer porn.'

'Right, cos you know all about that,' said Donna, as she put her foot on my bum to get more purchase. 'Is that tight enough?'

I checked out my cleavage. Usually it's pretty much non-existent, but with my trusty bustier's help I could conjure up some semblance of a rack.

I turned to Rich. 'What do you think?'

He paused, as if in deep consideration. 'Tits.'

'Indeed they are. Well noticed.' I looked at him impatiently. 'Well? Do I look all right?'

He sniffed, barely looking at me. 'Course you do, babes. You look gorgeous.'

I rolled my eyes. 'Donna?'

She stepped back and took it all in. 'Perfect,' she said approvingly. 'Different, sexy, fierce . . .'

Despite myself, I did a little skip. 'Aw, fanks, Don . . . Let me look at you?' She did a twirl for us. She was wearing ridiculous four-inch spike heels, black satin treggings and a sheer orange kimono top, and she looked incredible. The orange practically glowed against her brown skin.

'Shit, Don, I can't even put it into words,' I said, ogling her, and she beamed with delight.

'Yeah, really sexy,' added Rich. He held up his phone. 'Jack's just texted. Him and Ollie are on their way to Marv's.'

'Right, let's go then,' said Donna. 'Gis some more, Rich.' She held out her hand for the hip flask, took a couple of gulps then passed it to me. 'Leave the mess,' she said over her shoulder as she left the room. Rich smirked at me. She always said that and I had literally never seen her room tidy.

By the time we got to Marv's, the hip flask was empty and I was full of good-feeling, ready to party. Ollie and Jack were standing outside the house.

'Aw, guys, you waited for us.' I gave them each a smoochy kiss on the cheek. '*Très* sweet of you, darlinks.'

'All right, Ash?' said Jack, grinning. 'Looking amazing, as ever. You too, Donna.'

Don put her arm round my shoulders and smooshed her face up to mine. 'We *are* looking rather spesh, innit though?'

I laughed and squeezed her bum. 'Totally.' And on that bombshell, we made our entrance. 'American Boy', which had been the sound of the summer holidays between Year Ten and Year Eleven, was blasting out of Marv's living room. A few people were already dancing and they smiled at me and Donna as we joined them, singing along with every word. I love a welcoming dance floor.

We threw hip-hop shapes at each other while rapping along with Kanye. The man's a dick IMHO, but you had to respect someone who could rap about Ribena.

When the track had finished and the dopey vocal stylings of Snoop Dogg took over, we lolloped out to the kitchen to get the drink we'd normally have sorted as soon as we arrived. Marv's house wasn't huge by any means, but somehow his parents had managed to squeeze a sofa into the kitchen. It was a big, squashy thing in old-fashioned brown velour with a shaggy cream rug on the floor in front of it. And on it, his long legs stretched across the rug, his dark hair standing out in glossy relief against the brown of the sofa, drinking a bottle of alcoholic ginger beer like some sexy Enid Blyton hero turned to the devil, was Dylan. I think it's fair to say that my heart skipped a beat.

Marv stuck his hand in the air as he spotted us. 'Hey! Good to see you.' Without putting his hand down, he pointed at the kitchen table. 'Grab a drink and join us, yeah?'

We did as we were told. There wasn't much room on the sofa, so after Donna and Rich had squeezed themselves next to Marv and Dylan, me and Jack had to take the floor. I sat cross-legged on the rug, Dylan's foot inches away from my knee. I rubbed his calf in a friendly fashion. 'All right?'

'Yeah, good thanks.' He smiled at me, but then kind of looked away over my head. I wasn't giving up that easily.

'My sister loved you, by the way. Thanks for being so nice to her.'

He brought his eyes back to mine and shrugged slightly. 'She's cool, I liked her too.' Then Marv asked him something about something – I don't know what – and that was that.

I just didn't get him. How could he be all friendly and outgoing one day, then completely shut down the next? I turned my gaze towards Donna, who was already looking at me. She shrugged as if to say, *Don't ask me*. As I finished my first drink and fetched another, more friends of Marv's arrived and we all moved into the living room. There was Aiden and Jamie from the night at the cinema when I'd first met Dylan, and a few others I didn't know.

'You know my cousin Donna, right?' Marv said to them as they turned up. 'And this is Ashley and . . .?' He paused and looked quizzically at Rich, Ollie and Jack, who provided their names too. He swept his hand across us. 'They go to Woodside, so be nice to them.'

I raised an eyebrow. 'What, in case we whup your sorry asses with our superior intellect 'n' shit?'

He laughed. 'Yeah. That.'

I grinned. 'Right, we'll try not to do that, then.'

A bit later, Dylan left the room, I guessed to go to the loo. I'd had a couple of drinks, which was enough to give me the courage to try for an 'accidental' meeting. It wasn't that I was delusional, I just wasn't ready to completely give up on him. And I was drunk, etc. Anyway, I genuinely needed a wee so it wasn't totally stalker. The downstairs loo was empty, so I continued upstairs to the bathroom and tried the door. Locked. I hung around outside, chewing the sides of my nails and trying to look casual. There was a full-length mirror on the wall that led from the stairs to the bathroom, so I killed time by checking my outfit from all angles and doing a couple of catwalk struts. I was in the middle of a Keira-Knightley pout when the bathroom lock scraped, so I quickly reverted to my usual, non-mental demeanour.

'Oh, hey, Ashley,' he said.

'Hey,' I said back and was about to say something else – I hadn't quite worked out what – when he walked straight past me and jogged down the stairs. Shit. Those damn long legs. He covered more distance with a single stride than I did with five.

Sighing, and feeling like a total idiot, I went to the loo. The seat was warm. As I released several drinks' worth of wee, two thoughts went through my mind: (1) Dylan's perfection was such that his shit actually didn't stink; and (2) this was probably the closest I'd get to his naked butt. Neither thought made me feel any better.

As the general atmosphere got drunker and merrier, I tried to forget about Dylan and just enjoy myself. I did a pretty good job, too. Donna, Ollie and I danced a bit – even Rich joined in at one point – and we just messed about with Marv's friends, talking shit and having a laugh.

As the night went on, Donna disappeared with Marv and a couple of others to watch some American drama DVD box set Marv had been raving about, but I stayed put. I don't even know why I was so desperate to be where Dylan was. He was obviously a total lost cause.

Inevitably it got to the stage in the evening when everyone started fighting over Marv's iPod, each wanting to choose their own track, and someone – I think it was Rich – put 'Dirrty' on. I quite like Christina Aguilera, I don't care what anyone says, so I got up and started dancing. I was hammered on Baileys, crap wine and vodka. I knew I'd feel like shit in the morning, but for now I felt pretty damn good.

The boys started whistling and whooping as I

pelvic-thrusted away like a good'un, my arms snaking above my head.

'Oi, oi!' shouted Aiden. 'Get your tits out for the lads!' I shot him a look of pure scorn and gave him the finger, turning away from him as I danced, but on my way back round I inched my top down to reveal a glimmer of nipple. Everyone hollered but I whipped it back up super quick.

'In your dreams!' I yelled. I noticed Rich frowning at me, looking worried. I blew him a kiss and he sort of smiled, but I was too pissed to care.

'More! More!' chanted another of the boys. They were grinning at each other as if Christmas had come a day early. I closed my eyes and shook my head, but slowly started inching my skirt up. They started clapping and whooping, but as soon as a hint of girl-boxer appeared, back down it went. Honestly, boy-baiting was so easy. I felt powerful, like a frickin' warrior queen. One of the boys stood up and started dancing with me. I grabbed his arse and pulled him towards me. Over his shoulder I watched Dylan stand up and walk out of the room. Perfect timing. In for a penny . . . As we danced I pulled the boy's head towards mine and we started kissing, big, thick snogs. He tasted of booze and fresh sweat, in a good way. But, just as things were really steaming up, Rich grabbed my arm.

'Ash, can I have a word?'

I tried to protest, but he pulled me away. I didn't really care, so I drunkenly waved bye-bye, laughing at the disappointment on the boy's face, and let Rich lead me into the hall.

'For God's sake put your coat on,' he hissed. 'You're making a tit of yourself. Again.'

I stuck my bottom lip out. 'Ash is horny.'

'Ash is always bloody horny,' he grumbled, helping me into my coat. 'Ash needs to invest in some bloody love eggs or something.'

I giggled and Rich took my hand, pulling me after him. It was freezing outside and the shock of the cold air sobered me up enough to trundle home beside Rich without falling over once.

'Right, here you are,' said Rich, as we got to my house.

I snaked my arms round his waist and rested my head on his shoulder. 'Stay over?'

'Ash, love. It's Christmas Eve. I think my parents would have something to say if I wasn't at home when they woke up.'

'Oh yeah. Forgot.' I burped loudly as Rich searched in my bag for my keys, unlocked the door and gently pushed me inside.

'Go and sleep it off,' he said. 'And merry Christmas.' He gave me a kiss on the cheek and then left, closing the door behind him. I stood for a minute, the house silent except for the sound of my own laboured, drunken breathing. I hiccuped and started crying. Here was the lonely stage of drunkenness, then. I dragged myself upstairs to my bed and curled into a ball, pulling the duvet over my head. What happened to the me who used to get into bed on Christmas Eve so excited I thought I might burst? A rhetorical question, obvs; one of the shitter things about growing up is the realization that life sucks, and Christmas sucks even more. With such chirpy thoughts trudging around my addled brain, I fell asleep.

'Ashley! Wakey wakey! It's Christmas Day!'

I prised apart my eyelids and groaned. Mum and Frankie were looming over me, beaming like they'd won the Lottery. 'What time is it?' I mumbled.

'Gone nine!' said Mum incredulously.

I groaned again. 'Too early.'

Frankie sat on my bed, shoving me out of the way with her bum. 'Please wake up, Ash. Mum says we can't open presents without you.'

'I hereby give my permission,' I said, closing my eyes again and turning away from them.

'No way, madam,' said Mum firmly, pulling my duvet off me. 'You are not going to spoil Christmas. If Sasha and Toby can get here all the way from Kent by nine o'clock, the least you can do is get out of bed.'

I wanted to grab the duvet back and tell her I didn't ask them to get here that early so would she kindly piss off and leave me alone, but she'd go mental and it would have been shit for Frankie. So instead I sighed from the depths of my soul and told her I'd be down in twenty minutes.

'Good.' She chucked the duvet back on top of me and stalked out. Frankie followed her, but not before giving me a hug and whispering 'Happy Christmas' into my ear, which for some reason made my eyes prickle. That's hangovers for you.

I sat up in bed, noticing for the first time the bulging stocking at the end of it. According to family law, these presents were allowed to be opened without an audience. Kneeling up, I dragged the stocking towards me. My haul consisted of a chocolate selection box, a three-pack of M&S knickers, a bag of nuts and raisins, a Jackson Pollock calendar, a fizzing bath bomb, a notebook and some lip balm. Not bad. Pulling a pair of the knickers out of the packaging and finding yesterday's bra from the pile of clothes on the floor, I grabbed my ripped skinny jeans and oversized skull jumper from the wardrobe and went into the bathroom.

Twenty minutes later I appeared in the living room

to find that I was severely underdressed, the theme for today apparently being 'Sunday best circa 1950'. Frankie had on a velvet skirt and black V-neck, Sasha was wearing wide-leg trousers with a slim jumper, Mum was doing smart slacks and heels – even Toby had his shirt tucked into his jeans.

I raised a weary eyebrow and flopped on to the sofa. 'Happy Christmas, everyone.'

'And same to you, Ashy,' simpered Sasha. 'I'm guessing you had a good time last night, then?'

'It was all right.' I scratched my eyelid and sighed. All I wanted to do was go back to bed. Mum so shouldn't have bothered getting me up – they'd have a much nicer time without me.

'I recommend Coke,' piped up Toby, not quite looking me in the eye. 'The full-fat variety.'

I kind of smiled. 'Thanks. I'll bear that in mind.'

'Well,' said Mum sunnily. 'I'll do the honours, shall I?' She started handing out presents until we each had a pile and there was nothing left under the tree except shitloads of needles.

Another gruesome festive tradition in our house was that everyone had to open their presents in turn. As she was the youngest, Frankie went first. She started with Mum's present, ripping open the paper excitedly. Her eyes widened as she pulled out a long, narrow box. 'GHDs! Wow, thanks, Mum!' She opened the box and had another squeal when she saw they were shocking pink. 'Oh my God, Emily's going to be sooo jealous.' She got up to give Mum a kiss, who beamed. You couldn't help smiling at Franks's excitement.

Next she opened the Topshop scarf she'd chosen on our shopping trip and threw her arms round my neck. 'It's even better than I remember it.' I hugged her back and tried not to tear up again. Bloody Christmas hangovers.

Sasha and Toby had got her an iPod Shuffle, which put my scarf in its place. But although Franks gave Sasha a hug and thanked them both enthusiastically, she didn't seem like she loved it any more than my scarf. Not for the first time I wondered how such a lovely human being as my little sister could have been born into our family.

'OK, your turn, Ash,' said Mum, picking up one of the presents in my pile and handing it to me. I tried for a smile and tore open the wrapping on the excellent skull key ring Frankie had chosen for me. It was solid and heavy, and made of the kind of metal that makes your hands smell like money. I hugged Franks and gave her a kiss. 'Bloody brilliant, Frankie-Pank. I love it.' She shrugged and smiled modestly, but I could tell she was pleased.

I took a breath before opening the next present. It was from Sasha and Toby, and not iPod-shaped. 'Wow.

Thanks,' I said, holding up a pair of novelty zebra slippers. 'They're, uh, quite something.' They were, of course, completely hideous.

'You're welcome, Ashy,' smiled Sasha. 'We thought they were very "you", didn't we, Tobes?' Toby nodded, his gaze fixed on his hands, which were clenched between his knees.

My own sister thought I was a novelty-animal-slippers kind of person. Brilliant. Resisting the urge to shove them up her stupid, complacent arse, I moved on to Mum's present: an envelope containing fifty pounds in cash. I looked up. 'Nice one. Thanks, Mum. Really.' I smiled and she smiled back.

'You're welcome, love. I hope you get something nice.'

Relief that the present ordeal was over for another year washed over me. 'Take it away,' I said to Sasha. She clapped her hands and giggled excitedly.

'OK if I open the first one?' she asked Toby. He pretended to think about it, while she stuck her bottom lip out and put her hands together in prayer. Excuse me while I vomit.

'Go on, then,' he said at last. She clapped again and tore open the paper on her present from me and Franks.

'Olive oil, brilliant,' she said brightly. She read the label. 'It's not extra virgin, but that's OK. I can use it for cooking.' She held it up. 'Look, baby. It's our favourite.' Toby raised his eyebrows and made a kind of *ooh, so it is* noise. Frankie looked at me worriedly and I shrugged. So we'd got the wrong olive oil. The brand Sasha had specified on her list was so expensive that we'd just gone for the cheapest bottle. Nice of her to point it out.

Next Sasha opened the envelope we'd attached to the bottle. Her face took on a kind of fixed, waxy look as she pulled out the card from Oxfam informing her that instead of a present, we'd bought new books for schoolkids in Nairobi on her behalf.

'Oh. Excellent.' She smiled and blinked rapidly, totally failing to hide the fact that she was a bit gutted. 'Brilliant idea to give to charity, guys.'

'It was your idea, Sash,' I reminded her.

'So it was,' she said too brightly. 'Well, there's far too much materialism around these days.'

Ha ha. Sasha was the most materialistic person I knew. Silly cow. She shouldn't have put it on her list if she didn't really want it. That'd teach her to make the big altruistic gesture. Anyway, she soon perked up when she opened the grey-blue silk pyjamas that Mum had got her. 'Oh, Mum. They're gorgeous,' she breathed, rubbing the material against her cheek. 'Thank you.' She gave her a hug. 'You always buy such wonderful, thoughtful gifts.'

Which, as subtle digs go, wasn't very subtle. Not that I gave a shit.

Mum opened her iPod from Sasha and her earrings from me and Frankie, and made her well-practised exact-same responses to each, which is to say almost insultingly super-enthusiastic. Sasha lapped it up, though. 'You deserve it, Mum,' she simpered. 'You don't get treated enough, in my opinion.'

FFS. 'Yeah, we thought the earrings would really set off your hair, didn't we, Franks?' I said. That took the wind out of Sasha's sails.

'You're all wonderful. I'm a very lucky mummy,' said Mum. Blee.

So that was that for another year. Thank the newborn baby Jesus. As soon as Mum disappeared to get a bin bag for the wrapping and Franks turned the telly on, I sidled out of the room and back upstairs to bed. Unless something went wrong in the space–time continuum, Christmas dinner would be at two, which gave me four whole hours to sleep. Bliss. Setting my alarm for 1.45 so Mum wouldn't have to get arsey with me again, I gratefully shut out the world.

And it's a good thing I did or I'd never have got through the rest of the day.

Dinner was OK. Mum had rustled up a damn fine turkey with all the trimmings. Talk flowed pretty easily, I felt a million times better after my extra sleep, Sasha and Toby actually managed to refrain from talking about their brilliance for a bit and pre-dinner sparkling wine had put Mum in a great mood. So that was all good.

But then came the main event. We'd finished dinner and Mum had just brought in the coffee when, without warning, Toby cleared his throat and tinged his glass with a spoon. 'Could I have your attention for a moment, please?' Bit ostentatious when there were only four of us and we were slouched in over-fed silence, but anyway.

So. First I thought he was going to make a speech, but then he pushed his chair back and got down on one knee. My heart started pounding with embarrassment for him. Seriously, what a tit. Then he took Sasha's hand and, looking deeply and ever so meaningfully into her eyes, said: 'Sasha, I love you and I want to spend the rest of my life with you. Will you do me the honour of being my wife?'

Firstly: vomit. Secondly: I honestly thought she'd say no. Surely nobody gets married at twenty-four unless they're religious and it's the only way they can have sex without burning in hell. But she said 'yes' and burst into tears. Then Mum burst into tears, Frankie followed suit, and I was left feeling like a total party-pooper, not only dry-eyed but also fairly sure this was the biggest mistake Sasha would ever make. After the initial hysteria had passed, Toby hugged Mum, then Frankie. As he turned to me, I quickly hugged Sasha.

'I'm so happy!' she sobbed into my ear. I gave her a squeeze and managed to choke out congratulations. How evil was I that I couldn't even feel pleased that my sister was so happy?

'Oh, this is the best Christmas ever,' said Mum, sighing and wiping away a tear. She threw her hands in the air. 'We should have saved the fizz!'

'One step ahead of you, Karen,' said Toby with a smile. He went over to the fridge and pulled out a bottle of proper, expensive-looking Champagne. 'I smuggled this in while you were serving dessert. It should be chilled enough by now.' Grabbing a tea-towel from the oven door, he opened the bottle with an ostentatious pop, and of course Sasha, Mum and Frankie cheered. Usually the lameness of it all would have made me want to gouge my eyes out, but I felt drained of emotion. It was like I was made of lead.

With Sasha perched on his knee, her hand entwined in his hair, Toby proposed a toast to his 'beautiful fiancée'. And that was it. I had to leave the room.

Seriously, what was wrong with me? I was truly

evil. A selfish, evil bitch. Guessing that I wouldn't be missed, not now, I went back upstairs to bed. My hangover was long gone, but I felt like I could sleep for years.

9

Donna, just left voice
msg. SO sorry bout xmas
eve. Can I come over n
explain? Axxx

It's ok i forgive u. again.
Mum wants mummy-
donna time so no visitors
2day. Can u go on FB?
Could chat then . . . x

Gimme 5 mins x

Facebook Chat

Donna Dixon: Helloooo?

Donna Dixon: Ash?

Donna Dixon: OI, GREENE!!!

Ashley Greene: Yes yes I'm here. Was being distracted by Sasha
trying to organize family game of monopoly.

Donna Dixon: Fun fun fun!!!

Ashley Greene: Exactly. So what d'u get?

Donna Dixon: Money from dad, ipod speakers from mum, slippers from Jess . . . You?

Ashley Greene: Weird. sasha got me slippers too – ZEBRA ones, with a gift receipt, thank god. mum gave me money, frankie got me a key ring . . . that's kind of it. Spent most of yesterday in bed with hangover anyway. Sasha v disapproving naturellement.

Donna Dixon: I can well imagine *wags finger*. So where d'u end up on xmas eve then? who'd you shag this time lol.

Ashley Greene: Lol my arse. Didn't shag anyone thanks to Rich. He pulled me away a la knight in shining armour. Prob for best.

Donna Dixon: Go Rich. And what about Dylan??????

Ashley Greene: What ABOUT Dylan????? He barely said a word 2 me all nite then pissed off. He def doesn't like me.

Donna Dixon: Sure he's not just shy???

Ashley Greene: He wasnt shy when me n franks saw him in town the other day.

Donna Dixon: Oh yer forgot bout that. Hmm.

Ashley Greene: Hmm indeed. Gotta go. Apparently i'm spoiling xmas with my moodiness. Obvs being told that has cheered me right up :p

Donna Dixon: Bummer. Later dude xxx

Ashley Greene: Later xxx

Facebook status update:

Ashley Greene thinks family board games should be illegal.
  Monopoly, this means you.

Comments

Ollie Glazer: No way! Boxing-day Pictionary ROCKS!

Ashley Greene: It really doesn't.

Sarah Millar: We're playing Pictionary as we speak! Just done
  amazing clue for Return Address. Yes, we Millars like to live on
  the edge. How was xmas eve btw?

Ashley Greene: Hmm . . .

Sarah Millar: Riiiight. I'll call u later, yeah?

Ashley Greene: Yeah.

Rich Jones: Surprised you can remember any of xmas eve, Greene ;)

Ashley Greene: Oh a-ha-ha-ha. You made a funny.

Rich Jones: Many a true word spoken in jest.

Ashley Greene: Did you just QUOTE at me??

Rich Jones: Certainly did. *buffs fingers on jacket*

Ashley Greene: Wow. I'm impressed. No, really. I am.

Cass Henderson: If you think Monopoly's bad, you should try Trivial Pursuit with the most competitive people in the WHOLE WORLD i.e. my family.

Ashley Greene: Peace on earth?

Cass Henderson: Totally. Not.

> Donna answer ur phone!!
> Forgot 2 tell u something
> earlier xxxx

> Can't babes. Mum says no
> phone calls. TEXT ME!!

> Sasha n toby r
> ENGAGED . . .

> NO FREAKING WAY!!

> Yes freaking way.

> But she's like 22??!!

24. Silly cow. Mum
practically came with joy.
Had such rubbish xmas.

Aw babes. Come n see
me tomorrow xxx

Shit, just arranged to see
Sarah. Can i bring her
too?

Yeah course. Will call in
morn to arrange, yah?xx

Yah. Can't f-ing WAIT to
get out of this house. Got
to get thru Toby's parents
coming for 'afternoon tea'
today ffs. HELP! Am about
to commit familycide x

Hang in there, babes. C u
tomoz xxx

10

Toby's parents were rich. No other word for it. Proper old-school, country-pile toffs. I already knew that, because Toby had told us. Not in so many words, obviously, but by subtly dropping into conversation that he and his four older sibs had all gone to boarding school, or that they used to spend their summers in their holiday home in Italy, blah blah. So obviously I was all set to hate them and for them to hate me. But that's not quite how it turned out.

They rolled up in a battered old Range Rover for a start. I'd been expecting something shiny and ostentatious. Me and Frankie watched them from my bedroom window.

'She looks nice,' said Frankie, as Toby's mum got out of the driver's side of the car and walked round. She was wearing boot-cut jeans, a blue shirt and white lace-up pumps. They could have been M&S for all I knew. She had shoulder-length greying hair and didn't look like she was wearing much make-up, if any.

'And he doesn't look scary at all,' she added, as Toby's dad got out of the car and opened the boot.

He lifted out a Sainsbury's carrier and a bunch of flowers. He was wearing chino-type trousers with a cord shirt and loafers and had thinning brown hair.

'Yeah, well, we haven't met them yet,' I said darkly, turning away from the window as Mum bellowed for us. Frankie skipped downstairs and I followed at a statelier pace, not exactly looking forward to a few hours of polite chit-chat, watching Sasha posh it up with her future in-laws. I was wearing my skinniest black jeans, an oversized cream shirt and a black blazer I'd found in Oxfam, y'know, to make our aristocratic guests feel at home. Sasha had taken one look at me this morning when I came down for breakfast and rolled her eyes so massively I momentarily worried that she was having some kind of medical emergency.

'Do you have to dress like that today?' she asked. 'That coat smells.'

I sniffed the sleeve. 'It's just a bit musty. It'll wear off. Anyway, I like it.'

She pursed her lips. 'Mum, tell her.'

Mum turned round from the worktop, where she was buttering her toast, and looked me up and down. 'Ach, she's all right.' Ha! I shot Sasha a triumphant look, but she pretended to be engrossed in reading the back of the muesli box.

And then, when Toby's parents arrived and Mum had shaken their hands but his mum had insisted on giving her a hug instead, and Sasha and Toby had kissed them both, and Sasha had introduced me and Frankie, and we'd shaken their hands too, his mum looked at me and said (drum roll, please): 'Can I just say, I *love* your coat. You look amazing.'

It could have sounded totally crap and try-hard, but it didn't. It sounded like she loved my coat and thought I looked amazing. I raised an eyebrow at Sasha, but again she pretended not to notice. So, yeah, I was warming to his mum ('Call me Wendy'). His dad hadn't said anything much yet, so I was reserving judgement on him.

'Sash, take Wendy and Martin through to the living room,' said Mum. She took their tea and coffee orders and bustled through to the kitchen to get the tea things ready. Sasha had made scones that morning and we were inflicting mine and Franks's mince pies on them as well as Christmas cake, also made by Sash. Cakes for tea was OK by me. Silver lining, innit.

Back in the living room, Sasha was showing off her engagement ring to Toby's parents, who made all the right noises. To be honest, it was quite a nice one – it was a solid band with three diamonds kind of set into it rather than sticking out. It was made of platinum, not white gold. No idea what that means, but Toby thought it was important enough to tell us twice.

'Have you thought about where you might want to get married?' asked Wendy. 'Charlie, Sam and Amelia –' she turned to me and Frankie – 'Toby's brothers and sister – all chose to have their wedding receptions in a marquee in our garden, and you're more than welcome to do the same. But it's entirely up to you.' She waved her hand casually. 'Daisy – Toby's other sister – always says if she ever gets married it'll be in Vegas, so there's honestly no pressure.'

Toby's dad piped up then. 'We were more or less forced to do the whole church thing, weren't we, Binks?' (Binks??) Wendy nodded and he continued. 'What we really wanted to do was pop down to Chelsea Register Office, grab two witnesses off the streets and do it quietly, but it would have been, shall we say, frowned upon.' He and his wife looked at each other and smiled.

'Well, I do have a few ideas,' said Sasha.

Toby laughed and squeezed her knee. 'Of course, when she says a few ideas she actually means an entire spreadsheet, don't you, babe?' Sasha tinkled away prettily, but you could tell she wasn't entirely chuffed to be mocked, however affectionately.

'I just like to be organized,' she said.

Wendy gave Toby a look. 'Ignore him, Sasha. He needs someone to keep him in line. Don't you, love?'

Toby smiled and shrugged. 'I just need Sasha.' He

gazed into her eyes and she leant forward to kiss him. It made a disgusting lippy squelch. And I swear Wendy wrinkled her nose in distaste. And that was it. She was officially my second favourite posh person after Bridget the old lady.

Thinking about that must have put her in my head, because as the afternoon went on and we tucked into scones with jam and cream, me and Wendy got talking and I ended up telling her all about my interview with Bridget, and about her experience in the war.

'She sounds wonderful,' said Wendy. She took a sip of tea. 'I wonder if she's spending Christmas alone.'

'Actually, I've been thinking that myself,' I said. Much as my family drove me mental, I didn't want them living on the other side of the world or, y'know, dead.

'Have you thought about phoning her?' she continued. 'She'd probably love to hear from you.'

'I kind of have,' I admitted. 'But I thought it might be weird.'

Wendy shrugged. 'She's an old woman living on her own. I'd guess that any friendly phone call would be welcome . . .'

As soon as she said that, I was desperate to talk to her. As if reading my thoughts, Wendy said, 'Go on, do it now. Don't stay here on my account.' She drained her drink and smiled at me over the rim of her teacup.

I stood up. 'OK, I will.'

As I went upstairs I did reflect a bit on the weirdness of phoning an OAP I'd met once because my sister's fiancé's mum told me to. But whatever. I found Bridget's number in my Contacts and it was ringing by the time I got to my room and flopped on my bed.

'Hello?' She sounded weary, and what had happened to the perky 'Bridget Harper speaking' of the first time I'd called her?

'Oh, hi, Bridget. This is Ashley Greene? I interviewed you for my school project?'

'Yes, of course. How are you, Ashley?' I was beginning to wonder if this was a good idea. She really didn't sound in the mood for a chat.

'Yeah, fine, thanks. Uh . . .' I paused, not sure what to say. 'This might sound silly, but I was wondering if I could visit you this afternoon . . . "Just to say hello" type thing.' I closed my eyes. That had sounded fucking ridiculous.

'Well, that would be just lovely!' said Bridget. I smiled at the change in her voice. 'When would you like to come?'

'I was thinking maybe . . . well, now, basically,' I said. 'If that's OK.'

'That's perfect. I'll see you soon.'

However crap my Christmas had been, Bridget's must have been truly shit for her to get so excited about a visit from *moi*. Anyway, it wasn't like I was being all saintly and selfless, doing my good deed for the day. I really wanted to see her again.

Mum let me go without complaint when I told her where I was going. She even looked slightly smug and proud. Not an expression I ever thought I'd see on Mum's face unless it was aimed at Sasha, although maybe I did big up the lonely old lady thing.

Even in my coat, scarf, beanie and gloves, it was effing bitter out, with a heavy, grey sky and biting wind. Too cold for snow and all that. I shoved my hands deep into my pockets, stuck my chin into my scarf and semi-ran round to Bridget's. Her house was in darkness except for the light coming from her living-room window. It was dark outside, but her curtains weren't drawn. It made the place look empty and uninviting. I rang the doorbell and stomped from one foot to the other on the chipped tiles of her front step. Sound effects from inside told me she was on her way and approximately five years later, as my feet had just about gone completely numb, she sloooowly opened the door.

'Ashley, my dear, how lovely to see you!' she said, smiling brightly. She was in full make-up, just like before, although her lipstick was a bit wonky as if she'd put it on in a hurry. She was wearing exactly the same trousers and blouse as when I'd interviewed her. 'Come in.' She gestured for me to lead the way. In the living room, a tray with a teapot, a pint of milk, a sugar bowl and two mugs on it was waiting on the table by her chair, which was tipped forward, ready for her to sit down again. Bridget settled herself leaning against her chair and pressed the button to lower it back to sitting position. 'Be a dear and pour the tea, will you?' she said. 'White no sugar for me, please.' I did as she asked, then poured my own and sat down in the other armchair. I suddenly felt awkward. What the hell were we going to talk about? I mean, there was loads I wanted to talk about – her life, basically – but it seemed a bit crass to fire questions at her. And 'Tell me about your life' just sounded corny. But Bridget was a pro. She knew how to make small talk. We started with the weather, of course, then she asked what I'd got for Christmas and then I asked her about hers.

'Oh, I was just here,' she said, dismissing my question with a wave of her hand. 'They tried to persuade me to go to some god-awful pensioners' Christmas gathering at a church hall.' She grimaced. 'No, thank you. I have no desire to spend the day eating dry turkey with a room full of old people.'

I laughed, then stopped sharpish when I saw she wasn't joking. She gave me an arch look. 'You're as old as you feel, Ashley.' She carefully put her empty mug down, her hand shaking slightly, making it rattle against the tray. 'I may be old and decrepit on the outside, but inside I feel exactly the same as I did when I was your age. Exactly.' She sucked her teeth and shrugged slightly, as if to say: *C'est la vie.*

'You don't have any family nearby?' I asked. 'I know your son's in New Zealand . . .'

Bridget shook her head. 'My husband died twelve years ago. My daughter lives in Scotland with her partner. They don't have any children. She's a lesbian, you know.'

'Oh. Right,' I said stupidly.

'I know nowadays gay people have children,' she continued. 'But it didn't happen when Lorna was the right age and now she's too old.' She slowly stirred her tea. 'She comes to visit every six months or so, but it's a long way, and expensive.'

'You must miss them. Your son and daughter, I mean,' I said.

'I do,' she said simply. She cleared her throat and slapped her gnarly hands against her knees. 'Anyway, tell me about your documentary. Is it finished? Can I see it?'

So I told her all about it – probably in extremely

tedious detail, although she was too polite to look bored – and, after looking over at the TV table to check if she had a DVD player, I promised to bring her a DVD.

'Oh, please do, I'd love to see it . . . I really enjoyed talking to you, you know.' She slapped her hands on her knee again. 'I'm *glad* you telephoned today.'

I smiled. 'Me too.' Obviously by rights there should have been a humungous awkward silence at this point, but again Bridget came to the rescue, instantly asking me if I wanted another cup of tea. I said no, and that I had to go. I'd promised Mum I'd be back in time to say bye to Toby's parents. I had no idea if I would be – it was getting pretty late – but at least I was showing willing.

'Come and see me again,' said Bridget brightly as she opened the front door.

I turned back and smiled. 'I will. Thanks for the tea.'

She nodded and smiled. 'Cheerio.'

'Bye, Bridget.' She shut the door and I walked home feeling something that, if I hadn't known better, felt suspiciously like contentment.

Slightly randomly, Donna, Sarah and I ended up meeting at the art museum the next day. I'd only been

there once, on a school trip, but apparently Sarah
went there 'all the time'. (Whatever. She had a crush
on Andrea, her art-history teacher, is all.) Anyway, it
was free, so it suited me. Although frankly I'd have
paid anything to get out of the house, with Sasha and
Mum squealing over wedding plans and Toby strutting around all manly, like his balls had trebled in size
just cos he was going to have a *wife* now. *beats chest*
Honestly, it was all I could do to keep down my
breakfast. At least the good feeling after seeing
Bridget hadn't gone away. It was a relief not to feel so
ridiculously low any more.

So me, Sarah and Donna arranged to meet in the
fashion galleries, where I walked in to find the other
two staring at a display case with a Victorian lady's
outfit in it: all shiny material and buttons and ruffles.
I walked up behind them.

'Made for Mary Eliza Gibbons,' murmured Sarah
as she read the description. 'Weird to think a real,
normal person wore this.'

'I know,' agreed Donna. 'And that she's been dead
for years.'

'Yeah.'

'Yeah,' I added, making the two of them jump and
screech in v. amusing tandem.

'Shit!' Donna spun round, putting her hand on her
chest *à la* drama queen.

'Sorry,' I said. 'Didn't mean to make you jump.'

'Freaky quiet person.' She gave me a hug. 'Good to see you.'

'You too.' A quick hug for Sarah, and we started off on a mooch around the gallery, although we didn't look at much. It was an ideal place for a catch-up: free, warm and quiet. A bit too quiet, judging by the disapproving looks we got, but they could piss off. It's not as if we were shouting.

'So. Christmas Eve, then . . .' began Donna.

'What about it?' I asked innocently.

'Well, no offence, babes, but what were you *doing*? Rich said you practically got your tits out.'

Sarah went all wide-eyed and gasped. 'You didn't tell me that!'

I gave her a look. 'That's because it didn't happen.'

'What *did* happen then? Like, I'm assuming Rich didn't lie . . .?'

So I told them. And as I did, it struck me that, actually, I *had* pretty much got my tits out. And shown them my pants. It was like a five-year-old lifting her dress over her head to get attention. It was kind of mortifying.

When I'd finished my sorry tale I looked at the duo of furrowed brows and realized they couldn't think of anything to say that wouldn't either hurt my feelings or piss me off.

'Yeah, I know,' I said. 'It did get a bit out of hand . . .'
I sat down on a bench in the middle of one of the
galleries and the others sat either side of me. 'I
couldn't get my head around Dylan going all quiet
again . . . I just wanted to forget about him and have
a laugh.' I glanced at Sarah. 'Not that I care that much
either way, but I do like to know where I stand. Anyway, he must really hate me now, so . . .' I scuffed the
heel of my shoe against the shiny floor, making it
squeak, then stood up. 'I'm thirsty – let's go to the
cafe.'

As we bought our tea I decided not to dwell on any of
this. It had happened; I kind of wished it hadn't; time
to move on. I added a banana and oat bran muffin to
my tray to celebrate my no-nonsense attitude to life,
and the three of us sat down.

'So what's the plan for New Year's Eve?' asked
Donna as she tore into her flapjack.

I groaned. 'Oh God, I hate New Year.'

'Course you do, babes,' she replied matter-of-
factly. 'Everyone does, so let's plan something quick
so we don't end up topping ourselves, yeah?'

'That's the spirit,' said Sarah wryly. 'Nothing like a
positive attitude.'

'So . . . what?' I said. 'I would say you could all
come to mine, but Frankie and my mum'll be there.'

'No, let's go out,' said Donna. 'I want to do some-thing different. Isn't there a party we can crash?'

Sarah looked up from her hot chocolate and smiled, a vaguely porno-looking splodge of whipped cream above her top lip. 'Actually, I might know of one.'

'Whoa. Sarah the party animal,' I quipped. 'Go on . . .'

'I'm still friends with one of Joe's friends on Facebook.' She looked at me. 'You know, Will? With the massive house? Who you shagged?'

'Oh yeah.' I nodded. 'Crap in bed.'

'Yeah. Him. Anyway, he's having another house party.'

Donna narrowed her eyes. 'Sar, tell me you're not stalking Joe.'

'No! Course not.' Sarah managed to look both scornful and hurt that Donna could even think such a thing. 'According to Facebook, he's spend-ing New Year's Eve in Thailand with Mimi.' She broke off to mime sticking two fingers down her throat. Walking in on Mimi and Joe having sex was what finally woke Sarah up to his total wankertude. 'So we're safe. Big house, free drink, no Mimi or Joe . . .' She spread her hands. 'I think it could be a win-win sitch.'

Donna grinned. 'I think you could be right, babes. And you're sure Will won't mind us all rocking up?'

Sarah shrugged. 'He probably won't even notice.'

'Yeah, the house is, like, obscenely massive,' I added. 'Nice one, Sar.'

She smiled. 'Go me.'

I was about to go upstairs after getting home from the art gallery, when Frankie came out of the living room looking weird.

'You all right?' I asked, eyebrows akimbo.

She smiled, kind of. 'Yeah. Er . . . this is Freddy.'

She turned and a ridiculously good-looking kid with messy blond hair, olive skin and blue eyes (a strange yet alluring combo), edged out of the living room. His eyes darted around, never once actually getting anywhere near to making contact with mine. 'Hey,' he said.

I widened my eyes at Frankie and grinned. 'Hey, Freddy. Nice to meet you.' He sort of grunt-nodded.

Franks cleared her throat. 'Anyway. We were just going to the kitchen to get some crisps, so . . .'

'Cool. Have fun.' I gave them a wave and carried on up the stairs, although I was itching to eavesdrop. I was really happy for Frankie that she and Freddy were . . . well, whatever they were. Maybe I was a *tiny* bit jealous that she had someone, but mostly I was happy.

*

An hour or so later I was messing around on the Internet when I heard the front door slam, and a second later Frankie appeared in the room.

'So?' she said, biting her lip. 'What did you think of him?'

I smiled. 'He's gorgeous, babes. Maybe a bit lacking in the conversational skills department . . .'

She frowned at me. 'Don't be uncharitable, Ashley. He's just shy. It's very nerve-wracking meeting your girlfriend's big sister, you know.'

I did a comedy sharp intake of breath, although actually I hadn't meant it to be comedy. 'Oh my God, he's your *boyfriend*?'

She giggled. 'I know! Emily's soooo jealous.'

'But how? When? You haven't even seen him since school broke up.'

Franks twisted her mouth sheepishly. 'Well, actually, I kind of have. You know before Christmas when I said I was going to the cinema with Emily? I wasn't really. I was seeing Freddy. Please don't be cross with me, Ash.'

I shrugged. 'I'm not cross. It's your life. We can't always tell each other everything.'

'Really? I just felt a bit bad because you don't have a boyfriend . . .' She started biting her nails nervously and I resisted the urge to slap her hand away from her mouth.

'Oh God, don't worry about *that*,' I said. 'I'm not so insecure that I need a boyfriend to feel like a worthy member of society. Seriously, it's cool. Don't worry about it.' But I was gutted. And I did feel jealous. Don't hate me.

'So . . . how was the kissing?' I asked, bunging on a loony grin.

Franks hugged herself. 'It was lovely. Really warm and . . . yummy. And you were so right – it did just happen.'

I raised an eyebrow. 'Francesca, do we need to have the sex talk?'

She covered her ears. 'Ew, nooo!'

'Because, if you want to talk penises . . .' I got up from the computer and started following her as she turned to leave the room.

'LA LA LA CAN'T HEAR YOU!' she sang, running away.

'Wait! We haven't talked about foreskins yet . . .' 'Foreskin' was, like, Frankie's most hated word in the English language. Don't ask me why. She ran up the stairs, laughing hysterically, and I went back to the computer, smiling to myself.

My new night-time routine: get into bed, put headphones on. Sasha and Toby had apparently decided that as a token of their love for one another they'd treat the whole house to their sex sound effects, so I needed to drown out the ridiculous am-dram moaning. Even Frankie was getting pissed off with them. She came into my room early the next morning and climbed into bed beside me. I woke up just enough to make room for her.

'Whassamatter?'

'Nothing,' she whispered. 'Go back to sleep.' So I did. When I woke up, a bright winter sun was streaming through the gaps in the blinds and Franks was snoring softly beside me. I got out of bed as quietly as I could to go to the loo, but when I got back she was awake and staring at the ceiling.

'All right?' I got back in beside her. 'Did you have a nightmare last night or something?'

She shook her head. 'Nope. Just didn't want to sleep on my own. It's not fair that Sasha gets to sleep with Toby every night.'

I waggled my fingers in front of her face. 'Why, d'you want to sleep with Freddeeey?'

'No!' She slapped my hand away. 'You know what I mean.' She rested her head against my shoulder. 'I wish I didn't have to sleep on my own, that's all.'

'Sleeping on your own's great, believe me,' I said. 'There's a lot to be said for having the whole bed to yourself.'

She leant on an elbow in order to give me a *stop*

being patronizing look. 'There's a lot to be said for shar-ing it with someone, too . . . When I share a bed I won't ever care if I can't get to sleep. I'll just stroke my partner's chest till I drop off.'

I laughed, but I kind of knew where she was com-ing from.

'Think of Mum, though,' I went on. 'She's got no one to sleep with and *she's* forty-two.'

'S'pose.' Franks didn't say anything for a minute, then grinned. 'Maybe she'll marry that man from work.' She gasped. 'They could have a joint wedding with Sash and Toby!'

I sat up. 'What man from work?' It was the first I'd heard of it.

'You know. Duncan or Kieran or whatever it is. The material man.'

'What bloody material man? Franks, I haven't a clue what you're going on about.' My stomach felt tight.

'Yeah, you do,' she insisted. 'He brings all the fab-ric samples and stuff to the shop on Mum's admin days, then he and Mum go out for lunch. Ask Sasha – she's met him.'

I felt like crying. Why didn't I know about this? What was wrong with me that I was the only single one in the family? I threw off the duvet and got out of bed.

Frankie started to follow me. 'Ash? Where are you going?'

I waved her away. 'Get back into bed. I'll be back in a minute . . . I'm just going to the loo.'

I checked to see if she'd done as I said, then stomped into Mum's room without knocking. She was sitting up in bed watching the old portable TV she kept on her chest of drawers.

She looked up, surprised. 'Oh, all right, Ashley? Sleep OK?'

'Who the fuck is Duncan?' I glared at her.

Mum shook her head, looking confused. 'I've no idea. Who *is* Duncan?'

'Duncan the material man?'

'Oh. You mean Kieran.' She tried to look unfazed, but the way she was spinning the TV remote over and over in her hands told a different story.

'Duncan, Kieran. Whatever,' I said. 'Who is he and why am I the last to know that you've got a bloody BOYFRIEND?'

Mum patted the bed beside her, but I stayed where I was. 'He's not my boyfriend, Ashley. He's a friend who I have lunch with once a week. It's no big deal.'

I blinked and tried to breathe more slowly. 'If it's no big deal, how come Sasha's met him? And how come you felt the need to keep this from me?'

Mum sighed. 'Ashley. Honey. I wasn't keeping anything from you. I just . . . I suppose I thought you'd be scornful. He's quite a lot older than me.'

Tears pricked my eyes. 'Mum, I'd never be scornful of one of your friends.' I was gutted – *gutted* – that she could think that.

Mum smiled slightly unconvincingly. 'Well, that's great. Come and sit down and I'll tell you about him.' I didn't move, but I was properly going for it now. Tears, snot, the works.

'Ashley, sweetheart. Please don't cry. Come here.' Mum lifted the duvet and, still booing like a kid, I got in beside her. I couldn't remember the last time my mum had cuddled me – it must have been years.

Mum stroked my hair. 'I'm sorry I didn't tell you about Kieran, but honestly – there's nothing to tell. Sasha's only met him because she surprised me at work one lunchtime.'

I sniffed. 'OK . . . You do fancy him, though?'

Mum smiled. 'Don't hold back there, hon'. You just say what you think.'

'I'll take that as a *yes*, then.'

She raised an eyebrow. (Yes, it's a family trait.) 'You can take it however you like. So, what do you want to know?'

'I dunno. How old is he? What's he look like?'

Mum pulled the duvet up closer to her chin. I

smiled to myself and closed my eyes. I used to love being in Mum's bed when I was little. It was the cosiest place in the world.

'He's sixty,' she started, then broke off when I snorted. 'Do you want to hear this or not?'

'Yes. Sorry. Go on.'

'He's sixty,' she repeated. 'He's recently divorced from his wife of thirty years. He left her after he discovered she'd been cheating on him for years.' I resisted the urge to snort again. 'He's about, I don't know, five foot ten?' she continued. 'He's got blue eyes, he's clever and he makes me laugh. That enough for you?'

'Ho, yes,' I said. 'Enough to know you totally fancy him.'

'You're impossible,' said Mum, sighing campily. Whatever. She was loving this. I wasn't sure how I felt about her getting a boyfriend (oldmanfriend), but on the whole I thought it was probably an OK thing, as long as he didn't move in and get all fatherly. Ugh. Perish the thought.

'Ashley, I thought you were going to the loo?' Franks burst in all accusingly. She stomped over to the bed and got in with me and Mum. 'Budge up, then . . . What are we watching?' She snatched the remote from Mum and started flicking through the channels, stopping at some crappy 1990s American sitcom repeat on ITV3. I was obviously in a vaguely hysterical mood, because it actually made me laugh. In fact, before long the three of us were all chortling away like halfwits.

'What's going on in here?' Sasha appeared at the door, dressed and with her hair still wet from the shower. 'Looks cosy!' She smiled. 'Ach, now I wish I hadn't got dressed, so I could join you.'

Mum put one arm round me and the other round Frankie. 'It'd be a bit of a squeeze, love,' she said, laughing. 'You can snuggle up with Toby.' Sasha gave us a tight little smile.

'Is the kettle on, hon?' Mum continued.

Sasha cleared her throat. 'No. I'll put it on now. Tea all round?'

'Yeah, thanks, Sash.' I beamed at her.

'Right. Well. Don't say in bed too long, lazybones!' She wagged her finger at us, but she wasn't fooling me. She wasn't used to being left out.

'This is the life, eh, girls?' said Mum, snuggling further down under the duvet. 'D'you think Sash would mind if I asked her to bring up some toast too?'

As she called downstairs I made a face at Frankie, who giggled from behind the duvet. Weird morning. I wasn't complaining, though.

Mum went into work that afternoon, but just to do adminy stuff, so she didn't need me. (She wasn't meeting Kieran. I checked.) I was looking forward to Frankie's and my appointment with microwave popcorn and an ITV re-run of *Annie*, but then the traitor pissed off to go swimming with Emily. Much as I could never get enough of stage-school kids belting out 'Hard Knock Life', watching on my own wasn't an option. I flicked through the channels, but nothing grabbed me. I tried to do some homework, but after twenty minutes chewing my Biro and staring into space I gave up on that too. At just gone three I decided it was definitely afternoon snack o'clock, so I pootled downstairs to the kitchen, where Sasha was chopping vegetables and listening to the radio.

'What you making?' I asked, stealing a bit of carrot.

She frowned. 'Don't, Ash. There isn't enough as it is.'

Ooh. Stressed Sasha. I got a yogurt out of the fridge, took a banana from the fruit bowl and sat down at the table. No need for a spoon: I was going to dip 'n' suck. Tasty, nutritious and no washing up.

'That is revolting.' Sasha looked at me, her lip curled in disgust. 'For heaven's sake, Ashley, does everything have to be sexual with you?'

'It's not my fault bananas look like willies,' I said evenly. 'And we've run out of apples.' I closed my eyes in ecstasy and licked yogurt off the banana, throwing in a porno moan for good measure.

'So immature,' muttered Sasha, and she turned back to her chopping board.

I rolled my eyes at her back. 'You started it.'

She looked over her shoulder, throwing a thin smile in my direction. 'I rest my case.'

Neither of us said anything for a couple of minutes, the only sound the easy-listening pap coming from the radio and Sasha clattering around in the cupboards. I got up to chuck my yogurt pot in the bin and banana peel in the compost bucket, then stood and watched Sasha frying mushrooms in butter. She ignored me, so I attempted conversation. It's not as if I had anything else to do.

'Where's Toby?'

'He's having a nap. He's a bit short of sleep.' She smirked to herself. And she thinks *I'm* sex obsessed?

'Oh. Right . . . What's for dinner?' I started absentmindedly kicking the loose door on the cupboard next to the oven.

'Pork and mushrooms with cream . . .' She hunched her shoulders. 'Actually, can you stop that? It's really annoying.'

'Gosh, we are in a jolly mood today.' But I stopped kicking the door. See? Not immature.

Sasha banged her wooden spoon down and turned to me, folding her arms. 'Haven't you got a wall to spray or something?'

'What's that supposed to mean?' I said, staring her out, but her eyes didn't waver.

'Well, you're obviously not going to do anything to help – as per usual – so maybe you could go and waste time somewhere else instead?'

The volcanic pool of tension that simmered in my stomach whenever I was with Sasha started bubbling dangerously. 'You smug bitch,' I said, keeping my voice quiet cos she'd love it if I lost control. 'You have no idea what goes on here when you're not around.'

'Oh, I think I have a pretty good idea.' And, I'm not joking, she literally looked down her nose at me.

'Oh, do you,' I mimicked. 'Well, you can think what you like, but hard as it is for you to believe, we get along just fine without you.'

She sniffed. 'That's not what Mum says.' And that was it. Fury flooded through me like molten lava.

'Fuck you, Sasha.' Hot tears sprang to my eyes. 'You don't know anything.' I should have screamed at her. I should have slammed her against the wall and scratched her eyes out. But instead I just stood, shoulders shuddering and nose streaming. I angrily rubbed the water away from my eyes and glared at my sister. She was staring at me impassively.

'Oh, aren't we angst-ridden,' she said, shaking her head. She leant into me, lowering her voice to a murmur. 'For all your "alternative" clothes and free-love attitude, you're nothing, you know that?' She jabbed her finger at me. 'It takes more than black nail varnish to make a person interesting, Ashley.'

And with that she calmly turned back to her frying pan. I felt like I was falling down the rabbit hole, and not in a good way. She was right, of course. That's what made it so unbearable. I wasn't particularly clever or particularly pretty or particularly nice. I was nothing. Of course Dylan didn't like me. Why would he?

I walked numbly into the hall. I had to get out. Toby came down the stairs as I was putting on my coat. He was dressed for the outdoors in puffa jacket and beanie, his car keys jangling from his fingers.

'Do you need a lift somewhere?' he asked. I shook my head, not trusting myself to speak. 'Hey, are you OK?' He bent down to see my eyes, then seemed to think about something for a sec. 'Come on, let's go.'

'Where are we going?'

'I'm giving you a lift into town.'

It was the longest conversation we'd had for years. I shrugged and followed him out of the door: town was as good a place as any. His and Sasha's car was a sleek, purring thing with nice-smelling leather seats. I could have fallen asleep as soon as Toby started the engine, but just as my eyes were drooping he said, 'Do you want to talk about it?'

I didn't think people spoke like that in real life, or

at least not without a fake American accent or something to show they were being at least slightly ironic, but he was straight-faced and earnest. Him and my sister were made for each other.

'Not really. Thanks,' I said.

He coughed. 'I'm guessing . . . well . . . does it have something to do with Sasha?'

Had he overheard us? I snapped my chin up to look at him, but he didn't move his eyes away from the road. I sighed. 'It's just sister stuff, no biggie.'

'Oh, right. Yeah, I'm sure it is,' he said. He paused for a moment, then said, 'But whatever she said, I wouldn't take it to heart. She'd kill me if she knew I was talking to you about this, but she's been a bit stressed lately . . . It looks like she might lose her job.'

'Oh. Right.' I didn't feel sorry for her, but I didn't feel happy either.

He shot a glance at me. 'She's feeling a bit like she's got the weight of the world on her shoulders, and she sees you going out, having fun . . .' He tailed off.

I cleared my throat. 'I'm not having that much fun at the moment. You can tell her that from me, if you want.'

He kind of laughed. 'Well, I won't. Like I said, she'd be very upset if she knew we'd been chatting.'

I picked at my nails. 'Don't worry, I won't say anything.' We sat in silence again.

'Where do you want me to drop you?' asked Toby after a minute.

I looked around. We were just outside the centre. 'Here's fine.' He pulled the car up to the kerb and parked, keeping the engine running. As I went to undo my seatbelt he put his hand on mine. 'You'll be fine, Ashley.' He smiled sort of sadly, and I tried to smile back, now pretty much totally weirded out.

He took his hand away and, without looking at him, I got out of the car, thanked him for the lift and slammed the door. I watched, motionless, as he pulled away, merged into traffic and then disappeared round the next corner. Then I started walking.

11

I walked for hours, earphones in and my music on so loud it was like I was watching the world with the mute button pressed. I suppose I wandered the streets lost in thought, etc., etc., but I didn't come to any big conclusions or anything. Dylan and Sasha and Toby – they all went round and round my head, but I still felt numb. There was no substance to it. Sasha tried to call me a couple of times, but I sent it straight to voicemail. I got a text, too, but it was from Ian the Stalker asking if I'd had a good Christmas. Then Mum called, I guess when she got home from work and found me not there. I answered that one.

'Where are you?' she asked, her voice giving nothing away.

'In town.' I pressed my fingers into my eyes and imagined Sasha standing next to Mum in the hallway, her back against the wall by the photo of us that Mum had taken when Franks was a few months old. In it, Sasha is neat in floral dress and cardi, smiling prettily; I'm frowning, all scrunched face and mousey hair; and Frankie's fat and cute. Thinking about it made me tear up. Seriously, I needed to get a grip.

'Are you coming home?' she said.

A strange question. What the hell had my sister told her? I took a breath. 'Yeah, of course . . . But not while Sasha's there.' I didn't care about her job woes, I couldn't face her. Not yet, anyway.

Silence. 'Right. Sure you're not overreacting?'

'Yes.'

Mum sighed. 'Well, they're leaving tomorrow.' I heard a voice in the background – Sasha's I guessed – but I couldn't hear what she was saying. I didn't really care.

'I'll stay at Donna's, then,' I said. 'Do you need me at the shop?'

'Well, yes. I was hoping –'

I interrupted her. 'Fine. If you don't mind bringing my clothes, I'll see you there.' She agreed, and that was that. I ended her call and clicked on Donna's name in my Contacts, but as I was giving her my sorry tale she interrupted.

'Ash, babes. I'm at my mum's, aren't I? You know I'd say yes in a heartbeat if I was at home . . .'

I slapped my forehead. 'Shit, of course you are. Don't worry about it – I'll try Rich.'

'Wait, though,' said Donna quickly. 'Tell me what happened. You had a row with Sasha . . .?'

'She went for me, basically,' I said, walking over to a bus stop so I could sit down. 'She more or less told me I was pathetic, boring and worthless. Which was nice.'

Donna gasped. 'She said that?'

'Yup. Or words to that effect.' I cleared my throat. Thinking about it was making me feel wobbly.

'That's horrible.' She paused. 'And you've been, like, wandering the streets ever since?'

I kind of laughed. 'How did you know?'

'Guessed . . . Listen, don't even think about taking all that shit to heart,' she said fiercely. 'You're cleverer than that. She just wanted to hit you where you're most vulnerable . . . And I know you don't do vulnerable,' she added quickly so I couldn't interrupt. 'But that's what she did, right?'

I mumbled something that might have been agreement.

'Right. Don't let it hurt you, Ashley. That's exactly what she wants!'

'Yeah, but she has a point,' I protested pathetically.

'No, she fucking doesn't!' she almost shouted. 'I swear to God, if you start getting all low self-esteem on your own ass I'm disowning you. I don't want to cuss your family, but your sister's a dullard, babes, and she always will be. It's just jealousy. She's the pathetic one, not you. You're . . . you're amazing, not wanting to kiss your arse or anything. Don't let that . . . that *frump* tell you otherwise.'

I laughed out loud. 'Oh my God, she's totally a frump!'

'I know,' said Donna seriously. 'That's what I'm saying.'

I paused for a sec. 'You so love me.'

She snorted. 'Piss off. I think you're a skank.'

'Yeah? Well, you reek,' I shot back at her.

'Of niceness.'

'Anyway,' I said, taking my phone away from my ear so I could check the time, 'since you've heartlessly turned me away, I'm off to Rich's.'

Donna sighed airily, in the manner of one blowing on her nail varnish. 'Good. You were boring me anyway.'

I cleared my throat. 'So. Thanks for –'

She interrupted me. 'Anytime, babes. Have fun at Rich's.'

'Cheers, dude. I'll call you tomorrow.'

I ended the call and sat on the stupid too-high bus-stop bench for a bit, shoulders slumped but feeling a hell of a lot better. It was almost scary how much I hearted my best mate right now. Donna totally got me, in a way that Mum and Sasha never would. I might be fruit of my mother's loins (vomit, obviously), but there was a whole messy pile of genes to

choose from when she and my dad went about con-
ceiving me. And who knows what shit went down on
his side of the family? Our family tree probably has
plenty of mean, gnarly branches going back through
the ages. As I opened my phone Contacts again and
clicked on Rich's number I mused that I should probably be grateful that graffiti and bitching was all I had
to put up with – five hundred years ago I'd have been
burnt at the stake. As would Rich, I guess. The witch
and the homo. Or whatever he was. I got so caught
up with the idea that I forgot I was calling him, and
he had to say hello twice before I twigged his voice
was coming from the phone and wasn't just in my
head.

Two minutes later I had a bed for the night. Result.

As I walked to his house my phone beeped with a
text from Sasha.

> Hey Ashy, can we be
> friends again? :p

Bloody emoticons. I hated them. And WTF did the
sticky-out tongue one mean, anyway? If my sister
wanted to apologize, that was one thing. But no way
was I going to roll over like a sap for a colon and the
letter effing p. I was gagging to text something rude
and pithy back, but she'd only use it against me.
Ignoring it would really piss her off. So I ignored it.

What with that and Donna's pep talk, I was feeling almost OK by the time I got to Rich's.

He was the miracle only child. His parents were in their late fifties – I think his dad was even older – and were nice and everything, but more like grand-parents. When Rich's mum retired a few years ago from her pretty high-powered job, she instantly morphed into the world's most amazing housewife. She cooked and cleaned. A lot. Rich always had a home-cooked meal at the table (no TV dinners in his house) with pudding. And I'm not talking a Fruit Corner. It was apple crumble or sticky toffee pud-ding or trifle. By rights he should have been the size of a house, but he was from skinny stock. His par-ents were like beanpoles. His dad worked for the Post Office, doing something or other. I wondered if his parents were the reason Rich was coy about whether he fancied boys or girls (or both), but they seemed pretty cool to me. Although what did I know?

Anyway, his mum answered the door with her usual super-enthusiasm. 'Ashley! What a lovely sur-prise! Come in out of the cold. Brrr, it's freezing out there, isn't it?'

It was a bit like being bombarded with inflatable exclamation marks.

Rich appeared at the bottom of the stairs as his

mum was taking my coat, and as soon as she'd confirmed that no, we didn't want tea and yes, we were sure, and no, we didn't want any leftover cake and yes, we were sure, she left us to it.

'I think I'm a bit in love with your mum,' I said as I followed him back up the stairs to his loft room.

'Yeah, she does have that effect on people,' he said. 'But you should see her when no one's around. Covered with bruises, I am.'

I laughed. 'Right. Mummy's boy.'

He gave me a behind-the-back one-finger salute, but didn't contradict me. It was amazing he hadn't turned out a total arsehole, what with all the love and attention his parents showered on their beloved only child. Actually, he had two half-brothers from his dad's first marriage, but they were, like, forty years old and he never saw them.

'She's always so cheerful, but in a totally non-annoying way,' I continued. 'How does she do that?'

'Dunno, babes,' said Rich. 'Quite a lot of it's just her being polite. She's still grieving for my nan, isn't she?'

'Oh yeah. Of course.' Rich's Nanny Blue had died suddenly last month. He was devastated. They'd been really close.

'How are you doing on that score?' I asked as we reached his bedroom. I sat down at his desk and Rich threw himself on to his bed and put his hands behind his head.

He shrugged. 'Not great. I can put it to the back of my mind when I'm at school or out with you lot. But otherwise it's just . . . I can't stop thinking about her.' He bit his lip. 'I still can't believe I'm never going to see her again.' With horror I watched his eyes fill with tears. Rich wasn't the type to hide his emotions, but still. Crying in front of people is horrible. And I'd had no idea he felt like this. You'd literally never know, he was usually so bloody chipper. It kind of put my own problems into perspective.

'I guess it's not going to get better for a while,' I said, because it's what popped into my head. Great. Way to be supportive, Greene. I didn't know anything about grieving. But Rich rubbed his eyes and smiled.

'Thank you. Really. I feel like people think I should be over it by now. She was only my nan: it's not as if one of my parents died.'

'Yeah, but she wasn't like a normal nan. She looked after you for years while your mum worked, right?' He nodded. 'Right, so she was more like another mum.' I picked up a pen and started to doodle on an English worksheet he'd already scribbled on. I'd been pretty close to my mum's mum, who'd died of cancer when I was ten, but I'd never known my dad's parents and my mum's dad had been in a home with early onset dementia for years. His world was a blank – he didn't remember any of us. Maybe that's why I felt so close to Bridget. Maybe she was like a nan substitute. I'd be gutted if she died, and I'd only met her twice. I couldn't imagine how devastated Rich must be feeling. 'You know you can be sad in front of me whenever you like,' I continued. 'I won't be bothered, like.'

'Thanks, babes. But I'm OK. It's good to forget about it when I'm around you and the others.' He scratched his eyelid. 'Well, not *forget* about it . . . You know what I mean.'

I nodded. 'I do.'

'So, anyway, why d'you need to stay here tonight?' he asked, pushing himself up into a semi-sitting position. 'Lock the door, will you? And just kind of wedge my dressing-gown along the bottom.' He reached under his mattress and pulled out a small tin. 'You don't mind if I skin up?'

'Well, no,' I said, doing as he asked. I pointed at the dressing-gown. 'But this can't be enough to stop your parents smelling the weed?'

'No,' he admitted. 'But I've told them it's incense.'

I gave him a look. 'Rich, your parents were young in the nineteen sixties. I think they'll be pretty *au fait* with the marijuana thing.'

He smiled and shook his head. 'Really not. Seriously, they've always been ultra square.'

I wasn't convinced. 'And, anyway, since when are you smoking at home?'

He shrugged. 'Since Nan.' He lit the spliff, took a puff and offered it to me. I shook my head. I haven't touched the stuff since I overdid it one time and puked so much I burst a blood vessel in my eye. You know how you go off the last thing you ate before you get sick?

'So how come you need to stay here?' he repeated.

I lifted my feet up and swung round on his desk chair. 'Oh, pfft. It's nothing, really. I had a row with Sasha. She said some shitty things, so I'm not going home till she's gone.'

Rich frowned. 'Bummer. What did she say?'

'Stupid stuff – I won't bore you with it . . . Let's talk about something else. Like New Year's Eve. Are you coming out with us?'

He suddenly beamed, his little face all lit up. 'Yes! What are we doing?'

'Sarah's found us a house party.' I laughed at the expression on his face. 'Yeah, Sarah: who knew? But it's all good. I've been to a party there before – it's massive.'

'That is excellent news, young Ashley!' Rich slapped his thigh, not at all camply. 'I'd been getting a little concerned about the lack of a plan . . . Chuck us my phone, will you?' He nodded at the desk, where his phone was plugged into his computer. I did as I was told and he started texting, the spliff hanging out of the side of his mouth. Attractive. 'I'll let Jack and Ollie know.' When he was done he dropped his phone over the side of his bed. 'So, I hear Donna bumped into your fancy man today.' He blew smoke towards the ceiling, all casually like. 'I also hear she was totally bigging you up.'

'Aw, nice Donna . . . although it won't help,' I said, chewing the inside of my cheek to stop myself leaping on top of him and pounding him over the head with a pillow till he told me exactly, word for word, what Donna had said and how Dylan had replied. Why hadn't she mentioned this to me when we were on the phone? Dylan had probably told her he wasn't interested and she hadn't wanted to tell me when I was already upset about Sasha.

Rich nodded. 'Yeah, maybe not. Anyway, you can ask her about it yourself tomorrow.'

'What's happening tomorrow?' I asked, ignoring the distinct and rather hurtful lack of support re. Dylan.

He took another puff of the spliff, inhaling deeply and leaning back with his eyes closed. 'We're meeting at the pier. Didn't she tell you?'

I must really have gone on about the Sasha thing. Don obviously hadn't been able to get a word in. 'No, but anyway, I can't. I'm working.'

Rich shrugged as well as he could in his increasingly monged state and said, 'Don't sweat it, honey. We'll just meet later on instead.'

And on that bombshell I went off to the spare room to get an early night and leave Rich to his spliff and his memories.

I had a rubbish sleep. It was one of those nights when it feels like you haven't slept at all, but you probably have. You know, you check the time, then check it again half an hour later to find that actually two hours have passed. I kept thinking about Dylan and how Rich obviously thought the situation was hopeless, and about Ollie's party, and the graffiti, and Christmas Eve at Marv's, and Ian the Stalker, and wondering just what the hell was wrong with me. Suffice to say, I felt crap by morning. Rich was out cold when I had to leave to get to work, but his mum was up and insisted on making me eggs and bacon for breakfast. It'd have been rude not to, so I was half an hour late by the time I got to the shop. I'd texted Mum to let her know, but she wasn't best pleased.

'Lucky for you, the client's late,' she hissed, shoving my clothes at me. 'Go and get changed, quickly. And

do something about your hair. You look like a pikey.'
Nice. Lovely bit of casual racism from my mother,
there. But I did as I was told, reappearing ten minutes
later with hair tied back and disgusto-suit on. I'd
expected Mum to be pacing, readying herself for the
big sell, but she was sitting on the sofa reading the
Mirror.

'What are you doing?' I asked.

'They cancelled,' she said, her voice a monotone.
'They've found the perfect dress on eBay.'

'Classy.' I sat down at the other end of the sofa.
'They couldn't have afforded one from here anyway,
then.'

'Possibly.' Mum licked the tip of her finger and
turned the page. Why do people do that? Very strange
behaviour.

'So . . .' I began, waiting for Mum to tell me the rest
of the day's schedule.

She neatly folded her paper and put it on the floor.
'Yes, I suppose this is the ideal time to discuss what
happened yesterday.'

Huh. How subtle. 'I didn't mean that, but whatever.' I gave her the floor. 'After you.'

'Sasha's terribly upset . . . Where are you going?'

I stood up and straightened my top. 'I knew you'd
take Sasha's side. You just can't help yourself, can
you?'

Mum slammed her hand on the arm of the sofa. 'Agh! You drive me *insane* sometimes.' She rubbed her forehead manically. 'D'you know what? Fine. If you're going to be childish about it, go home. Sasha and Toby have gone, thanks to you, so you're safe. We haven't got any more appointments today anyway.' Mum's eyes flashed with anger. 'Go on, get out!'

'Don't worry, I'm going,' I snapped back. 'You and Sasha are fucking welcome to each other.'

'Don't you DARE speak to me like that,' shouted Mum, her face turning brick red.

'Oh, fuck off.' I grabbed my bag and wrenched the shop door open, sending the bell jangling like a leper warning.

Outside the shop I fumbled in my bag for my phone and called Donna. 'I've finished work early. Can we meet now?'

'Uh, yeah, I guess. Are you OK?'

'Never better. I'll meet you at the pier.' I finished the call, turned my phone to silent and marched towards the pier. I speed-walked with my head down, hoping my work clothes would stop anyone recognizing me, and wailed and gnashed, letting the tears come so they'd be gone by the time I saw Donna.

Mum and me didn't see eye to eye on most things, but we hardly ever argued like that. I knew I got on her nerves, and I guess she knew she got on mine, so we kind of skirted around one another, avoiding contentious topics, i.e. pretty much anything except work and the weather. And even those could be tricky. Usually I could pretend we rubbed along OK, but not now. Could I even go on living with her? If I hadn't known that Frankie would be devastated, I'd have been on my way home to pack.

At the pier I bought a magazine and sat in a cafe, drinking tea and mindlessly flicking through the pages.

'Ash, what the frig?' Donna appeared at my table. I hadn't seen her come in. She sat down opposite me. 'What's with the drama-queen stuff?' She bent her head so she could see my face. 'HELLO? What gives?'

I attempted an airy smile, but just about managed a watery grimace. 'Had a row with my mum. Nothing exciting.'

'Not about that Sasha stuff? You're having a right *EastEnders* time in your house, innit.'

I nodded glumly. 'Innit.'

'Come on, then. Tell Auntie Donna all about it.' I opened my mouth to speak but she held up a finger to stop me. 'Actually, babes. Hold that thought. I'll just grab a drink.' She sped up to the counter, bought a can and slid back into her seat.

'Sorry, I'm parched from practically sprinting here

in case you were about to leap off the pier.' She gave me reproachful cat's-arse mouth. 'Anyway. You were saying . . .'

So I told her all about it. And Rich too, after he turned up. 'So, my mum and my big sister hate me. Looks like I'll be moving in with you, Rich,' I said in conclusion. A slightly panicked look appeared in his eye, replacing the sympathetic-but-not-empathetic one that had been there before. Parental rows weren't in his frame of reference. I gave him a *duh* look. 'I'm joking, you tit.'

'Yeah, I know,' he protested, his voice about five octaves higher than normal. 'So what *are* you going to do?'

I shrugged. 'Just go home. Avoid my mother. Never speak to my sister again as long as I live. The usual.' There was a moment of silent sympathy, then Donna shifted in her chair and womanfully changed the subject. Fair enough. I suppose it was a bit of a conversation stopper.

'So, anyway. Dylan's been asking about you.' She stuck her tongue into her cheek and smirked.

'Oh yeah, what'd he say?' I asked, making sure *don't really care* seeped lethargically from every pore. I so should have done theatre studies with Donna. But she looked at me through heavy eyelids, blatantly not fooled.

'Well, to be honest . . .' She suddenly looked slightly less smug. 'Well, he was asking if you're always like you were at Ollie's party, and at Marv's on Christmas Eve. But I don't think he was judging you,' she hurriedly added. 'It was more like he was . . . fascinated, maybe?'

I attempted a laugh. 'Nice try, babes . . . But I think it's safe to say my reputation precedes me.'

Rich put his empty mug down with a clatter. 'Yeah, except it's not really your reputation, is it? It's how you actually were, right in front of him.'

'Excuse me?' I said angrily, my face getting hot. 'What's that supposed to mean?'

Rich shrugged. 'Exactly what I said. He saw you coming out of the loo after shagging a stranger, then he watched you show your tits to different strangers: you make your own reputation, Ashley.'

Was everyone going to have a go at me today? Fuck's sake. 'So it's OK for Ollie to sleep around – that just makes him a loveable rogue. But it's not OK for me. Is that what you're saying?' I snapped.

He shook his head. 'Not at all. You can do what you like, babes, although I don't *think* I can recall Ollie ever getting his dick out.' He stroked his chin, hamming it up all contemplative, then said, 'Look, all I'm saying is, you can't blame other people for spreading rumours when Dylan actually saw you do what you do. I'm not saying it's bad or not bad, I'm just saying that's how it is.'

I glared at him. I was fuming. 'You *are* bloody saying it's bad. "Show your tits to strangers" is a value judgement, and you know it. You could have said, "Show your tits to friends of Marv's," and it would still have been true. And what about the graffiti – are you saying I deserved to have lies written about me on the wall for everyone at school to see?'

He impatiently scratched his forehead with both hands. 'Of course not. But you're missing the point. You need to love yourself a bit more. You treat yourself way worse than anyone else treats you . . . For God's sake, Ash, you're an amazing person, but that's despite the fact you shag for Britain, not because of it.' He made, like, little frustrated karate-chop actions in the air. 'Have a bit of respect. I'm serious.'

I swallowed, my eyes kind of bugging with the effort of listening to yet another person tell me how shit I was. I pushed my chair back. 'You know what? Piss off, Rich. Maybe you should look in the mirror, Mr Suppresses-his-emotions-with-drugs. And at least I'm open about my sexuality.' And I stormed off without looking at Donna or waiting for Rich's reply.

*

As I walked vaguely in the direction of home, my anger rapidly turning to sadness, my phone pinged with a text. It was from Ian the Freak Stalker.

> Hi when r we goin 2 hav
> that drink?????

I turned the screen off without replying.

Who the hell did Rich think he was? But the further I walked, the more I started to think that maybe he was right: Ollie wasn't like me. Ollie never showed off, he just was. I think he was still friends with every single girl he'd slept with – an impressive feat considering how many there were. I'd be hard pushed to recognize some of my conquests in a line-up. I still believed that I should be allowed to take it when I wanted it, I really did. But how many times had I genuinely wanted it: genuinely fancied the guy and genuinely thought we'd be good together? Hardly ever. And what had it left me with? A stalker and libellous graffiti on a toilet wall. Nice. Just what every girl wants.

It was shamingly *Jeremy Kyle*, but I probably did shag around because it made me feel wanted. I let my head drop back on my shoulders and stared up at the sky.

'What are you going to do about it, then?' I said aloud to myself.

There was only one thing I could do: stop. No sex unless I *really* wanted it, no getting so hammered I didn't know what I was doing, no showing my tits, no bloody lifting my skirt up to show my knickers. I cringed at the memory. Rich had been right about that too: it was my fault that Dylan didn't want me. If the boot had been on the other foot I wouldn't want him. If the boot had been on the other foot I'd think he was a try-hard, attention-seeking loser. How very sobering. It really hurt that I'd lost out on Dylan, but maybe it was the kick up the arse I needed.

I sighed. No time like the present. I got out my phone again and opened the text from Ian the Stalker. Hitting Reply, I tapped out:

> Hi Ian. i won't be meeting
> u for a drink. It wouldn't
> work between us. I
> enjoyed our time but it's
> over. I'd appreciate it if u
> stopped getting in touch.
> I'm really sorry if i led u
> on. Thanks and best
> wishes for a happy life.
> Ashley.

I read it through a couple of times, then hit Send. I hoped it was respectful enough. Mostly because he wasn't a bad person – just strange and deluded – but also because I didn't want him to turn into Mental Stalker and start sending me, like, pubes in an envelope. Or worse.

So that was that. The big test was tomorrow night: the New Year's Eve party. 'New year, new Ashley' type thing. I sighed to myself. The thought of not getting drunk made me nervous – what if without booze I didn't like dancing or forgot how to talk to people or sat in a corner with a weird half-smile on my face so nobody would know I was desperate to go home?

Only one way to find out.

So – *yay* – I had a plan. Shame I couldn't say the same about my family sitch. Going home to a house where fifty per cent of the occupants hated me was like going into an exam you know you're going to fail. As I turned into our road I checked the time: still too early for Mum to be home. I had a few hours of freedom.

But when I opened the door she came straight out of the kitchen and stood in front of me, arms folded.

'Excuse me.' I tried to push past her to go upstairs, but she didn't budge.

'No. We need to talk.'

I stared somewhere over her shoulder and tapped my foot, waiting for her to bloody move.

But she stayed where she was. 'You can huff and puff all you want, honey, but you're not going anywhere until we've sorted this out.'

'Sorted what out?' I said, turning ultra-bored eyes on her. 'What a brilliant daughter Sasha is and what a massive disappointment I am?'

'Oh, stop being so oversensitive,' Mum snapped. 'Come into the kitchen and, for God's sake, get over yourself.'

Nice. But I did as she asked, sitting at the table and staring expectantly, one eyebrow stuck in raised position.

'As I was saying,' said Mum, as if only a moment had passed between this morning's set-to and now, 'Sasha is upset that things got so out of hand. She told me that, whereas usually she's able to rise above your comments, yesterday she just saw red.'

I snorted. 'Well, that's bollocks for a start. I know you won't believe me, but I didn't say anything. I made one minor comment about her being in a mood, and she went mental.'

Mum saw my elevated eyebrow and raised me a disappointed sigh. 'It might have been a minor comment to you, love, but Sash obviously saw it differently.'

I shrugged. 'You should have heard what she said to me.' And, like the total lame-ass I seemed to have become, I started to cry, dropping my head on to the tabletop.

For a moment neither of us said anything, the only sound my increasingly grotty sniffing. Then Mum said, 'OK. What did she say?'

I shook my head. 'It doesn't matter.' Admitting to Mum that I knew she'd been slagging me off to Sasha was not something I ever intended to do.

'Yes, it does,' Mum said sharply. I looked up in surprise. 'Tell me. Please.'

'Well . . .' I tugged at a loose thread, the hem of my skirt soon to be a distant memory. 'She said that you think that I never do anything to help and that things are only fine when she's around, and that I'm "nothing" and . . . stuff,' I finished lamely. I sneaked a look at Mum, who'd gone sort of pale.

'Are you telling me the truth, Ashley?'

I looked her in the eye. 'What do you think?'

I saw her throat move as she swallowed. 'I think you are.'

'Thank you.' And I started tearing up again, this time with the relief of telling her, and of her believing me.

Mum reached across the table and circled my wrist with her hand. 'OK. Well, firstly, I may once or twice have mentioned that you don't help much around the house – which you don't, by the way. But

I have never, ever said that things are only fine when she's around. Perhaps this is unkind, and you are never to repeat it, but I think possibly she'd like to believe that's the case. And I certainly do not –' Mum stopped as her voice became strangled with tears. She took a breath and continued. 'I do not think you are nothing, Ashley. I find you difficult and confusing and frustrating, but I am so –' she choked up again – 'so proud of your strength and your individuality. I don't know where you get it from. It's certainly not me.'

You probably don't need me to tell you that I was sobbing like a baby by this point. Talk about emotional rollercoaster. I didn't know whether I was happy or just deeply traumatized.

'Don't just sit there blubbing, for God's sake,' said Mum through her own tears. 'Come and give me a hug.'

So I did.

'I do love you,' said Mum into the top of my head. 'And I know it's rubbish that you have to work in the shop for free. I really do appreciate it, Ash.'

I sighed and did an attractive sniff-hiccup. 'I love you too, Mum . . .' I paused. Oh well, in for a penny. 'It just really feels like I can't win sometimes. It's like Sasha can do no wrong, and I can do no right. I do try . . .' *Bloody* hell, I was going to cry again. 'I do *try* to make you proud of me.' Oh, for fuck's sake, somebody give the girl an Oscar. The words just came out. I didn't ask them to.

'Oh God, Ashley, I *am* proud of you,' said Mum. 'I just told you that, didn't I? All that work you did for your documentary, going to see the old lady on Boxing Day . . .'

I honestly tried to suppress what came out next, but I just couldn't. It welled up inside me and burst out like a tsunami. I hadn't even known I felt that strongly about it. 'SO WHY DIDN'T YOU COME TO MY SCREENING?' I wailed. And I burst into tears all over again.

'What? I thought you said you didn't mind?' said Mum, pulling back so she could see my face.

'Of course I *said* I didn't mind,' I sobbed.

'But I thought you'd prefer it if I wasn't there. I thought you'd think it was embarrassing if I showed up.' Her eyes were wide with shock and confusion.

I growled with frustration. 'For God's sake, Mum, will you stop with the embarrassment stuff? You. Don't. Embarrass. Me. OK? I'm not that lame, seriously.'

She hugged me to her again. 'If you'd have just said, I'd have been there like a shot, and I'd have been the proudest mummy in the room.'

'That's good to know.' And it was. I sniffed. 'Although

if you keep calling yourself "mummy" I might have to rethink the embarrassment thing.'

She laughed. 'OK, baby girl . . . Joke.'

I rolled my eyes. 'Ha ha.'

12

It was New Year's Eve and I was standing outside Will's huge house waiting for Donna and, I guessed, Rich too. I was never the first to arrive, but as changes were afoot I thought I might as well add punctuality to the list. Wasn't convinced I'd stick with this one, mind. I felt a right Billy No Mates, looking up and down the road as if I'd been stood up, so I kept my head down and fiddled with my phone. Ian the Stalker hadn't replied to my text, which I took as a good sign. It was strange to be sober. Normally I'd have had a couple of drinks at home while I was getting ready, but obviously not today, since saintly new *moi* was off the good stuff. It was soft beverages all the way for me tonight. Sigh. But I felt pretty good in what I was wearing (black vintage bell-sleeved maxi dress with multiple-strand purple beads) and I'd told Donna about my plan, so she was poised to be all supportive.

There was the small matter of Rich, though. We hadn't spoken since our little chatette, and I had the horrible feeling that he'd been right and I'd been wrong. Humble pie sucks. I just wanted him to arrive so I could get the apology over with. That's assuming he still wanted anything to do with me – I wouldn't blame him if he didn't.

'All right, Ash?'

I looked up at the sound of Donna's voice and momentarily forgot how to breathe. Marv and Dylan were with her. Dylan! What the hell was he doing here? He was wearing grey skinny jeans, his pied-piper shoes and a frock coat. Seriously, he was like my fantasy man made flesh. My heart went all free-form jazz, thudding in crazy rhythms as my emotions veered from joy to despair and back to joy again. It was amazing to see him, but agony too. Yet again I mentally kicked myself in the head for spoiling any chance I might have had with him.

Excruciatingly, I was too embarrassed even to look him in the eye, let alone talk to him. He didn't say anything to me either, and before I knew it the moment had passed and he and Marv had gone into the house. Meanwhile, outside in leper land, I was left with Donna gawping at me in disgust.

'Ash, seriously. What are you *doing*?'

I winced. 'I couldn't talk to him, Don. I just keep thinking about running into him straight after shagging that Year Twelve.' I shuddered. 'He hates me, I know it.'

Donna put the back of her hand to her head and

swooned *à la* movie queen. 'Oh, he *hates* me, I just *know it*.' She straightened up and gave me heavy eyelids. 'He doesn't hate you, dumb-ass. He's shy and, anyway, he doesn't even know you . . . Oh, and by the way, you're welcome.'

'For what?' I said.

'Bringing him here! Who knows what the night will bring?' She grinned saucily.

'Whatever. Oh . . .' I looked over Donna's shoulder. Rich.

'"Oh" indeed,' said Donna. 'I'll see you inside, babes.' She patted my arm. 'Godspeed, young Ashley.'

'Yeah, thanks for that.' I watched her disappear up the steps and through the front door, then turned to face the music.

'Hey, Rich.'

'Hey.' With dead eyes he looked somewhere past my right ear, but I took it as a positive that he hadn't actually walked straight past me.

I took a breath. Here goes . . .

'I'm so sorry, Rich. You were right, about everything. I do need to respect myself more, and I'm really going to try. Starting tonight . . . And I'm really sorry I said that thing about your sexuality.' I almost mumbled the last bit, I was so ashamed.

He tried to stay looking serious and cross, but a slow smile crept across his face. 'Oh, that's OK, you daft bitch. I'm glad *you've* forgiven *me*. Not that I did anything wrong nor was anything other than deeply wise and insightful.'

'Totally.' I said earnestly, then threw my arms round him. 'Love you, babes.'

He hugged me back and kissed the top of my head. 'Love you too, sweetpea. Although if you start getting your privates out tonight I'm going to drag you away by your hair. And that's a promise.'

'What, even when I need a wee?'

He closed his eyes and nodded seriously. 'Even when you need a wee.'

'Wet pants it is, then.' I sighed.

Rich smirked. 'Well, a leopard never changes its spots.' How rude. And reassuring. We were back to normal. Go me and my excellent apologizing skills.

Fending off my punch to the upper arm, he grabbed my hand and led me into the house. 'Let's do this.'

The house was done out like something in one of Sasha's interiors magazines. No ancient primary-school-made decorations and straggly tinsel here. It was all decorated in white, blue and silver, and I mean everything. Even the Christmas tree was white, although it was so extravagant and lush that somehow it managed not to look tacky. But the kitchen table, which had been pushed back against a wall to make more room, was covered messily in bottles, with splashes of spilled booze drying to form a sticky layer. The owners of the house – Will's parents, I guessed – must have been away. New Year in the Bahamas or summink. Rich and I poked our heads into every room. A band was setting up in the living room, complete with logo-on drum and mahoosive amp, but there was no sign of everyone else. Then I spotted a gigantic glass conservatory off the living room, *et voilà*. Everyone was there: Cass and Adam (boo), Jack, Ollie, Sarah and Donna. They were sitting on an enormous wicker corner sofa, with Ollie and Sarah on beanbags on the floor. Seeing them made me have to blink a bit – I had to swallow back the kind of wet-eye you get when you watch, like, an advert for an abandoned-dog charity or something. Don't ask me why. There was no sign of Marv and Dylan. I hadn't expected there to be, but that hadn't stopped a pinch of anticipation forming inside me. Even now it didn't go away. At this stage it would have almost been enough just to gaze upon Dylan. Any port in a storm and all that.

I did a round of cheek-kissing and sat cross-legged on the floor.

'So, good Christmas?' asked Jack, who was wearing new dark jeans I hadn't seen before and looking pretty buff. Not my type, but I defo appreciated him in a kind of art-appreciation way.

'Not really,' I said. 'Sasha got me zebra slippers.' I showed my palms in an *I rest my case* kind of way. 'How about you?'

'Yeah, really good . . . I got a snowboard, a course of lessons, and an IOU for a skiing holiday next Christmas' He grinned and shrugged modestly.

'Oh my God, that's such an amazing present!' enthused Cass, while Adam curled his lip disdainfully.

'I know! It's the best..'

'I did quite well too, actually,' said Cass, smiling prettily. 'I got a car.'

'A brand-new Polo,' added Adam proudly, as if his girlfriend's car reflected on him as a boyfriend.

'Did you give it her?' asked Donna.

Cass shook her head. 'My parents did.' She put her hand on Adam's knee. 'He gave me a Tiffany necklace.' She held out the silver chain that was round her neck. It had a heart pendant on the end. Adam nodded smugly and slouched further down in his seat, spreading his legs slightly wider.

'It's white gold,' he explained. 'Two hundred quid's worth of kit, there.'

Seriously: 'kit'?

'I'm worth it, though,' said Cass, smiling and ruffling Adam's hair. 'You're lucky to have me, aren't you, babe?'

'Not as lucky as you are to have me.' Cue soppy

smiles and little kisses. I happened to catch Sarah's eye and she ever so subtly puffed out her cheeks *à la* about-to-vom. Funny.

I cleared my throat. 'Anyway. I have news.' And I told them all about Project Find-Inner-Beauty-and-Respect-Self, making sure I credited Rich with starting me off on the straight and narrer. There was a slight pause afterwards, as if people were finding it hard to take in the enormity of such a life-change.

'So you haven't had a single drink?' asked Jack disbelievingly.

I shook my head, eyes closed in saintliness: 'Nope. And I'm not going to.'

'What, *ever*?' said Sarah, eyes the size of saucers.

'God, NO!' I said. 'I'm not looking to become a nun.' I shuddered at the thought. 'Tonight's a one-off, just to see if I can. But I do want to stop getting hammered every single time we go out.'

'Thought you didn't believe in New Year's resolutions,' said Cass, looking slightly triumphant, as if she'd finally uncovered my inner conventionalist.

'I don't,' I said, giving her a super-arched eyebrow. 'It's just coincidence that my personal epiphany happened at this time of year.'

Donna raised her hand: 'Long-word five!' I duly high-fived, adding a pointed finger clicky-wink into the mix.

'Well, I think it's brilliant,' said Sarah. 'Good for you.'

Ollie tapped me with his foot. 'Me too.' The others all chimed in to the same effect, which was nice and all but did kind of make me wonder whether they'd thought I was a drunken slag all along. Anyway, it didn't matter, not now that I was turning over new leaves 'n' shit.

Meanwhile, Adam started fidgeting and sighing long-sufferingly. He nudged Cass. 'Babe, we should make a move.'

'Where are you going?' asked Ollie.

Cass looked sheepish. 'We've got another party to go to. One of Adam's friends.'

'But you've only just got here,' complained Sarah. 'C'mon, hon, I haven't seen you properly in ages.'

Cass turned to Adam, her face all hopeful like she was a kid begging its mum for sweets. He sucked his teeth. 'Sorry, babe. I told Ryan we'd be there early.'

'You've got to be kidding,' said Donna, banging her hand on her thigh. 'Seriously, Cass, is this going to happen every single time?'

Cass went red and stuck her chin up defiantly, but her eyes were worried. 'I can't do *everything* with you.'

'Yeah, fair enough. But your argument would be slightly more convincing if when Adam said "jump" you didn't always say "how high".'

Sarah put her hand on Cass's shoulder. 'We're supposed to be your best friends.'

'We deserve better, babes,' I added.

Tears sprang to Cass's eyes. 'Stop getting at me!' she said loudly. 'If you had boyfriends, you'd understand.'

I shook my head in disbelief. 'Ouch. Nice one, Cass.'

'Cass, listen . . .' started Jack, his voice gentle, but Adam broke in.

'Er, no. Don't think so, mate. You can stay out of this . . . C'mon, Cassie.'

'I won't stay out of this actually, thanks, "mate",' said Jack. He turned to Cass again. 'The only reason they're getting angry is because they care about you . . . We all do.' He smiled. 'Why don't you stay another half an hour, then meet Adam at the other party?'

'Nice try,' said Adam before Cass could say anything, then he muttered something under his breath that may or may not have been 'Tosser'. He stood up, stuck his hand down his jeans for a quick sort of the old bollocks – *très* attractive – and pulled Cass up. 'Let's go.'

Cass stroked his arm. 'You go, honey. I'll be out in two minutes.' He shot us a filthy glance, as if I were corrupting his girlfriend, and she added, 'I promise. Two minutes.' She gave him puppy-dog eyes and kissed him lightly on the lips, and he swaggered off.

'Bye then!' I sang. 'Don't be a stranger!'

'Don't, Ash,' said Cass. She turned to us all. 'Look, I'm not stupid. I know how he comes across. But do you think I'd be with him if he was like that all the time? I know you care about me –' she shot Jack a quick smile – 'and I care about you too. But I love Adam, and he's not going anywhere, so . . .' She trailed off. 'Anyway. Enjoy the rest of the party.' She hesitated, then kissed and hugged each of us in turn. 'Happy New Year.' We all said it back and, with a weird little wave, she left.

Ollie exhaled loudly. 'Why do I feel like a total bastard now?'

'I know, she totally turned that one round,' said Rich. 'Although Adam's still a pecker.'

Donna nodded. 'Totally.'

And then, with perfect timing, the band started up and distracted us by being actually quite good. They were a kind of indie/rock/pop mix, which sounds shit, but they threw themselves into it and you couldn't help feeling the joy.

After an hour of dancing, talking, drinking and picking at bowls of Bombay mix and nuts, we took to a bit of people-watching. Not wanting to generalize or nuffink, but the place was heaving with self-consciously cool students leaning against the walls, drinking red wine and laughing too loudly. They either had really posh accents or really Northern accents. Nothing in between, as far as I could make out.

'Look at that girl's top,' said Sarah, nodding at a whippet-thin bird with long dark hair and a fringe. She was wearing black skinny jeans, grey Converse boots and a grey wide-neck top with 'Fashion is Fascism' written on it.

'What, is that supposed to be ironic?' asked Ollie. 'Shit, the long winter evenings must fly by.'

Jack laughed, then pointed out a guy who was earnestly taking photos of random things like someone's foot or the corner of a table or a cigarette butt upended in a glass. 'What about that one?'

'Oh. He is *arty*,' said Donna, sighing sarcastically.

'To be fair, you don't know what he's doing,' said Sarah. 'Maybe he's . . .' She searched around for an explanation.

'. . . a pretentious wanker?' I offered, although TBH I was quite intrigued to know what he was doing. She looked at me reproachfully, but laughed.

'Anyway, we shouldn't be too smug,' she added. 'That'll be us come September.'

'Don't think so,' said Jack. 'Not with sports science.'

And, just to prove his point, he added a puffy-cheek belch.

'Don't give me that,' scoffed Sarah. 'Mr Predicted-three-As.' Jack shrugged, but looked pretty pleased with himself. He was fully expected to walk his A2s in sports studies, maths and chemistry. You'd never know he was a brainiac to look at him, or at his slightly dyslexic spelling and rubbish handwriting, but then that was one of the reasons why he was such a cool person to be around. Quietly brilliant, that's what Jack was.

'Oop, dinner's served,' said Donna, as people started appearing with plates piled high with food. 'Who's coming?' The boys stayed to save our seats, while Sarah and I followed Donna up for first sitting. The kitchen surfaces were covered with Chinese takeaway cartons. There must have been over a hundred quid's worth.

'Bloody hell, this is some party,' said Sarah, as she started dolloping noodles, rice and various fragrant vegetable and chicken-based dishes on to a paper plate.

'It so is,' agreed Donna. 'Actually, have you even seen that Will guy?'

Sarah grinned. 'Nope. I noticed a few people giving us quizzical looks, though.'

'We should gatecrash a rich person's party more

often,' I said, inspecting a carton of brown stuff with vegetables to make sure it wasn't duck-based. I don't do duck. Anything that waddles so cutely doesn't deserve to be eaten. And, yes, I know that doesn't make sense, but that's the way it has to be.

When we'd all piled our plates obscenely high, we trooped back to the conservatory.

'Hang on, where's Rich?' asked Sarah, as Jack and Ollie started walking in the direction of the kitchen.

'Still not back from the loo,' said Ollie over his shoulder.

'Oh, oh!' Donna suddenly started jumping up and down. 'Oh my God, I saw him! Just now! He was with a boy!'

'Really?' asked Sarah. 'What, *with* with?'

Donna gave her a look. 'Well, they weren't ripping each other's clothes off in gay abandon, if that's what you mean. But there was definite talkage and laugh-age. And they were standing quite close together . . .' She shook her head. 'Can't believe I've only just twigged the significance.'

'Oooh!' Sarah jumped up and down and did little excited claps. 'What was he like? Where are they?' She ran to the living-room door and poked her head out, one leg stuck out behind her as she leant to see round the corner.

'He was gorgeous and blond,' said Donna triumphantly, as if that just about clinched it. 'And they were at the bottom of the stairs.'

'Ooh, they're not there now!' sang Sarah. 'Do you think they've gone *upstairs*?' We all had a bit of a girlie squeal at the thought.

'Go, Rich,' I said with a smile. It would just about make my year if he got together with someone. He deserved a bit of . . . well, a bit of what he fancied.

Sarah suddenly went all big-eyed and breathless. 'Oh my God, he's the new Ashley! He's gone upstairs for a drunken shag!'

'Thanks for that, Sar,' I said. 'But I don't think I'm the only one who's shagged someone in a bedroom in this house, hmm?' I pursed my lips and looked at her over imaginary glasses. She'd had it off with Joe at the same party that I'd had my, ahem, dalliance with Will.

She blushed. 'I wasn't drunk, though.'

I rolled my eyes. 'Nit-picking, Sar Bear.' Although I was being a bit unfair. She'd only ever had one sexual partner, as they like to say down at the sexual health clinic. But she giggled anyway. Having any kind of sex story was quite a novelty for our Sarah, and I think she quite enjoyed it. Fair play to her.

'What are you lot gossiping about?' asked Ollie, as he and Jack got back with their food.

'Rich has gone upstairs . . . *with a boy*,' Donna whisper-shrieked. Jack didn't say anything. I guessed Rich might have confided in him and he didn't want to speak out of turn. But Ollie shook his head and grinned. 'Whoa, Rich. You dark homo horse.'

'We don't actually know that, though,' protested Sarah. 'He could have been asking the boy the way to the loo or something.'

'Yeah, yeah,' said Donna. 'But let's assume it's this until we hear otherwise. Much more fun.'

'I hope it is,' said Ollie. 'He deserves a bit of fun. He hasn't been himself since his nan died.' Ol could be really sensitive when he wanted to be. Until I'd spoken to Rich the other night, I'd had no idea he was anything other than totally fine. Was I the only one? I looked at Sarah and Donna, and was relieved to see them looking surprised too.

'God, yeah. I suppose he has been a bit quiet,' said Sarah. 'I sometimes catch him kind of staring into space.'

Jack nodded. 'He is suffering a bit, but he doesn't like to talk about it.'

'Gorgeous blond's just what he needs then,' said Donna approvingly.

And I couldn't tell you what was said after that because I spotted Dylan in the kitchen. He was talking to a statuesque blonde girl.

'Er, Ashley?' Donna tapped me on the shoulder and I snapped back to reality. I shook my head rapidly to bury both the image and the galloping envy.

'Sorry. I'm back in the room.'

'Excellent. Now, who's for a dance?'

13

For the next couple of hours we ate our bodyweight in the chocolate brownies that had appeared in giant bowls around the house, had a laugh and generally enjoyed being together. Not knowing anyone else at the party was kind of nice, in an us-versus-the-world kind of way. Every now and then I'd spot Dylan and I'd will him to look my way, but he never did. A little bit of me died every time, but at least I didn't see him talking to that girl again. And, in other news, Rich *still* hadn't reappeared. Jack had just gone off to make sure he was OK (hmm, could be awkward), which left me, Sarah and Donna watching Ollie throwing shapes on the dance floor. He was a bit pissed and totally into it: closing his eyes, biting his bottom lip, hunching his shoulders. All that. You had to love Ollie.

'Uh-oh, she's back.' Sarah pointed at a drunken bint who'd been walking past/staring at/accidentally-on-purpose bumping into Ollie for the past hour. She was wearing a flippy skater skirt, platform stilettos and had her hair in bunches. You just knew she liked to think of herself as 'quirky' and 'a character'. She'd clearly decided to step her campaign up a notch, winding herself round him, giving him sultry looks over her shoulder and doing slow hip-swings to the ground and back right in front of him. It was both hilarious and totally embarrassing.

'Oh God, I can't watch!' squealed Donna, watching.

'That's it, I'm going to rescue him,' said Sarah, but Donna pulled her back down. 'Don't. It's funny.'

'C'mon, Don, look at the poor bastard,' I said, as Bunches Girl started running her hands through his hair and skilfully blocking every one of his attempts to duck out of her way. Donna looked disappointed, but she let Sarah go. We watched Sar dance up to Ollie, whisper in his ear, then say something to Bunches; at which point Bunches gasped and covered her mouth with her hand, said something to Ollie and then hurried out of the room.

'This girl is a genius,' said Ollie, as he and Sarah came back to join us.

'What did you *say* to her?' asked Donna, grinning in anticipation.

Sarah shrugged. 'Told her he was gay.'

'She was most apologetic,' said Ollie. He put his arm round Sarah and kissed the side of her head. 'Cheers, flower. I owe you one.'

Then a rush of people came into the room, Rich

and Jack among them, and someone turned the telly on. Big Ben filled the screen: it was nearly midnight. The boys sprinted over to us and we counted down to 2013, throwing ourselves at each other as on the TV Big Ben chimed, streamers filled the sky and people cheered.

'Happy New Year, babes!' shouted Donna into my ear. I shouted it back, but I wasn't really feeling it. Christmas had been too crap, and that business at school, and the waiting to see if I could get on to a film course . . . It was all just a bit rubbish. I was glad I was doing the turning-over-a-new-leaf stuff, but it still sucked to be toasting the start of 2013 with a glass of flat lemonade and no one to kiss. But I wasn't about to put a downer on everyone's New Year by moaning as the clock struck midnight. Attention-seeking much? It was like someone choosing a place right in the middle of the school field to have their private breakdown. So I pushed all that away and instead caught Rich's eye and raised a questioning eyebrow. He just smiled and shrugged. Annoying. I'd get it out of him later.

After everyone had muddled their way through 'Auld Lang Syne', duh-duh-duh-ing where they didn't know the words, and the hugging and kissing had given way to a full dance floor as the band struck up the feel-good choons, I broke off from the others to grab another Coke. The kitchen looked like a bomb site, with bin bags overflowing with empties and spills all over the place. The empty Chinese cartons were still there, and someone had dropped a bottle of milk by the fridge. I grabbed my drink and went back to join the others, but stopped outside the kitchen to look at a group of old black-and-white family photos on the wall: grim-faced Victorians in sepia, kids in white flounces. Maybe it was because I didn't know anything about my dad's family that I was so fascinated by hard evidence like photos. Anyway, I was in some kind of reverie when I felt a familiar hand on my arm. I knew who it was before looking up.

'Hi.' Dylan smiled his ridiculous, gorgeous smile, his eyes deep and dark. 'How's it going?'

I swallowed, my heart thumping so hard I wouldn't have been surprised if it had shot out of my chest *à la* Bugs Bunny when he sees a girl bunny.

'Yeah, good,' I said.

'I've been wanting to talk to you all night . . .'

'Have you?' was all I could manage. (*HAVE YOU???!!!!* went the voice in my head.)

'I'm a bit drunk,' he explained. 'Not very. Just enough, you know?' He smiled again, and I nodded. I knew.

'So, anyway. Shall we go for a walk?' He held his

hand out to me and I took it, my heart still racing. His threaded his lovely long fingers through mine and I tried not to worry that I hadn't had a chance to wipe the sweat off my hand first. He led me into the massive back garden. There was a summer-house thing at the end, which we could just make out in the light coming from the main house. He looked at me questioningly and I nodded, and we walked mutely across the frozen lawn. The summer house was unlocked, but dark and bitterly cold inside. Using his phone as a torch, Dylan looked around. There were two wicker sofas, just like the ones in the conservatory, a glass-and-wicker coffee table and a small wooden shelving unit with dark shapes on it – books and, weirdly, what looked like seashells. On the top of the unit was an old-fashioned oil lantern, which Dylan lit using a lighter from his pocket. One of the wicker sofas had a blanket over it. I pulled it off and wrapped it round one shoulder, then held out the remainder for Dylan to use. He came and sat beside me, and pulled the blanket round his own shoulder.

And there we were, snuggled up under a blanket in the early hours of New Year's Day in a lantern-lit summer house. It was deeply surreal, and throughout every second of the few minutes since we'd bumped into each other outside the kitchen I'd wondered what the hell was going on. Was this another Debenhams?

('*We'll always have Debenhams*' went through my head, and I smirked into the semi-darkness. Luckily Dylan didn't notice – dunno how I could've explained that one without sounding mental.) Was he going to be really nice to me tonight then practically ignore me until the next time he decided to pay me some attention? I was confused, but I wasn't going to waste too much time analysing it. Not till later, anyway. It's not like I was going to declare undying love. For now, it was enough to be close to him, and talking to him.

'Well, this is nice,' I said, smoothing the blanket over my legs camply.

He laughed. 'It is.' He stuck his hand out awkwardly. 'Hi, I'm Dylan.'

I shook his hand. 'Ashley. Nice to meet you.'

'You too.'

Dylan cleared his throat. 'So. I saw an amazing film the other day. *Towards the Light* or something?'

My mouth fell open. I couldn't have been more shocked if he'd whipped off his top and informed me he was a girl. 'You were there?'

He grinned. 'Yep. Donna invited me. I loved it.'

I squished my hands between my knees with chuffedness. 'Really?'

'Yeah, totally. It was thoughtful, insightful . . . beautiful to look at.'

'Wow. Thanks.' I grinned in face-cracking stylee. 'How come you didn't say hello?'

He pulled the blanket a bit tighter round himself. 'I'm not sure. I guess, since you didn't talk to me at Donna's theatre studies thing . . .' I didn't say anything to that, because what could I say that wouldn't make me sound ridiculous or needy or both?

'Are you into films, then?' I said, mainly to change the subject but I did want to know.

'Actually, I want to be a screenwriter,' he said, almost sheepishly. 'I write short films. Like, really short. Just ten minutes or so. But I'm trying to learn "the craft".' He waved his hands to show he realized it sounded wanky.

Oh God, could this boy be any more perfect? 'So are you going to do that at uni?' I asked.

He rocked his shoulders from side to side, which forced him even closer to me. My head only reached his upper chest, but I could smell his shampoo as he moved. 'Nyeh . . . I don't know. I'm in two minds. I'd love to, but at the same time it's kind of a difficult industry to get into, you know? Maybe it'd be better to do something more . . . I dunno. Useful.'

'I reckon you should just do it,' I offered, shrugging. 'Unless you do, like, nursing or medicine or engineering or something, hardly any degrees are actually useful. Do something you love, that's what I reckon. Even if you don't end up being a screen-writer, you'll have spent three years doing the thing you really love. Not many people can say that.'

He looked at me. 'That's so exactly what I think!' He started agitatedly running the satin trim round the edge of the blanket through his fingers. 'The idea of stumbling through life, not doing much, getting by, doing what you think is expected of you, then ending up on your death bed thinking, *Fuck, I didn't do ANY-THING . . .*?' He shook his head. 'It scares the shit out of me.'

I almost started bouncing up and down, I was so feeling what he was saying. 'Exactly. Ex*act*ly!'

We fell into a slightly embarrassed silence, the summer house suddenly extremely quiet, then after a minute Dylan cleared his throat and said, 'Actu-ally, there was something in particular I wanted to say to you.'

'Oh, yes?' I said, all casual, while my insides started sprinting from one end of my body to the other and back again.

He looked down at the floor for a moment, then up at the ceiling, then he laughed. 'Even with a few drinks, this is still hard.' I smiled encouragingly, hardly daring to believe what I thought I was hearing.

He started to say something, then stopped, then started again. 'I think you're beautiful . . .' He kind of winced like I might laugh in his face, but I smiled. 'Smile' isn't even enough of a word to describe it. I beamed, I grinned, my mouth stretched so wide with joy my cheeks ached. Dylan thought I was beautiful!

'You're beautiful and clever and really funny,' he went on. 'But there's something I don't understand.'

'What's that?' I whispered, hope turning me shy.

He paused, then said – quietly and devastatingly – 'Why do you get drunk and do dumb stuff with guys when you don't even like each other?' My heart sank and I started stuttering, trying to say something but completely failing to do anything because my body was just about shutting down with disappointment, but he turned to me and said: 'I only ask, because . . . here's one boy who does really like you. So why do you ignore me?'

I almost laughed. 'I thought you were ignoring me!'

Dylan grinned and shook his head, and looked so deep into my eyes – the lamplight making them even deeper and darker – that I thought I might pass out with lust.

And then we kissed.

14

Honest to God, it was the best kiss I'd ever had. But that's where it ended. I was sober, so while it was really hard to resist the urge to try to take it further, it wasn't impossible. Anyway, maybe there was no hurry this time. Maybe where me and Dylan were concerned, there was all the time in the world.

'For the record,' I said, after we'd gently pulled away from the kiss and were grinning like idiots and gazing into each other's eyes, 'I really like you too.'

He reached into his pocket and pulled out his phone. 'What's your number?' I told him and his long fingers flew over the buttons, the display casting weird light around the summer house. 'I've texted you, so you've got mine too.' He ran his hands over my shoulders. 'Please can I see you soon?'

I pretended to think about it. 'Yeah, go on, then.'

We went back into the main house, me leading the way this time. I could see Donna standing in the conservatory, her hands on her hips, but she didn't see me until I reached the door. She slapped her forehead. '*There* you are. Listen, we're all . . . Oh, hello!' She stopped in her tracks as Dylan came up behind me, then turned to me with eyebrows so high they practically had their own airspace. I smiled, giving nothing away.

'Hey, Donna, happy New Year . . .' He turned to me. 'Actually, I have to go. I promised Marv I'd share a cab with him.' He met my eyes and smiled. 'I'll see you soon.'

'You will,' I agreed. And Donna and I watched him lope away, his frock coat swinging.

'Something you want to tell me?' she asked casually.

'We kissed,' I said equally casually, then winced as Donna screeched.

'NO WAY! Oh my God, Ash, I'm so happy for you. Oh my God, this is immense. Shit . . . I mean, *shit*, this is BIG!'

I giggled like a kid. 'I know!' I still couldn't really believe it.

'Aw, Ash. This is the best thing *ever.*' Don clapped her hands and squealed again. 'Tell me EVERY-THING!'

'There isn't much to tell,' I said. 'He said he really liked me, that I was beautiful . . .' I broke off for another bout of face-stretching beaming. 'And that he wants us to meet up really soon.'

Donna threw her arms around me again. 'I KNEW he liked you!' She so didn't, but I let that one go. 'Anyway, we were all about to make a move. Are you coming?' I nodded and we went to find the others.

'What's the story with Rich?' I asked, as we weaved our way through the groups of hammered people. It was strange being the only sober one, but funnily enough I didn't give a flying frig. I was high on Dylan, baby.

She shrugged. 'He won't say. He keeps smiling enigmatically and tapping the side of his nose. It's really effing annoying.'

'I'll get it out of him,' I said. 'I'll call him tomorrow.'

Later, after I'd got home and was in the kitchen having a cup of tea, contentedly staring into space, I remembered that Dylan had texted me. I quickly pulled my bag towards me from where I'd dumped it on the edge of the table and fumbled around for my phone. As I clicked the button to bring the screen to life, his words were lit up like a neon billboard.

> Hi beautiful. This is me.
> And don't you forget it.
> Dxxx

15

The morning after the night before usually went something like this: wake up with banging headache, stagger to bathroom, throw up, stagger down to kitchen, neck two Nurofen and a gallon of water, stagger back to bed, remember snippets of previous night's drunken snogs and fumbles, groan, go back to sleep.

But today was different. New Year's Day 2013: the day Ashley Greene woke up bright-eyed, bushy-tailed and with total recall of the night before. The day I woke up happy. Tra la laaa! (If my life were a musical I'd be breaking into a life-affirming song ending in rousing finale with cast of thousands right about now. Just so you know.) I checked the time – half ten – then snuggled down under my duvet, stretched my toes out and wiggled them in contentment. I could hear the wind in the tree outside my window, making my bed seem even cosier. Every now and then the clouds would clear a space for the sun and light would stream through my blinds. All I needed now was for Dylan to burst in with a basket full of pastries and my morning would be complete.

Dylan.

Even though I'd been stone-cold sober I couldn't help doubting myself. He'd said he was a bit drunk, but what if he'd been a lot drunk? He hadn't seemed it, but maybe he was one of those people who hides it well. I bit my lip and turned slightly cold at the thought of him waking up this morning and cursing himself for giving me his number. Or, even worse, not remembering it. I didn't know what to do. Should I contact him or wait for him to get in touch with me? I didn't do dithering, but this was different. I was no Ian the Stalker: there was no way I was going to text him if he was busy regretting.

My phone chirruped a text alert and I rolled my eyes in a totally unsuccessful attempt to tell myself it wouldn't be from him. But still, I forced myself to count to twenty before I checked it.

It wasn't from him.

I swore under my breath. Donna wanted to know if I'd spoken to Rich yet. At 10:45 on New Year's Day? Not likely. I texted back to say as much, and a minute later another text arrived. Bloody Donna.

But it was from Dylan. Yes! I actually said it out loud, then tried to control my breathing in case it wasn't good news.

Let's meet up xxx

How much did I dig his short and sweet messages? I replied:

Let's xxx

2pm outside
Debenhams?? xxx

Oh my God, we had Our Place! We totally had Debenhams! OK, it wasn't exactly Grand Central Station or whatever, but still. With my heart skipping like a kid in the sun with a rope, I replied.

See you there xxx

But before that I had three hours to kill. First things first: I phoned Rich.

''Lo?' he croaked.

'Oop, sorry, did I wake you?' I heard the sound of bed springs and grunting as he sat up in bed.

'Yeah. What time is it?'

'Nearly eleven.'

'Ugh.' I took that to mean: *Gosh, about time I woke up then. Please continue*.

'So. How are you feeling?'

I heard the sound of glugging water. 'I don't even know yet, Ashley. I'm still asleep.'

'Soz, babes . . . though it *is* nearly the afternoon.'

'S'pose . . . How are you, anyway? Heard from Dylan?'

I grinned. 'Uh-huh. I'm meeting him outside Debenhams later.'

'Romantic,' he said, sniggering.

'Piss off . . . Anyway, *Richard*, what happened to *you* last night?'

He coughed. 'How d'you mean?'

'Don't come the innocent with me, young man,' I said briskly. 'You were seen talking to a, I quote, *gorgeous blond*.'

'Ooh, hold the front page,' he said, deadpan. 'There's nothing to tell, I'm afraid. You and Donna'll have to find someone else to gossip about.'

'Oh, come on, Rich. Please?' I wheedled.

He sighed dramatically. 'His name's Jamie and we used to hang out when we were about ten cos his mum's the same age as my mum and they got talking in Tesco one time about how they were always being mistaken for our nans.' He took a breath. 'Then they moved away but now he's back and he recognized me and we got talking. The end.'

'You were talking for a very long time,' I said, trying not to sound suss.

'Yeah, well. We had a lot of catching up to do.'

'Are you going to see him again?'

Rich laughed. 'Yes, Ashley, I probably will. We were really good friends for like a year, so . . .'

'Oh. Right,' I said, kind of disappointed. 'We thought —'

'I know what you thought,' he interrupted. 'And I'm sorry to disappoint . . . So, anyway. How was the Night of No Drinking? Have you decided to go permanently teetotal?'

I got to Debenhams at exactly one minute past two and there was Dylan, hunching his shoulders against the cold and looking delicious in a long army surplus coat, the skulls scarf and a black beanie. He smiled at me as I approached, then leant down and kissed me on the lips, his mouth soft and warm. He smelled kind of woody and spicy, and his chin was ever so slightly stubbly. The kiss was like electricity, making my whole body zing. This is what they mean (whoever *they* are) when they talk about chemistry. We were like . . . well, whichever two chemicals react with each other to make an explosion. I hadn't done chemistry for years. Anyway, it was amazing, is all.

'Hey,' he said. 'How are you?'

'All right, thanks . . . You?'

'Not bad.' We both looked slightly embarrassed at the stilted small talk, then caught each other's eye and smiled. We were so on the same page, it was ridiculous.

'I thought we could go for a walk on the beach, if that suits you?' he continued, putting his arm round my shoulders as we started walking.

'Sounds good.'

I leant into him, and he didn't move his arm from round my shoulders. It didn't feel awkward or uncomfortable, like it sometimes can. We fitted together all perfect like a jigsaw. At the deserted beach we bought takeaway coffees and walked along the pebbles, the wind buffeting us. It was a New Year's Day kind of day, or at least the kind you might see in a film or read about in a book. Blowing away the cobwebs, expanse of empty shore and restless sea, some kind of metaphor for clean slates and fresh starts and simmering potential – all that guff.

As we ambled along, I watched the sea rolling, blue-grey and choppy.

'I nearly died in the sea,' I said, without thinking. An original conversational opener, I think you'll agree.

Dylan stopped and looked down at me. Every time his eyes met mine my heart skipped a beat. 'I know. You talked about it at your screening. What happened?'

I smiled at the thought of him remembering things about me. 'We – Donna, Rich and that lot – went to Devon in half term. I went swimming in the sea. It was cold.' I shrugged. 'Turns out it was a stupid idea. Sarah and Jack had to come to my rescue.'

Dylan laughed delightedly. 'You're unbelievable.'

'In a good way, I hope,' I said, raising an eyebrow.

He pulled me round so I was facing him. 'A very good way.' And he leant down and kissed me again – a long, slow, gorgeous kiss, our tongues lazily moving against each other. If he wanted to think I was all cute and crazy for winter swimming that was up to him. I wasn't going to contradict him. Especially not if this was what it got me.

I wrapped my arms round his waist, resting my head against his chest. 'You're just lovely,' I said into his coat so he couldn't hear me.

'You're lovely,' he said, kissing the top of my head. I pulled away and grinned up at him. 'I was just think-ing the same about you.'

We started to walk again. It was freezing, but the sea spray lashing against my face making my cheeks burn was invigorating and the crazy biting wind just made me feel more alive. The combination of about fifty layers of clothing along with hot coffee and hot Dylan was enough to keep me warm. I could hardly believe we were together. Things like this didn't hap-pen to me. I felt so happy I was almost scared.

'Actually, I nearly died once, too,' he continued. 'While we're sharing tales of almost-tragedy.'

'What happened?'

'It's not as exciting as yours. I was stung on the tongue by a wasp when I was seven. It swelled up so much I nearly choked to death . . .' He smiled at me. 'I had a near-death experience and everything.'

I snapped my head up. 'No!'

'Yeah. I saw the tunnel, the bright light, all that.' He shrugged, his whole coat moving up and down with his shoulders. 'Back then I was convinced I'd seen heaven . . . though not any more.'

I told him about applying to film school and he told me that he'd pretty much decided to apply to screenwriting courses, then I told him about Frankie, and a tiny bit about Sasha and Mum. 'You can tell me to shut up, if you want,' I said, after I'd talked non-stop for about ten minutes. 'In fact, I will shut up. Tell me about you.'

'What do you want to know?' He moved his arm so he could sprint over to a bin and chuck our coffee cups, then took my hand when he got back. The feel of his palm against mine was more erotic than sex. Or at least the sex I'd had so far. The anticipation of what might be to come with Dylan made me weak at the knees. I couldn't believe how different this was from my usual experiences. I was loving it.

'I want to know everything,' I said.

He grinned. 'Hmm, that might take some time.'

I raised an eyebrow. 'Got any plans?'

'I have now.' He stopped and drew me to him again. 'Kiss me, Ashley.'

So I did.

Epilogue

In case you were wondering, I got an A* for my documentary. As to whether I'll get into film school: who knows? I've only just applied. But, if I get in, nothing – and nobody – will stop me. And Dylan knows that.

Don't miss the next fantastic book,
coming soon in paperback
and ebook:

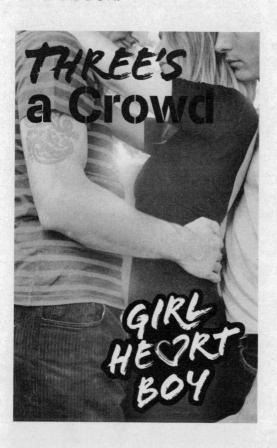

Turn over for an exclusive extract . . .

1

I awoke with a start, and a weird dream in which Richard Madeley was my dad disappeared with a *pouf*. I looked around blearily to find out what had disturbed me. For once Adam was sleeping silently, so it couldn't have been his snoring. I squinted at a glow coming from my bedside table. *Ah*. Stretching my face to Scream-mask proportions to force my eyes to focus, I picked up my mobile. It was a text from Sarah, my best friend.

Happy NOO Years!

Oh yes, it was New Year's Day! My insides did a little flip at the realization that 2012 was gone for good. 2013: the year things were going to get difficult. Not pessimism but reality. I'd known it for months. Banishing bad thoughts, I read on.

Fab party, hun. Wish u'd
been there. Ashley got
with DYLAN!!! Rich went
off with gorgeous blond

> BOY!!! See what you miss
> by not being with moi?!
> How was yours? Xxx

I actually gasped. This was big news! I was tempted to sneak out of bed and call her, but she was probably still asleep and it would only get on Adam's nerves. I quickly texted back.

> OMG I need to know
> more!! Call you later. I
> had fab night too, thanks
> xxx

I always got a pang when I missed a night out with the girls, which was silly because being with Adam totally made up for it. And we *had* had a lovely time. We'd shown our faces at the girls' party before going on to Adam's friend Ryan's house. Ryan's fiancée, Lucy, had made this amazing chicken and chorizo pasta bake with garlic bread, and I'd made chocolate pudding. We drank loads of wine and chatted and watched Big Ben on TV at midnight. It was nice. My friends Ashley and Donna would rather have slit their wrists than spend a New Year's Eve like that, but I'd always liked low-key nights – maybe more than mental ones. My dad sometimes joked that I was born adult, and I did wonder whether I was missing some kind of teen gene. I mean, I wasn't a total lost cause. I got drunk and danced like an idiot with the best of them, but there wasn't much that could make me as contented as a night in with good food and good friends. I just don't think you need to get completely off your face to have fun.

I guess that was why I'd ended up with a boyfriend four years older than me. His friends were now my friends as well, especially Ryan and Becky. Becky was lovely. She was twenty-one – the same age as the boys – and was a manager of some kind at Topshop in town. She let me use her discount a couple of times, although I felt slightly bad about it. It's not like I couldn't afford to pay full price (yeah, guilty, I get a pretty generous allowance from my parents), but I figured Sir Philip Green – that's the Topshop guy, right? – wouldn't have to cancel his Christmas in Barbados just because I got a fiver off a jacket.

So, yes, it'd been the perfect way to spend New Year's Eve, and I'd been able to kiss my lovely boyfriend as the clock struck midnight, but still – it wasn't a party with dancing and laughing and friends partaking in gossip-worthy incidents.

I looked at sleeping Adam again. He had one arm curled round his head, the muscles of his shoulder and upper arm involuntarily flexing. The smattering of hair on his chest and under his arms gave me a little thrill. I was going out with a man, not a boy. He really was gorgeous. I felt lucky every time I looked at him. I blew lightly on his nipples and sniggered as they instantly stood to attention.

'What's so funny?' mumbled Adam, without opening his eyes.

'Nothing, babe.' I smiled. 'Just your hair-trigger nipples.'

He opened one eye and grinned at me. 'Hair-trigger nipples? Crazy bunny.'

He threw back the covers and got out of bed. He's always been able to do that: asleep to awake in one second flat. He stood naked for a moment, looking around for something to put on, and grabbed a pair of jeans from the floor. (I'd long since stopped trying to get him to at least fold his clothes. The tidiness issue was going to be a big one when we moved in together, but we'd cross that bridge.) Leaning over, he kissed me on the forehead. 'Stay there, baby. It's a breakfast-in-bed day.'

I raised my eyebrows. 'Ooh! What have I done to deserve this?'

He smiled. 'Just been your usual adorable self.' Another kiss, on the mouth this time, then he padded along the hallway to the kitchen, his bare feet slapping against the floorboards. He didn't feel the cold like normal people. I was always freezing in his flat.

I bit my lip. My sexy boy. I sent Mum and Dad a quick text to wish them a happy new year and tell them I'd be back later, then grabbed the remote from Adam's bedside table and turned on the news. I have a bit of a weird thing for news channels. I like to flick between them to see the different ways they're reporting the stories. Maybe I'm just paranoid but I find it kind of mind-blowing that TV producers have the power to decide what the rest of us should know about. I mean, newspaper editors are the same, and I guess Twitter means nothing much is secret, but whereas loads of people don't read proper newspapers (and, I'm sorry, but anything tabloid-sized isn't a proper newspaper, whatever my dad says) or use Twitter, *everyone* watches telly. Anyway. Adam's TV only had BBC and Sky, and for some reason the signal was scrambling, so I clicked the telly off and snuggled under the duvet to wait for my breakfast. I could hear clattering coming from the kitchen. Adam didn't really do cooking, so I knew tea and toast was the most I could expect, but it was lovely all the same.

'What are you smiling about now, mentalist?' he said, putting a tray with mugs of tea and a big plate of toast on the end of the bed.

'I was just thinking about what a nice boyfriend I have,' I said, reaching for a slice. I smiled at him. 'I love it when you make romantic gestures.'

Adam stepped out of his jeans and got back into bed. "'S the kind of guy I am, Cassie.' And he took a massive slurp of tea followed up by a lavish belch, just so I didn't start thinking he'd gone totally soft and metrosexual. I gave him a half-hearted punch on the arm, but really there was no point. To stop Adam from burping would almost be a cruelty, it gave him so much pleasure. Sometimes, after a particularly long and sumptuous expulsion of mouth gas, he'd beam like he'd just won the lottery. At least I'd managed to stop him blowing the result in my direction. That really was gross.

'Happy New Year, by the way,' he continued, leaning over for another kiss.

'Happy New Year to you too, sweetie.' I reached for another slice of toast. 'Why am I so starving? We ate loads last night.'

'Better watch yourself,' Adam joked. 'I don't want my girl getting a muffin top.' He playfully squeezed my – very svelte, thanks very much – waist.

'I might say the same for you,' I retorted, but he just laughed. Adam was buff and lean, as was his dad, still, at the age of forty-seven. My boy had genetics on his side. My mum, on the other hand, while extremely stylish and – like me – a carrier of the list-maker gene, was softer and rounder.

'Hello?' Adam waved a hand in front of my face.

'C'mon babe, I was only joking. You know I think you're hot.'

I blinked. 'Oh, I know that. I was just thinking about Mum, for some reason.'

Adam grunted as he stuffed half a slice of toast in his mouth. A love of burping and of food go hand in hand, I guess. Which reminded me. 'You're definitely coming to Sarah's birthday dinner on Wednesday, aren't you?' I said.

'Yeah, course. I'd be a fool to miss out on a meal cooked by you, babe.' He leant precariously off the bed to put the empty plate on the floor. 'Don't think I'll stay afterwards, though.'

'Oh ba-a-a-be,' I whined. 'You promised.'

He put his arm round me, drawing me in to his chest. 'I promised I'd come for the dinner, Cass. I'm not going to spend a whole evening with your friends.' He shuddered. 'I'd top myself.'

I swallowed the rising irritation. Adam hated my friends. I hated that he hated them, but there was nothing I could do about it. They hated him right back, of course. Anyway, I knew why he didn't like them. He was jealous. They took up too much of my time. Or maybe that was really arrogant and it was a genuine clash of personalities. Either way, it was two really important parts of my life that were never going to join up.

I sighed and leant into him. Why couldn't he see that my friends weren't in competition with him? I was his — I would always be his. I reckoned it might have something to do with the choices he'd made. He left school at eighteen to work for my dad's building business. He seemed to love his job; he earned pretty good money, and my dad loved him (and he looked shamefully buff lugging bricks around wearing nothing but jeans and a sweaty sheen), but was there a chance he could be jealous of my friends? I mean, most of us were planning on going to university. I'd told him over and over again that I wanted to go to Sussex Uni to be close to him (we lived in Brighton), but he was obviously still nervous. Until now he'd seen my friends as school kids, but soon they'd not only be fellow adults but better qualified with better earning potential. Money's important to Adam — I suppose it is to all of us, to an extent. Personally, I want to be a lawyer, then an MP, then a Cabinet minister and then Prime Minister. (It's nice to dream . . .)

Anyway. There was no point worrying about the friends thing, and certainly no point talking about it. That would be a bad way to start a new year. I tilted my head back and Adam leant down to kiss me. Even if it was dark he could always — *always* — tell when I was moving in for a kiss. I relaxed into him and our kissing intensified, then he gently pushed me on to my back and smiled like he only ever did for me.

'Get 'em off,' he growled. So I did, awkwardly pulling off the Homer Simpson T-shirt of Adam's that I wore on cold nights when I was staying at his, mainly to stop him wearing it during daylight hours. 'Much better,' he grinned, and he started kissing my neck, then working his way downwards. 'Hello, biggie,' he said affectionately, as he kissed my right breast. He moved across to my left. 'Hello, smallie.'

Smallie? Er, what? My boobs were different *sizes*?! I wasn't confident about them at the best of times – Adam sometimes made jokes about buying me a boob job for my eighteenth – but the different-size thing was new. I already paid someone to yank most of my pubes out on a regular basis for Adam. Was I going to have to do something about the boobs as well? Well, not *have to* do something. It's not like he ever forced me to do anything. I just knew what he liked, and I wanted to make him happy.

Ugh. *Save it*, I thought. I closed my eyes and tried to tune in again to what Adam was doing. It wasn't difficult. As with most things, when it came to sex Adam was confident and capable. I'm not that into bedroom confessionals – unlike most of my friends – so suffice to say the next half an hour was intimate and gorgeous and the perfect way to see in 2013.

Adam had some kind of sixth sense as to when the time was right for romance, and when to just go for the gasping, athletic stuff. He was great at both.

Afterwards, as the orgasmic glow subsided and we lay entangled, the revelation of my wonky boobs fixed itself in my head again. I was about to say something to Adam – make some kind of jokey remark – but the rise and fall of his chest told me he'd fallen asleep. It was probably for the best. Some of Adam's friends' girlfriends were clingy and high-maintenance, constantly wanting reassurance. I was never going to be like that.

The moment I left Adam's later that afternoon I called Sarah, but it rang out. I left a voicemail asking her to call me back ASAP. I couldn't believe Rich got with a boy! (*Potentially* got with a boy, I reminded myself. The text hadn't been clear. Hey, lawyers need to be pedantic . . .) We all sort of knew that Rich wasn't strictly heterosexual, but there'd never been actual proof. Not that he needed to prove anything to us, but you know what I mean. And Ashley and Dylan! I was really pleased for Ash. I always thought that all the sleeping around she did was a sign of dodgy self-esteem, not that I voiced that to anyone other than Sarah. Ashley and Donna – Ash's best friend – would never see it like that.

I was just about to try Sarah again when she called back. I answered before the first ring had finished. 'Tell me EVERYTHING!'

She laughed. 'Oh, babes, you should have been there. It was the best night.'

(Of course it was! It got on my nerves when my friends went on about some amazing time they'd had when I wasn't there. It was never that amazing when I *was* there, so why should it be so great when I wasn't? But I didn't say that. Obviously.)

'It sounds it, hon,' I said. 'I can't believe Rich got with a boy!'

'Actually he didn't.' She huffed disappointedly. 'Or that's what he's saying. He told Ashley that it was just someone he used to know when he was little. They only "chatted", apparently.'

'Oh no!'

'I know! Gutted . . . But Ash definitely got with Dylan.'

'"Ash Gets With Boy Shocker",' I harrumphed. 'Not exactly news, is it?'

'Ah, but she didn't go home with him!' said Sarah. 'They. Did. Not. Shag.'

'Wow, was she ill?' (Does this sound like bitching? Because it really wasn't. Ashley happily admitted that she liked no-strings sex. It was almost a badge of honour to her. Actually there was no 'almost' about it. It was her Thing. I was the organized one, Sarah was the innocent one, Ashley was the sex-crazed one. End of, as she would say.)

'I know, right?' agreed Sarah. 'Rich told me that he told her that she needed to sort herself out. They had a massive row, but then she saw the error of her ways or whatever and apologized to Rich just before the party. It was really weird, Cass. Firstly, Ashley didn't drink –'

'What, not anything?' I interrupted.

'Well, she drank Coke and stuff, but no alcohol.'

'No!' This was proper news.

'I know! And then she and Dylan ignored each other all night, although she was obviously checking him out, and then all of a sudden they were together. They're seeing each other today, like for a proper date.'

'Has Ashley ever even been on a date before?' I asked. I couldn't imagine it: Ash and Dylan in a diner looking shyly into each other's eyes across the table, sipping milkshakes and then sharing a chaste kiss at the end of the evening.

'I know, right?' said Sarah, after I'd voiced the above. 'Dates only happen in fifties movies. But guess where they're meeting?'

I spent approximately one and a half seconds trying to come up with somewhere suitably offbeat and alternative, before giving up. I just wanted to hear the story. 'I dunno.'

'You'll love this.' I could hear the smile in her voice. 'They're meeting outside Debenhams.'

I snorted. 'Oh my God! That's so . . . conventional!'

'I know!'

I was weighing up whether to talk about Adam's boob revelation when Sarah had to hang up – her parents had family friends over. It was probably not such a bad thing I hadn't been able to discuss it. She tried to be nice about Adam, but she didn't need any more ammunition. It was entirely my own insecurities that were making me feel bad, but Sarah wouldn't see it that way. I tried to stop thinking about it, but every bus-stop advert I passed seemed to have a perfectly breasted woman smiling smugly at me. Obviously I knew all those images were airbrushed, but still. It was not normal to have one small boob and one big boob. If it was, they'd make bras with different cup sizes. I'd obviously been in denial for years. Like the opposite of that thing when anorexics see themselves as fat in the mirror, I looked in the mirror and saw someone with normal breasts.

This was stupid. I had a lot to be thankful for. I'd started the new year with breakfast in bed, for a start. Crossing my arms tightly over my chest, I counted each of my many blessings with every step, until that got irritating and I just pulled myself together.

My mum came bustling out of the kitchen as soon as she heard me open the front door. 'Happy New Year!' she sang, kissing my cheek. 'Did you have a lovely evening?'

'I did.' I was slightly taken aback by her enthusiasm. 'Looks like you did too.'

'Oh, it was *marvellous!*' she said, clasping her hands together. 'Your father surprised me with dinner at 9 George Street.'

'Wow.' 9 George Street was a restaurant in town that had recently been awarded two Michelin stars. I know this because it was all over the local news. Now you had to book months in advance to get a table, and yet my dad had managed to wangle a reservation on New Year's Eve. I wasn't surprised. In certain circles y dad was something of a local celebrity – self-made millionaire (in property and investments, at least. I'm pretty sure he didn't have a million pounds knocking around his bank account), did a lot for charity, larger than life, blah blah. Obviously I was ridiculously proud of him.

'Wow indeed,' my mum agreed. 'The food was just . . .' She paused to search for the right adjective. '. . . *delectable*.' She leant in as if about to tell me a secret. 'Dad ordered a ridiculously expensive bottle of Champagne. Oh, it was something special.'

I couldn't help smiling at her joy. Just not having to cook for once must have been a treat in itself and, as a rule, my mum was never the recipient of my dad's famously extravagant gestures. That accolade had always gone to me and my brother, Charlie. If there was a school prize to be won for the most raffle tickets sold, we'd win it. No need to flog them to grandparents – Dad would just chuck a couple of fifty-pound notes in an envelope for Charlie and I to take to school and exchange for fistfuls of annoying little tokens. We ended up with a LOT of toiletry sets and crap wine. He also threw us excellent birthday parties with such amazing party bags that girls who'd previously never said a word to me used to come up to me in the playground to blatantly beg for an invitation. One year I was obsessed with the Barbie Nutcracker movie, so Dad got every guest – all thirty of them – the DVD and a tie-in Barbie doll. I was the talk of the playground for a while, which I hated, but on the whole I wasn't complaining. I liked having a generous dad.

Mum was no downtrodden housewife, though. She had a degree from Cambridge, but she'd found out she was pregnant with my brother on the day she handed in her final thesis. My gran wasn't exactly thrilled, especially because the guy who'd knocked up her daughter was a local wide boy and not exactly academic. Anyway, Mum and Dad got married, Mum had Charlie, Dad got successful, a few years later I came along and, to cut a long story short, Mum had never had a job. And if you're wondering what happened to all that unfulfilled ambition, look no further. She seamlessly transferred it on to me: the female heir to the family brains. No pressure there, then.